W9-BMM-170

FIC
WIN

4864

WINDSOR, LINDA
Hi Honey, I'm Home

6/08

DEMCO

Hi Honey,
I'M HOME

Palisades Pure Romance

Hi Honey, I'M HOME

Linda Windsor

Palisades is a division of Multnomah Publishers, Inc.

HI HONEY, I'M HOME
published by Palisades
a division of Multnomah Publishers, Inc.

© 1999 by Linda Windsor
International Standard Book Number: 0-7394-0637-X

Design by Andrea Gjeldum
Cover art by Aleta Jenks

Scripture quotations are from
The Holy Bible, King James Version

Palisades is a trademark of Multnomah Publishers, Inc.,
and is registered in the U.S. Patent and Trademark Office.

Printed in the United States of America

For information:
MULTNOMAH PUBLISHERS, INC.•P.O. BOX 1720
SISTERS, OREGON 97759

To Suzie, Donna, and Annie, my own "angels," for encouraging me when I was down and sharing their love in Christ.

The Lord is my light and my salvation;
whom shall I fear?
The Lord is the strength of my life;
of whom shall I be afraid?

PSALM 27:1

One

FRIDAY NIGHT TRAFFIC ON THE BELTWAY WAS TYPICAL BUT nonetheless horrendous, particularly if one had a deadline. Kathryn Sinclair did. A glance at the clock on the dash told her she had exactly one hour to deliver her recalcitrant son to her neighbor's home. Then she had to make like the devil for her own, where her assistant manager was putting the final touches on their promotional brain child—an intimate open house to display the Emporium's latest imports. At seven o'clock, not only would her choice customers fill the spacious living room of her historic Georgian manor, but her employers would be there as well.

One dilemma at a time, Kathryn decided with a sidelong glance at her small companion. Despite herself, she couldn't help drumming her manicured fingers on the steering wheel and inadvertently rocking forward, as if that would speed up the long line of red brake lights moving at a snail's pace ahead of her. Beside her, eight-year-old Jason Egan stared at the menagerie of cars, trucks, and sport utility vehicles as though the red glow had lured him into some sort of trance.

Kathryn thought he was shaken by the parent-teacher conference, which was making his mother late for her business engagement. At least, she *hoped* he was! It was hard to tell. Jason was like his late father in that respect. He tacked off to more neutral ground rather than dwell on a troublesome matter. Drawing him back to the subject at hand required vise grips. She shoved a thick lock of dark hair behind her ear, checked the side mirror, and pulled over to the right lane, where traffic was coming to a stop.

"There will be no television this weekend. I expect you to make up all the homework you excused yourself from."

The computer-generated note, allegedly from her to his teacher, was a gem. He hadn't even used the spell checker!

"You already said that, Mom." Jason also possessed his late father's uncanny knack for undermining her momentum, which was amazing considering he'd spent a scant year and a half with the man. Most of the time Nick Egan had been a TV shot for thirty seconds here and there, hardly the real father a little boy needed and certainly not the husband she herself had hoped for when she'd fallen head over heels in love with him. She married Nick, but Nick married his job.

Kathryn mentally shook herself, refusing to be drawn back into the past when her future was about to become stalled on I-95. She resisted the urge to blow her horn as others were doing. It accomplished nothing, except to irritate those about her all the more. With her luck, some nut would break out a pistol and start taking potshots at them.

She stepped up the speed of the automatic delayed wipers instead. The wet snow that splashed on the windshield was coming down faster now, as if it hadn't made up its mind whether to make a liar out of the forecasters or not. Scattered showers was the prediction, not snow and freezing rain. But the roads were clear so far, Kathryn noted, hoping the bad turn in the weather wouldn't cut down on attendance. Last year's first show had been such a success.

"I did know all the material, Mom. Even Mrs. Himes said that," Jason reminded her, taking a stab at his defense. No afternoon cartoons was a serious penalty.

"Jason, you have to follow certain accepted rules." Kathryn held back the *unlike your father* that flashed through her mind and remained on the subject at hand. "Even if you know the work, you *must* do your homework!"

"Maybe if I had a reason to do it," the boy began, cutting cinnamon-hued eyes at her from beneath a forelock of sandy brown hair. It was the same color Nick's had been in his boyhood pictures, before it turned darker with maturity.

It was also shaggy again and needed cutting, although when she'd find the time for a trip to the salon was another story. From Thanksgiving to Christmas was the store's busiest time of year. She reached over and brushed the boy's bangs back, only to have them stubbornly resume their comfortable sprawl. Jason was so like Nick, even down to the long dark lashes that set off his eyes in a way a woman would die for. They had a lazy, pensive look at the moment, one Kathryn recognized from the past as well.

She felt a familiar anguish tear at her chest as she looked away from the mirror image of her late husband. Although their divorce had been almost final when Nick was killed in a terrorist explosion in some third-world city she couldn't pronounce, she hadn't been prepared for the grief that overtook her. After all, she'd been about to have him legally removed from her life.

At least that's the way it had appeared. Actually, she'd prayed that asking for a divorce would shake Nick up enough to make him realize how he was neglecting her and Jason. Good as her intention was, it backfired. When he agreed to it without a fight, she'd been so hurt and angered that she let it coast on its own momentum, against heart and reason.

Then he was taken from her forever. Nick's sudden death only drove home that there was a part of her that would always love him. He was her first, her only love, and God took him or allowed him to die, maybe in punishment for her foolish attempt to get her husband's attention. She swallowed back the sudden rise of bitterness from the past.

Somewhere she'd read that the human memory tended to erase the bad memories and highlight the good. While she'd contest the first part, the last she found to be true. Sometimes, when she was tired and off guard, a glance at Jason could wring the sweet images from the past and leave her undone.

Tonight she could not afford that regression. Nick always invaded her thoughts more at Christmastime. She'd married him and, three years later, said her final good-bye to him, both on Christmas Eve. With the same resolve with which she'd reassembled her life, borne Nick the second son he never knew about, and established herself as one of the lead import buyers on the East Coast, Kathryn willed the gnawing ache away. She never wanted her son to know the anguish he innocently brought her with his resemblance to his father.

"I can think of a reason to do all that work," Jason spoke up, bringing Kathryn back to the conversation at hand. He didn't look at her. Instead he concentrated on brushing away the crumbs of a snack he'd devoured while Kathryn met with his teacher.

He obviously was up to something, but that sudden emotional blast from the past dulled her ability to discern just what it was. She remained cautiously silent, wishing she had a windshield wiper for her brain.

"Soccer," the boy informed her when she glanced at him expectantly.

"I should have known." Jason also had Nick's tenacity, the ability to go after what he wanted if it took days, even weeks, until she either gave in from exasperation or forgot her initial objection. It had made his father one of the top network reporters. He always got his story.

"I'm a tough kid, Mom, and soccer's not as rough as football. I won't get hurt like Grandma says."

"You're too little! And what if you break your fingers? How will you play the piano?" Jason was a gifted musician, according to Madame Tremaine.

"I won't break my fingers! We're not allowed to touch the ball!" the child responded in grating condescension at her ignorance of the sport. "Dad was a football captain. He could have gone pro! I want to be like him, but I'll settle for soccer. Too late for football anyway."

Double wham! If Jason were any more like his father, she'd not be able to bear it. He had a sturdy build for an eight-year-old and could hold his ground like a rock according to Jim Anderson, their neighbor and pony league coach. Then there were those dark brown eyes with volatile flecks of gold that could flash with anger or dance with mischief. They'd drive some girl crazy someday.

"Jason, you know I can't take you to and from soccer practice this time of year. My time is limited even more by business." If only she weren't so worn out from getting ready for the show, she'd be quicker on her feet. As it was, Nick—no, Jason, she amended—had the advantage. "We'll discuss this later, okay?"

Kathryn would have closed her eyes in despair were the thinning cars ahead not approaching her turn.

"An' what am I going to do while the guys watch TV tonight?" Jason lamented, switching tactics smoothly. "I can't even go to my *own* room in my *own* house because of that dumb old party."

Why had she ever told the boys the house was really theirs, held in trust from their late father's estate? Dr. Spock never had a chapter on this situation. "But I am in charge of the house until you and Jeremy are twenty-one. Then you can kick me out and do what you will with it!"

Her knuckles whitened from her grasp on the steering wheel as she turned onto a county road boasting several swanky developments. Since Jason had gone into the third grade, he'd become more and more disagreeable and difficult to handle. He was learning exactly where her strings were and which ones to pull.

"In the meantime—" She broke off upon feeling her son's small hand close about her arm.

"I'd *never* kick you out, Mom. You know that."

The stricken look on Jason's face tugged at her heart. She could feel it melting beneath the contrition of his gaze.

Kathryn wanted to let go of the wheel and draw him into her arms. Instead, she shot into the right lane and passed a service van loaded with workmen. They'd obviously started their weekend celebration early, judging from the way they swerved over the line.

Her destination was just ahead. The name Brighton Heath was outlined in colonial blue and gold against a wood-planked background and illuminated by soft spotlights. Small white Christmas lights adorned the impeccably manicured plantings in the median dividing the entrance and exit to one of the metro area's more elite subdivisions.

"I know, Jason." She reached out to squeeze the boy's hand as she passed off-shooting streets marked with plaques bearing old English names of the same design as the entrance. "And you do have a point. A lot of the books you need to finish your homework are in your room."

"Does that mean I can play with the guys and watch TV?"

"Only if you give me your solemn promise to spend the rest of your weekend at home working on your catch-up work," Kathryn conceded. "Can you do that?"

She drew her free hand back to the wheel to turn into Meadow Green. As she did so, she gently tested the brakes. The car didn't lose traction, which meant that, so far, the wet snow wasn't sticking or freezing.

"Cool!" Jason's smile was back in place.

The Andersons' two-story home, designed in a French style, was aglow with Christmas candles in each window and beribboned swags of evergreen on the sills. As Kathryn maneuvered into the driveway, Karrie Anderson, clad in her typical battle-of-the-bulge

regalia—a sweat suit, sweatband, and running shoes—
opened the wreathed front door and waved, a steaming
cup in hand.

"New tea! Guaranteed to take off pounds! Not bad
either!"

"As if you need it!" Kathryn teased through the open
electric window of the car. Despite a slim figure, her
neighbor was always on some diet or exercise kick.

With the Andersons' two boys of six and eight, she
supposed it was too much to hope that her younger son,
Jeremy, would poke his little face through the open door
to greet her. Jason, however, did deign to give her a hasty
peck on the cheek.

"Thanks, Mom! Hope you have a good party!"
Bundled in a down-filled jacket, he practically rolled out
the car door and dashed for the house.

"Good luck tonight!" Karrie called out to her, backing against the glass storm door to let Jason barrel past.

"Thanks! And thanks for keeping the boys. I'll pick
them up as soon as the trucks take the goods back to the
store!"

Karrie's cheerful "Take your time!" faded as she
stepped inside and drew the door shut behind her.

Grateful for good neighbors like the Andersons,
Kathryn backed out of the drive and headed toward the
far end of Brighton Heath's boundary where the original
homestead, which belonged to the Egan family, lay on
the remaining four acres still in that name.

With the impending divorce, Nick had bequeathed

everything to his offspring, changing his will just before leaving on his last news assignment. Since their separation had been one of mutual agreement and was not bitter, at least on the surface, he appointed Kathryn as a trustee of the boys' estate along with their longtime friend and attorney, Paul Radisson. As trustees, she and Radisson felt it was in the boys' best interest to develop the land, which more than quadrupled the value and resulted in a considerable fortune to invest for the minors' future.

It was hard to believe that just over six years ago all this had been farmland and the house was a cold brick monster, isolated amid overgrown shrubs and trees. Nick's parents had bought the rundown place and worked it, but with their passing, the fields were rented for a pittance and the house became an oversized, under-modernized bachelor pad until she and Nick were married. Her mother was appalled at their living conditions, as Nick's career had not yet taken off and money to restore the house was not to be had.

Development had been a good decision, Kathryn thought as she turned into the large circle dubbed Egan Court. There the now-stately family home stood in all its Christmas splendor, as it might have appeared nearly two hundred years earlier when it had originally been built. Unlike its original state, however, it was insulated and boasted the latest indoor plumbing amenities as well as heating and air-conditioning. As one appraiser had put it, it was a two-hundred-year-old *new* home by the time Kathryn had finished restoring and remodeling it with some of the profits from the development.

Ordinarily she'd have taken time to appreciate the spacious yard, which was landscaped with its original ancient oak and walnut, as well as professionally restored beds and gardens. Egan Court had been featured in more than one of the house-and-garden magazines and now stood on the historical register as well. The restoration was a dream come true…a dream she and Nick had once shared. It saddened her that Nick had not survived to see it. No doubt, though, if he'd lived, he'd have spent more time reading about it than actually living in it.

Ah, no matter what was written about only good memories surviving a loved one's loss, the bitter still rose with the sweet from time to time. Kathryn pulled her minivan into the garage, an addition built on in the form of a carriage house. It was connected to the manor by a long mud/utility room. The last of the items they intended to show were packed in boxes in the back of the car, but her assistant David and housekeeper Ruth Ann would have to get them out. She had to shower and dress in less than forty-five minutes!

In the mad rush into the house, Kathryn didn't take time to seek out her partner in this unconventional show scheme. Knowing David was efficiently devoting his time to the great room, she told her housekeeper to advise him of her arrival and the items in the car. While she hated delegating authority, there were some times

17

when it was unavoidable, and, thanks to Jason, this was one of them.

The scent of the Cajun-blackened prime rib and its accompanying dishes being prepared by the caterers followed her as she scrambled up the servants' stairwell to the master suite. It reminded Kathryn that she'd missed lunch. Lying across the bed, courtesy of David, was one of the Parisian designs she'd purchased for Mrs. Whitehall's fashion department at the Emporium. It was still in its protective plastic. Coordinating shoes, purse, and gloves, as well as a short matching velvet cape, were beside the dress, although Kathryn doubted she'd need the cape or purse inside the house. Maybe she'd display them on the coatrack in the hall, since with the rush she'd been in, she was in an overheated lather as it was.

Fortunately, she wasn't one to linger in the shower. Life did not allow her the luxury of using the porcelain pedestal tub with the slanted back in the light of the flickering electric sconces hanging on the walls. Instead she showered in a tiled cove adorned with stylish curtains to match those hanging over the shuttered window, making quick work of lavishing scented bath gel on her smooth skin. After drying with a thick towel, she rushed through her after-bath toilette and dried her hair recklessly, since she was going to wear her hair up anyway.

The dark green velvet of the dress fit her figure like a sheath. By the time Kathryn drew on the matching long silk gloves, she looked quite the princess, especially after she fastened a jeweled velvet comb in her hair to hold her upswept locks in place. With one last breathless look in the mirror, she dabbed on a touch of new perfume imported from Demonde of the Virgin Islands and hurried down the main staircase just as the walnut grandfather clock in the central hall struck six.

Six! But it should be seven! Kathryn stopped halfway in her descent and stared at the face of the elegantly carved Swiss timepiece in confusion; then it dawned on her that she'd been running on the schedule of the clock in the dash of her car. It had not yet been set back for the end of daylight saving time. She was an hour *ahead* of schedule!

With a breath of mixed relief and exasperation over her unnecessary tizzy, she started downward again. Although thick oriental carpet on the grand staircase cushioned her steps, her descent drew the attention of the two well-dressed men conversing in the doorway of the great room. One was her assistant manager, David Marsh, and the other, Paul Radisson, her attorney and fellow trustee of the children's estate. The preparations must be completed or David would still be flitting about like a hyperactive hummingbird.

"David, you're a lifesaver!"

She stopped at the bottom of the steps to adjust her feet in the sequin-buckled high heels before she pulled a Cinderella act and left one in her wake. They were supposed to have been size 8, not 8½, but it was too late to do anything about it. They were designed to complement the rest of her ensemble.

Both men moved forward to steady her as she wrestled with the errant slipper, but David reached her first. "And you, Kathryn, are a work of art, not to mention an hour ahead of schedule. I take it you've solved the case of your little black sheep to the school's satisfaction?"

"For the time being, although this single working mother bit drives me batty at times. I'm only an hour early because I was rushing by a clock I hadn't set back yet."

"I'm willing to come to your rescue anytime," Paul Radisson spoke up. "Especially if you wear that dress! I'll wager that if the women coming tonight think they can look like you in it, you can't possibly have ordered enough of them."

"Only one of each style, dear." She patted his cheek. "It wouldn't do to have two ladies appear at the same function in the same dress." Aside from her, there would be models circulating among the guests for an additional peek at the new holiday apparel. "As for coming to my rescue, you already have by agreeing to act as my cohost. David and I will be frantically involved with sales if this works out the way we plan."

Paul had been Nick's best man at their wedding, and for a while he and his wife and she and Nick had socialized together. If only time could have stood still then— when they were all newlyweds, and, although struggling to make financial ends meet, so much in love. However, when Nick took the job of foreign correspondent and Paul graduated from law school to join his father's firm, the two couples drifted apart.

Upon her husband's violent death, Kathryn discovered that Paul had divorced his wife, although it didn't come as a complete shock. Word drifted down along her mother's grapevine that Paul had become something of a silver-tongued devil with the women in the elite social circles about D.C. He'd tried his charm on Kathryn, but to no avail...yet.

Even if he had truly had enough of his *freedom* as he claimed, she was not ready for a relationship beyond the one they had as friends and occasional escorts to thwart well-intentioned matchmakers like her mother and friends. Sometimes Kathryn wondered if she'd ever be receptive to another man.

She humored Paul with an absent smile as he made a gallant show of lifting her hand to his lips. While Nick had fallen short of her ideal of a husband, Paul was closer to it than any man she'd ever met. Maybe she was too picky, as her mother accused, but *once burned, twice shy,* as the saying goes. The most important requirement was that the man she chose had to be good father material for the boys, someone she and they could count on. They were the only men in her life that really mattered.

"Since I've a moment to catch my breath, I'd love a cup of the imported punch before the hordes arrive."

She withdrew her hand when he held it a moment longer than necessary. Yes, Paul would be perfect but for his discomfort around children.

"The alcohol-free English wassail," she requested

21

with a thoughtful upturn of her lips. "I'm saving the spiced ciders for dinner."

"At your service, madam." Paul broke into a toothsome grin and winked. He'd given away excellent tickets to attend the symphony with his senior partners without complaint, just to be at her side. Kathryn couldn't help but appreciate his attentiveness and dedication.

"You're a dear for putting up with me."

"*Us,*" David injected as Paul retreated to the bar set up in the front parlor. "I was in such a dither, I asked *him* to help unpack the Venetian glassware."

Kathryn grinned at the *last resort* implication in David's voice. Like her, he was very particular and preferred doing things himself. Still, she couldn't imagine having to put the show together without her employer's nephew.

David had joined the firm upon graduating from a European art school three years ago and seemed to soak up the knowledge she had to offer like a sponge. There was no doubt in her mind that the Whitehalls would leave the business to their only nephew, having no children of their own.

Then her assistant would become her boss, a prospect that didn't bother Kathryn in the least. The two of them operated on the same wavelength and with the same devotion to their trade. Too often they teased each other about being married to imports and not having time to seek personal relationships. David would no doubt make some young woman a delightful husband

when Paul was serious or teasing, although David told her the man only fell back on the teasing angle to avoid her rejection and save his ego.

"Crazy!" she accused playfully, allowing Paul that out. Could she ever bring herself to take him seriously?

Brandishing a brilliant smile to wash away her doubt, she opened the front door. The wind had picked up, and the icy air rushed in to assault her back and shoulders, bared by the halter design of her gown. Instead of her employers, however, she found herself face-to-face with only one individual. He stood, shoulders hunched in a beige topcoat. His brown hair whipped about his face, while his breath fogged the air before a mouth frozen in a thin white line.

Somehow an incredulous "Nick!" escaped her tightening throat as Kathryn stared at the mature version of her son Jason. Were it not for the fact that her heart seemed to have stopped cold, the expectant whiskey-colored gaze fixed upon her would have negated the icy air rushing in and warmed her from head to toe as it always had.

But it couldn't be Nick. Kathryn's strength drained as quickly as the blood from her face, leaving a pin-pricked trail of disbelief. *Nick was dead!* They'd sent home a few of his charred belongings, his body having been destroyed in the explosion beyond retrieval, much less identification. She buried them in his place. Pregnant with his second son, the one she hadn't told him about during the divorce negotiations, she'd wept at the small gravesite with guilt and grief until she could cry no more.

The memory reemerged with a terrible blow. Staggering a step backward, Kathryn blinked as if to erase this bizarre visitation of the ghost of Christmas past from her sight, but he remained there, studying her with an enigmatic gaze.

Suddenly he spoke, his voice as real as he appeared to be, the solemn line of his lips breaking in a poor attempt at humor.

"Hi, honey, I'm home."

Two

THE CUP IN KATHRYN'S HAND CRASHED TO THE FLOOR, ITS lead crystal shattering about her feet as she stood statue-like, staring at her husband—her *late* husband! She'd never fainted in her life, yet she felt her body sway like a snake beguiled by its charmer. Despite the sip of wassail she'd just taken, her mouth was too dry to voice the name that formed once more on her lips.

"Nick!"

"Easy, Kate."

The uninvited guest moved toward her. His arms, which had been burdened with luggage, were suddenly around her. Shaking her head as if to dispel this vision come to life, she had no choice but to accept the support. With her face now buried against his cold and damp wool muffler, her senses were again assaulted, this time by a light, spice-scented cologne, one that brought back a flood of memories.

"Y-you're…dead." She pressed her face against him. Yet, for a dead man, he felt very much alive. No lifeless corpse could hold her so tightly, nor breathe such warmth against her ear as he reassured her.

"No, Kate, I'm *not* dead. I wanted to tell you in person before you heard about my release in the news."

"Release?" she echoed lamely, her shock only beginning to thaw. She tilted her head back to look at him. This time the shot from Nick's intoxicating gaze began to work its old magic. She could feel the warmth stinging its way through her veins. Or was it the fact that someone had closed the door behind him, shutting off the winter draft?

Half fearful that he'd disappear and half that he was actually real, Kathryn touched the face that had haunted her days and nights without invitation for the last six and a half years. With a trembling hand, she touched his whisker-shadowed jawline where the muffler had fallen away.

"Nick," she whispered hoarsely. From out of nowhere, a tear slipped down her cheek. Questions collided in her brain, decimating each other and leaving her speechless. Instinctively, she sought the reassurance of his embrace to verify what her other senses reported to her.

Nick was here, alive and holding her as though he'd never let her go. A joy born of incredulous relief bubbled in her throat. "It's really you." She ran a finger over his lips in stunned fascination. "Tell me it's really you!"

"I'd rather show you."

Thanks to area matrons' matchmaking, Kathryn was no novice at dodging kisses, yet she stood grounded as Nick lowered his lips to hers. They were warm, wonderfully warm. Their adamant vitality spread, first to her face, then her neck, and onward until her senses were thawed from head to toe. Then in a pièce de résistance, he deepened the kiss with such intensity that her insides curled. Just when she thought herself on the verge of swooning again from sensory overload, there was a reprieve.

"Kate! It's been so long." His voice was low and filled with raw emotion.

Kathryn nodded in agreement. It *was* Nick. He was the only one who called her by the nickname that infuriated her mother. And it *had* been so long—six and a half years since she'd seen him staring at her coolly across the lawyer's conference table, where their life as one was being legally cleaved in two by the agreements being drawn up. She'd been so angry with him for not protesting that she refused to tell him she was pregnant, especially after he'd looked at her as if *she* were the deserter, not him; as if *she'd* been the one who had destroyed their happiness by absence.

But she'd been there, making a home for him and his son. He hadn't. She'd let her fine arts degree waste away and put her family first, while he pursued his dream and put them second.

"Blast you, Nick!"

Kathryn rallied with the onslaught of bitter recollections. Yet part of her demanded one last brush of her cheek against his stubbled one before she wrenched free of his grip. Beneath her feet, the shards of her punch cup crunched, causing her to stumble backward. If not for Paul, she'd have sprawled at the foot of the staircase in her fervor to get away from the disruptive embrace of a very much alive Nick Egan.

"I don't know what brings you here, Nick, but this is a fine way to break the news to Kathryn!" Paul's eyes snapped as he steadied her.

"It's good to see you again too, good buddy."

"Be careful, Kathryn, you'll cut your feet."

The sound of David's voice made Kathryn wonder how long she and Nick had had an audience. She'd not heard either David or Paul join them. All she'd been aware of was Nick. He affected people that way. He affected *her* that way. But how could he be here? Where had he been all this time?

"Mr. Egan, if you'll kindly move yourself and the luggage to the side, I'll have this swept up in a pinch."

Ever efficient, David knelt and hurriedly brushed the remains of the punch cup into a dustpan. "Why don't you gents help yourselves to the bar while I see to Kathryn." He handed the dustpan to Paul. "But first make yourself useful and put this in the kitchen garbage. Then take care of our unexpected guest."

"Who the devil are you?" Nick stayed the arm David sought to put about Kathryn's shoulders.

The sudden anger that sprang to her husband's gaze spurred Kathryn into action. This wasn't a nightmare, one where she was totally helpless to do anything except participate; but she had to take control before it became one.

"This is David Marsh, Nick. He's my assistant. David, this is my—my...husband, Nick Egan." What else could she call him? He'd never signed the divorce papers. All proceedings were dropped at his death.

Inadvertently, Kathryn reached for the back of her neck where muscles tightened in a threatening way, as they often did during the periods of high stress that went with her job. This crisis, however, exceeded any work-related distress. She shook her head. "I think Nick and I should speak privately."

Heaven help her, the last thing she wanted was to be alone with Nick, but she was about to burst with questions swirling about in a quagmire of raw emotion. Besides, it was evident that if he was going to be dealt with, it would have to be by her. At the moment, he looked as if he couldn't decide which of her two companions to punch first. Impetuous and physical, that was Nick. Her mother often said his years of playing football more than offset those spent studying journalism. More of a news maker than a news reporter, Stella Sinclair had once remarked with a cynicism reserved for when she was displeased with her son-in-law, which was most of the time.

31

"We'll go into the library." Kathryn was unable to keep her anxiety from her voice any more than she could blink away the smattering of tiny white lights that danced across her field of vision. A migraine! That was all she needed.

"Don't you worry about a thing, Kathryn," David assured her, as if reading her mind. "I'll run up to your bedroom and get your migraine tablets. Were you using your blue or green purse today?"

"Blue, but the guests…"

"Aren't here yet." He raised a silencing finger, then started up the stairs. His slight but meticulously Armani-clad figure moved with footfalls as quick as the beating of Kathryn's heart, which had now resumed with unprecedented haste. Nick eyed the younger man like a confounded lion trying to decide whether to pounce now or later.

Paul laid a supportive hand on her shoulder, garnering her attention. "Are you sure you don't want me to stay with you?"

"What the blazes *is* this?" Nick switched his attention back to the lawyer. "You'd think I was intent on hurting my wife, and, believe me, that's the *last* thing on my mind."

"Your soon-to-be *ex*-wife, and you could have called us, for Pete's sake!" Paul shot back in Kathryn's defense. "This is a fine way to break your resurrection from the dead to her!"

"You already made that point, Radisson…and what's this *us* business?"

Disconcerted by Nick's sharp observation, Paul straightened his tie unnecessarily. While one man was quick tempered and just as quick to act, the other was not one to back down. Paul resorted to diplomacy first, then action. It was only natural for him to be defensive of her, considering all they'd been through together since Nick's alleged death. Kathryn knew she had to do something and fast before yet another scene evolved.

"Paul, I need you here, to help David," she intervened, placing a placating hand on his arm to soothe his ruffled feathers before turning to the source of her problem and assuming a cool, take-charge manner.

"Now, Nick, if you will, come with me..."

More the ice queen than the princess, Kathryn led the way to the library. It was once Nick's study, replete with his sports trophies and awards and heavy pine furniture reminiscent of a hunting lodge rather than a historic mansion. Its paneled cabinets had been restored from an unimaginative beige to their original wood tone. Tasteful green moldings tied in the decor of oriental carpet, drapes, shutters, and reproduction wallpaper imported from England. Instead of the old gray metal desk with the attached rickety typing stand where Nick had written his first news story, a large cherry one wrapped in a half circle around an upholstered leather chair commanded the center of the room.

"Wait a minute, Kathryn, I have your medicine. We can't have you down with a headache tonight, can we?"

Kathryn stood back for Nick to precede her. The

look he shot at David nearly made her smile, but she maintained her aloof air. "Go in and make yourself comfortable, Nick. I'll be right with you."

As her assistant handed her a plastic cup of water from the master bath, she closed the door partially and lowered her voice. "Got a sedative too?"

"No, *I* took that!" David shot a nervous glance at the door. "Things sure are getting hot on the home front these days. You want me to go in with you?"

"Don't—" Kathryn nearly choked as a trickle of water invaded her windpipe—"Don't even think about it. I thought he was going to pound you as it was, especially when you ran up to my room. He doesn't know you put together the ensemble for me while I was at the meeting."

"Better me than you," David quipped valiantly.

"You needn't worry about Nick lifting a hand against me. His mistakes were more of neglect."

"And everything I'd ever heard about him indicated he was intelligent." David took back the empty glass.

"Thanks, David, but I'm a big girl. I can handle myself now that I know I'm not squaring off with a ghost."

At least she *hoped* she could. Upon entering the room she found Nick examining a gaming table of the same period as the candle stand and Queen Anne chairs on either side of a hearth the workers had uncovered during the restoration.

"It's an original," she informed him. Having hunted

antique stores for months, Kathryn was proud of the acquisition.

"You've certainly improved the looks of the place." Nick turned to face her. "It's almost as classy as you look."

"Thank you, Nick. I'll take that as a compliment." Kathryn strode past him, all too aware of the way his gaze followed her, sweeping over her from head to toe as if it had been starved for her image. Or was he looking for a crack in her armor?

"It was meant to be, Kate." His voice was softer now, like a brush of silk against the back of her neck.

Merciful heaven, get me through this night!

Self-conscious, she smoothed the velvet sheath of her dress over her hips before assuming the chair of authority behind the desk and wondered if God was even listening. *And whose fault is it if he isn't?*

She pushed the thought—and the sting of guilt—away. So what if she wasn't worshiping regularly lately? She was too busy. Sunday was the only day she could rest. That's what she kept telling herself anyway. At least she made certain the boys attended Sunday school with the Andersons. Hopefully that counted for something.

The edge of the leather cushion creaked beneath Kathryn's slight weight in warning, offering little friction against the material of her skirt. Ruth Ann and her polish! Even as the picture of her sliding unceremoniously to the floor flashed through her mind, Kathryn braced herself on the arms with an air of nonchalance. Once certain of her seat, she folded her hands primly in front of her and pointed an imperious finger toward the companion chair placed opposite her for her clients.

"I haven't time for small talk, Nick. I'm expecting guests at any moment…important guests, my employers among them. I would, however, like to know where you've been for the last six and a half years and why you're here now before you go on your way."

The slight semblance of satisfaction garnered from her recovery of seeing a dead man come to life flailed beneath the marked darkening of Nick's face. There was a time that snap of anger in his eyes had intimidated her, but she couldn't let that happen. She wasn't the same young woman he'd almost divorced. She was stronger, more sure of herself.

"*On my way,*" he repeated with a derisive crook of a smile. He ignored the chair she offered, deliberately passing it by. "Somehow I'd imagined my homecoming would be a little warmer. I've taken a chill since stepping inside."

The nerve of the man, trying to make her feel guilty when it was he who invaded her comfortable world unannounced! But that was Nick. Everything was her fault.

"Surely you didn't expect to be greeted with open arms, Nick. As I recall, we were all but divorced when we parted ways."

Kathryn refused to retreat, fixing a head-on glare on her companion while he shed his coat and tossed it casually on a Queen Anne chair. Like the gaming table, it too was an original, beautifully restored. So was Nick, she thought for a reckless moment—at least for a dead man. He looked as though he might have just returned from a health spa sabbatical, judging from his tanned face and the lean physique beneath his shirt and jeans. Nick had never been the muscle-bound jock, but he was hard and fast enough to cut his way through an opposing team like a steamroller.

She recalled his turning down the chance to pose in an underwear ad. *"Not overdone,"* a modeling agent at a pool party had once declared, eyeing the ridged plane of Nick's chest as he climbed out of the water. *"Just right."*

Kathryn steeled her relaxed pose against the back of the executive chair as he paced around the desk the same way Jason walked when he was upset. Except that Nick's expression was inscrutable, a gift her son, thankfully, hadn't yet mastered. He stopped next to her, forcing her to look up. Supporting his weight on one hand, he leaned over and cupped her chin with the other.

He still wore his wedding ring! The little flash of gold in the light of the desk lamp followed by Nick's touch banished all thought entirely from her mind.

"I remember a lot of things, Kate…good things."

He drew a line along her jaw. It was impossible to pretend indifference. Kathryn seized her bottom lip with her teeth, lest he trace her mouth as she'd so unwittingly done to his earlier. Then she'd been in shock. Now she was in control of her wits, if not her floundering reflexes, and he was evading her question.

"Now, where is my son?"

My son. The question cut through the warm turmoil brewing in her chest like a blade of ice, making her obsession with his prior whereabouts seem paltry compared to his present purpose. Surely he wasn't here to collect the children! He'd agreed to give her full custody without a fight. He hardly contested the divorce with any more than an "Are you sure this is what you want?" It was his unspoken words that put her through hell, those driven home by his accusing eyes from across the divide of the negotiating table over six years ago.

"He's spending the night with a friend, which is just as well, considering the way you fell in on us! I need to prepare him for meeting you. Children don't adjust well to sudden changes and Jason has been a problem of late as it is." Kathryn bit off the "He takes after his father" before it escaped. There was no point in antagonizing an adversary, and there was no doubt in her mind that that's exactly what Nick was. He'd skipped the parry and gone for the kill—Jason.

"He's a problem at eight?"

Nick's skepticism destroyed the last remnant of her attempt at psychology and reason. "Paternal genes. He can't help himself."

"So he doesn't live up to the high and mighty *Sinclair* standards. What will you do, give up on him too?"

Kathryn's knuckles grew white from the pressure

she put on the desk. She rose like a fury to meet her adversary eye to eye rather than suffer his looking down at her any longer.

"Don't be absurd, Nick! And I didn't kick you out. You never lived here in the first place. This was just a stay-over for you."

"Well, I'm home now, Kate, so get used to it."

"Fine, but not tonight! I have other plans, which do not include you, so gather up your bags and get out. We'll discuss your meeting Jason tomorrow—*by phone.*"

Nick smiled again, this time as though he took some devious pleasure in this cannonball conversation to disaster. Back with him came all those bitter feelings she'd tried so hard to put behind her, all fresh as the day they carried her through the divorce proceedings. *"Stay calm."* That was her family attorney's advice then and it would serve now.

Nick's characteristic smirk would not push her beyond control, no matter how much she wanted to slap it away. *He* was the intruder. She was on home turf.

The sound of the front door chime ringing in the hall gave her the opportunity she needed to escape without appearing the coward. Kathryn marched away from the desk, ending the matter.

"You can use the phone in here to call a cab. I have guests to welcome."

"I have no intention of going anywhere, Kate. As I recall, this house is mine now that I've returned from the dead."

"What...?"

"This house is mine" instantly replayed in her mind, answering her startled question before she even finished it. Her chest constricted as the validity of Nick's declaration registered. She placed a hand over her stomach, where a queasy weakness assaulted her.

Now she knew the source of his wry amusement. He'd let her forge ahead at full tilt for the pleasure of stopping her dead in her tracks. Why hadn't she seen it coming? Feeling more the puppet than the puppeteer, Kathryn leaned on the back of one of the wing chairs with the dawning of the knee-weakening truth. What was she going to do?

Her mind reeled from trying to separate fact from emotion, the result of her effort far from comforting. Nick was right. She was merely a trustee, living in the house he'd left to his offspring. Alive, the ownership reverted back to him. If anyone were to leave, by law it should be her.

"Don't work yourself into a migraine, Kate. I'm not nearly the monster you've conjured in your mind. You're welcome to stay here until you can find suitable lodgings." Nick waved magnanimously toward the door. "And continue with your little party by all means."

Bested for the moment, Kathryn glanced at the door where the cheerful voices of guests milling in the front hall epitomized the opposite of what she was feeling at the moment. She had to join the party.

"Rest assured, Nick, I'll not impose upon your hospitality any longer than I have to." From some reserve deep within, she regrouped beneath a regal facade. "If you would be so kind as to make yourself scarce until the show is over, we can finish this discussion then."

"I'll take the spare room. It's not occupied by one of your host of *protectors,* is it?"

"What?" She stared at him blankly, her mind such a quagmire of struggling reason and reaction that she overlooked the innuendo when it registered.

Where could she go at such short notice? How could she explain to the children, prepare them to meet a father neither one remembered? A new wave of anxiety washed over her, but this time maternal instinct rallied. She wouldn't let Nick disappoint the boys, not as he had her. *So help me...*

"The spare room, is it free?" Having closed the distance between them, Nick placed his hand on her arm with a hint of concern.

Kathryn withdrew from his touch as though it scalded her. "Yes, for the time being."

He'd always been physically affectionate with her, unable to keep his hands to himself. When they were happily in love, she'd adored it. Then she came to see it as a show put on to placate her during those infrequent appearances at home. Had he really loved her, he'd not have left her alone so much.

"If we both try, we can work this out, Kate. I'm not after blood."

"No?"

"No."

He'd already stated he wanted the house, which was paid for by her blood, sweat, and tears, even if the money for the restoration had come from Nick's estate. Now it belonged to a man who could not possibly appreciate it any more than he could the two fine sons she'd borne at the same cost.

Was Jason next? What would Nick do when he found out about Jeremy? By heaven, she'd fight him tooth and nail before she let him build up false hopes in her sons for the father they longed for.

"What do you say? Truce?"

Kathryn looked at his outstretched hand but dared not take it. She needed all her faculties at the moment. Instead she nodded stiffly and stepped into the hall. One day at a time, she counseled herself, schooling her face with a brightness she was far from feeling upon hearing Austin and Kitty Whitehall in the front hall. Her employer's wife had one of those unmistakable laughs, a high-pitched titter reminiscent of chalk squeaking on a blackboard.

Still in the cover of the arched divider separating the foyer from the back of the house, Kathryn glanced over her shoulder to see Nick picking up his belongings, his coat thrown over one broad shoulder. Her contrived cool wavered for a moment. She'd had an attorney serve him the papers and negotiate their separation before, but dealing directly with her estranged husband was entirely different, especially when he seemed so amenable. That was when Nick was most dangerous.

"You *will* take the servants' entrance to the second floor, won't you?"

"Black tie affair, eh?"

When Nick made that boyish face of disdain, it was like looking at Jason confronted with a healthy helping of brussels sprouts.

"My most important clients."

"Don't worry, Kate. I'll not embarrass you."

"I've worked hard and come a long way, Nick." She stood her ground as he came up behind her.

"So I see. I'm proud of you." With a reassuring wink, he nodded for her to precede him into the hall.

It wasn't until after he disappeared two steps at a time up the hidden stairwell reserved for servants that Kathryn recovered from the compliment. Nick Egan proud of her business accomplishments? She'd thought the only thing that made Nick proud was her wearing the domestic apron like a banner in the kitchen and absolutely nothing in the bedroom. He was Tarzan, the man of the house, the breadwinner. She was Jane, keeper of the house and dependent.

Now, however, Jane was the breadwinner, even if she was about to have no home to bring the bread to. And if she was going to earn enough bread to secure another home for her and her children, she'd best paste on a smile and promote the beautiful arts and antiquities on display like she'd never done before.

What she needed most and had the least of was time, Kathryn mused later over a perfectly prepared prime rib dinner. This was the first moment she'd had to really think about Nick's untimely arrival since joining her guests, despite the haunting headache, thankfully dulled by her medication. Orders had already been placed for the English silverware and bone china upon which she and her guests now dined. The decorative basket on the hall table was filled with orders from the small booklets provided each attendee by the Emporium.

Austin Whitehall told her one of the decorators had placed an order for the entire contents of the great room, provided Kathryn set up a similar display in his show-room. Kitty fairly beamed earlier when she'd told Kathryn in a stage whisper that this was the most successful show to date, while David kept giving her a thumbs-up every time he caught her eye. Perhaps the snow had evoked a shopping frenzy among her clients as it did in area grocery stores.

It would soon be over, she thought, gradually focusing on the conversation at hand. Her guests were a fair representation of the diplomatic variety of peoples found in and around the nation's capital. Most owned their own boutiques or gourmet shops. Others were interior decorators, while a select few were private buyers whose volume earned them distributor prices. At the moment, there was a friendly rivalry going on over the assorted spiced ciders she'd pegged for the Sharmas' private cellars.

"Now, wait a minute, Mohabir, my wife and I would like to have some for our gourmet shop, so don't take it all."

"But I will need at *least* as much for the New Year's Eve party I am giving at the embassy."

"I'm certain Kathryn ordered enough for you both," David intervened amid the friendly banter.

Kathryn gave her assistant a smiling nod of confirmation. "Once the ciders are served at the Sharmas'," she assured the Hampshires, "everyone in Washington will want to add it to their coffers, and where else could they purchase it but at your chain of gourmet shops?"

"Did you really think Kathryn was playing favorites, Hal?" Austin Whitehall wheezed with an asthmatic breath. "My girl takes care of everything!"

"If we didn't know better, we'd swear Kathryn had a crystal ball," Kitty chimed in.

Paul, having attached himself like a leech to her side once everyone had arrived, gave her hand a friendly squeeze.

"Her *crystal ball,* as you call it, is that she knows her clients, what they like and dislike."

"I'll bet she's even got a few unopened jugs in the kitchen!" her employer ventured in bold agreement.

Kathryn should have withdrawn her hand from Paul's. He meant well, completely unaware that his possessive nature was part of her immediate problem with Nick. It antagonized an already awkward situation. Nor did her admirer realize that her work was a bastion of renewal, despite the long hours. Times like these made it all worthwhile.

"Yes, as a matter of fact, I do."

Kathryn knew what her employer was getting at—a gratis gift set of the various flavors to those who placed orders. It was simply good business, even if it did cost over two hundred dollars per gift. They'd make that back many times over, she felt, her shaken confidence well on the mend.

"But you've ruined my surprise," she chided gently. "At least part of it. The set has all four flavors in it."

She was a born manager, Kathryn told herself, both of her office and her life. Nick couldn't take that away from her, even if he could take her home. She had what it took to move on *with* her boys.

"Since the cat's out of the bag, I'll go get them, Kathryn." David started to get up from his seat at the opposite end of the row of banquet tables, but Austin headed him off.

"No, *I'll* get them while you and Kathryn see our guests into the front salon for dessert. I need to take my asthma medication before these scented candles take my breath away."

Kathryn rose at the head of the table to dismiss the assembly and chatted with Kitty and Paul while David led the group from the dining room to the front salon. It had been a ladies' parlor at one interval of the house's past and ordinarily served as a family room, when not decked out in Ashley-Devlin reproduction Chippendale furniture.

The rich cherries and mahoganies with lighter inlay were interspersed in intimate groupings with upholstered pieces of modest but extremely comfortable design. On a gateleg table, a tempting mousse in pedestaled cut glass awaited them. One of the fashion models, a tall brunette attired in a scarlet lace chemise provided by the Emporium fashion department, stood by a tray of assorted coffees encouraging everyone to take samples to accompany the dessert.

Now was the highlight of the evening, at least for her and David. Kathryn picked up a book of drapery and upholstery swatches from the hall table and followed the crowd into the room. While their guests relaxed and enjoyed dessert, sampling the latest international coffee blends, the last of the orders would be placed and completed. If the night ended as well as it had progressed, by the middle of next week the brimming warehouse at the Emporium would look almost empty, which would make year-end inventory a breeze, not to mention make room for her spring purchases now in transit.

When the evening finally came to a close, it was accompanied by stacks of orders and an endless stream of compliments on the show. These were interspersed with hopes of attending another next year. There was no way, much as she wanted to, that Kathryn could avoid a small celebration afterward.

While the caterers removed all traces of their fine spread and Ruth Ann and David supervised the packing of the Emporium's display stock, Kathryn and her cohost sat in the great room with her employers and the

Grossmans—Kitty Whitehall's sister, who was the owner of a chain of exclusive gourmet shops in and about D.C., and her husband, a publisher from New York.

Although Nick had not shown his face, Kathryn hardly heard the animated conversation about the show. One battle was over, but how could she celebrate its victory when another more threatening confrontation loomed on the horizon? Her attention continually shifted to the stairwell, as if she expected him to casually saunter down at any moment. Since it was so late, perhaps Nick had gone to bed.

She took a healthy sip of the hot Russian coffee and nearly choked. While the brew was rich, its bite wasn't quite as smoothed by the whipped cream topping as she would have preferred. To think some people actually added vodka or a liqueur to it was incredible.

"Easy there." Paul patted her lightly on the back.

Kathryn dabbed an embossed napkin to her mouth. The last thing she wanted was Nick going to sleep under the same roof, especially when they'd not finished their conversation—not by a long shot.

"I'm fine," she reassured her company. "It's a bit too strong to my taste."

"It's made to see a body through those Siberian winters. Helps 'em stay awake!" Austin Whitehall joked. He breathed deeply and exhaled. "Not to mention it opens a body up better than any inhaler."

"Speaking of which," his wife spoke up, "you need another dose."

"Yes, well, we'd best be getting on our way anyway and it's in my coat pocket. Ready, folks?"

Austin rose, his twitching mustache reminding Kathryn as much of a Southern gentleman as the longish white hair he wore combed back off his face, away from long, neatly trimmed sideburns. All he needed was the linen suit and a bucket of chicken, she thought fondly, putting aside her coffee to say good-bye to her last guests.

She gave each of the Whitehalls a hug. Though Kathryn had been out of the art and decorative world during her marriage to Nick, Austin and his wife had given her a full-time position as Kitty's assistant. The woman's health demanded she take a less active part, and Kathryn had already worked part time for the Emporium while earning her degree, so it benefited all concerned. They were like a second set of parents and treated the boys like the grandchildren they never had.

"I've got a racquetball game at seven in the morning, so if you're sure you're all right, I'll be on my way as well."

"Of course I will...and thanks, Paul." Kathryn bussed him on the cheek and followed the departing group into the hall to collect their coats. "I'll not be thrown out tonight at least," she quipped under her breath.

"Thrown out?" Kitty Whitehall turned in surprise. "What on earth are you talking about, Kathryn?"

It was amazing the things Kitty could hear when she

wanted to, Kathryn groaned silently.

"Her *late* husband, Nick Egan, turned up not so dead just before the gala tonight with no advance notice," Paul informed the curious group before she could summon an evasive answer. "I wonder that she's held up as well as she has."

"Egan?" Natalie Grossman's husband repeated, raising his gaze toward the ceiling as though the files of his memory were displayed there. It was the first time that evening that he'd said a word, for the chain of gourmet shops was clearly his wife's interest, not his. Now, however, his publisher's instincts had been whetted. "Nick Egan...yes! He's that journalist who played football. I thought he was killed in a terrorist attack or some such thing."

"So did everyone until tonight." It was hard to tell which was more dour, Paul's voice or his expression.

"This is nothing I can't handle!" The last thing Kathryn needed was a barrage of concerned questions.

Kitty looked stricken, Austin grim. As for Paul, something about his grudging attitude over Nick's survival pricked at Kathryn's already frayed nerves. He'd been Nick's best man, for heaven's sake!

"Funny we haven't heard any news about this." Arnie Grossman's brow, heightened by a receding hairline, crinkled like a pleated shade.

"Goodness, now I remember, dear!" His wife finally caught up with the rest of the group. She put a hand on Kathryn's arm. "You two were divorced just before he

50

was killed, weren't you? But then," she amended awkwardly, "he actually didn't die in that explosion, not if he was here tonight! What happened?"

"We were *nearly* divorced, and I—we...haven't had a chance to discuss that, what with the show."

"Is he still here?"

Kathryn had seen the kind of kindling in Arnie's eyes before, except that it had been in Nick's gaze. It was a fever sparked by the scent of an exclusive. She supposed book publishers were no different in that regard than their newspaper counterparts. A reluctant yes teetered on her lips while her brain spun with the possible repercussions the affirmation might lead to.

"Yes, I am, sir, but I'd prefer no one know about it until the evening news on Monday, when the story is scheduled for release."

Kathryn turned in wary relief to see Nick making his way down the curving stairwell, an accusing expression directed at her and Paul for letting the story out. He'd changed into a pair of casual slacks and a sweater but blended into the elegantly attired group with characteristic ease.

"It's a political sticky wicket," he explained to his stunned company, "so I'm appealing to your patriotic sense of duty to keep mum until the authorities announce the news of my release."

"I smell a bestselling story here." Arnie stepped up to shake Nick's hand. "The name's Grossman. I'm with Gloucester Publishing in New York."

"Like I said, Mr. Grossman, it's *no* story until Monday."

"But you'll give me first offer on a book, once it breaks?" Arnie produced a business card with the finesse of a magician and flashed it in front of Nick's face. "Call me, Mr. Egan. If my hunch serves me correctly, I'm prepared to be generous."

"So what are your plans, *Mr. Egan?*" Kitty's pale blue eyes narrowed with suspicion and Kathryn almost smiled. Kitty had been there to pick up the pieces after Nick's alleged death. Of them all, perhaps the older woman was the only one other than Kathryn herself who could even begin to understand the bizarre volatility of the situation. "That is, regarding *our* Kathryn?"

"That's for them to work out, Kitty." Her husband's admonishment was as gruff as the look he gave Nick, a look that implied things had better work out to Kathryn's favor. "You heard Kathryn. She hasn't even had a chance to speak to the man, for heaven's sake."

Nick met Austin's look evenly. "We'll work things out, I promise." Just like Nick was working her guests.

Although Nick said absolutely nothing to indicate he wanted her guests to leave, he masterfully herded them toward the front door, so smoothly they hardly knew what he was up to. That winsome smile and manner enabled him to milk the substance from the most hostile interviews without his adversary even realizing it. *I can't allow him to lead me down a merry path—not again.*

"Kate's best interest is foremost in my mind, Mrs…"

"Whitehall," Kathryn supplied, still uncertain as to which of the two men had annoyed her the most—Paul for revealing Nick's presence or Nick for showing himself. "You remember, Nick. Austin and Kitty were my employers when I was in school."

"Of course, I apologize. It's been a while." Nick extended his hand first to Kitty, then Austin.

"And this is Kitty's sister and brother-in-law, Natalie and Arnold Grossman. Natalie is one of our best customers."

"Pleased to meet you."

"The evening's been a terrific success." Kathryn waved nervously at the box of orders David had placed on the hall table. She was blabbering like an overwound doll but couldn't help herself.

"Congratulations," Nick conceded, only momentarily distracted from the purpose she detected in his gaze, the nature of which she could only guess. "But as for Kate," he rallied in singular determination, "rest assured, contrary to what *some* people may think—" he directed a glare at Paul—"I am not tossing her out, even if I do own the house and grounds legally."

"I think a court will be a better judge of that issue."

Kathryn's breath froze at the sharp glance Nick gave Paul Radisson. The blow she fully expected him to deliver to Paul, however, came verbally, bowling her over with such impact that she barely registered the others' reactions.

"If I have my way, she won't be leaving at all."

Three

"HOW COULD YOU MAKE SUCH A STATEMENT IN FRONT OF ALL those people!"

Nick studied his wife, careful not to give in to the grin tugging at his mouth.

The guests had left, taking their assorted looks of curiosity and shock with them. With the staff clearing the front salon, Kathryn chose the great room to square off against him rather than suffer holding her tongue the moment longer that it would take to return to the library. Ignoring the seat he'd indicated she take with a magnanimous wave, she stood like a tall, svelte, velvet-clad lineman ready to take him down.

"I merely stated my intentions, Kate."

Nick had never seen her more beautiful...or formidable. His first encounter had been a disaster, failed by his irritation at the territorial overtones of her wet-behind-the-ears assistant and Radisson, a seasoned man about town. Nick had reverted back to his old self, the Nick who had gone through Christian motions since childhood but didn't really understand them; the Nick who failed to practice what he heard preached because his mind was on other things more important...or so he thought at the time. He knew better now. Or so he'd hoped. Then the minute he got alone with Kate, he forgot all he'd learned in the last six and a half years about turning his life over to God.

God, please don't let me blow it again. Help me with my temper...and the fact that I want her back so badly, I can't think straight.

He no longer was the same man, nor she the same woman. Kathryn had changed from the blushing bride he'd married. It became her as a woman. And she was all that. He took note of the way the soft material of her dress clung to her figure, challenging a man's imagination.

"Don't be ridiculous! There's no way I'll consider staying here a moment longer than I have to." She tapped her foot as though gathering steam. "I'll find a townhouse closer to work and move in there until you decide you're in a rut and move on. It'll be just a matter of time."

She was nervous, despite her magnificent bravado. Kate had a habit of toying with the material of her clothes when she was nervous, like she was doing now. That hadn't changed. Nick seized upon the innocent show of uncertainty, hoping she was guilty of protesting too much, that somewhere beneath that you're-the-last-person-I-want-or-need-in-my-life bluster was a remnant of the opposite sentiment.

"Kate, God pulled me through many years in a hole-in-the-wall prison. When I wasn't simply trying to survive, he gave me plenty of time to reevaluate my priorities."

Nick took a deep breath, measuring his words carefully. He'd practiced this a million times, but Lord help him say this right.

"I shouldn't have let my work come between us, and I certainly never should have given you the divorce so easily."

"There are a lot of things you never should have done, Nick, no matter how holy you've become since." She gave a short cynical laugh. "At least God was *with* you. He let me struggle on my own."

"Kate…"

"I've heard the 'I've changed' story before. We can't go back to the way it was. I'm not the same person. It won't work."

She reached behind her neck and squeezed as though she meant to rip the tendons out. Suddenly she looked up at him with delayed reaction.

"Did you say you were in *prison?* I suppose you got that tan in the pen spa?"

He'd hurt her terribly and now she was striking back with all she had, both at him and at God. Nick tried to think how to explain himself without breaking government confidence.

"Suffice it to say, the general who captured me was

a golf fanatic as well as a political one; that is, when he wasn't given to torture and isolation."

He detected a waning of color from Kathryn's high-boned cheeks and drew hope from it. She still cared. He went on, somewhat encouraged.

"I can't say more until Monday. Now, why don't you let me work on that headache. Even you agreed I had talented hands."

Nick checked further pursuit of that subject with his offer. State department and foreign policy rigamarole wouldn't tie his hands much longer. What he really wanted to do was kiss the slight trace of whipped cream that lined her upper lip so invitingly.

She sidestepped him. "I'd rather take a pill."

Reeling in his overactive imagination before the temptation carried him away, he held up his hands in mock surrender. "Suit yourself...about the pill that is. Go on and take it. I'm not going anywhere."

As if to drive home the point, he plopped down on the sofa and fitted a fringed needlepoint pillow behind his head. Nick wanted Kate to know he wanted more than her body. He loved all she was more than he'd realized when he agreed to the divorce without a fight. Admittedly, this new spunk would take some getting used to, but he never was one to turn from a challenge, particularly one so critical to his future happiness.

"That's the point, Nick. You *have* to...at least for a few days."

The smooth white shoulders she'd held at full

attention dropped to a softer pose, the sort that invited hands to caress them, a nose to inhale the faintness of the scent she wore. Nick steeled himself, cursing his overactive imagination. He was a charge-ahead creature by nature, but that tactic would not work. Not now, with this prickly side of her nature. He had to win Kate by proving how much he'd changed, how much she meant to him as wife, companion, and mother, no matter how much he wanted to add *lover* to that list.

"I can't imagine why," he said cautiously, "but I'm certain you're going to tell me."

"For the children's sake."

Kathryn felt her face blanch, her insides cringing at the slip. It was too late to retract her words. It wasn't that she was going to keep Jeremy a secret. She just hadn't planned on going into that tonight. She was tired. Her head was starting to throb with each panicked beat of her heart.

"Was that *children* as in plural?"

While he'd been in the process of making himself at home, Nick now sat on the edge of the sofa, all aggressor but for the telltale paling beneath his tanned face and the wounded confusion in his gaze. "You have another child *besides* mine?"

"I was going to tell you *Monday*."

Kathryn tried to shun the pang of guilt his reaction aroused in her. After all, he had no qualms about keeping secrets from her. Besides, she ought to be offended by his incredulity that she might have a child by someone else. It was beyond Nick, she supposed, to imagine she had actually built another life that did not include him. She almost wished Jeremy had been someone else's child, just for the sake of argument. But the fact remained that he was as much Nick's as Jason, despite the raven-dark hair and blue eyes he'd inherited from her.

"Not *besides* yours. Jeremy was…is yours. He was born six months after you…disappeared."

She watched the mental calculation stirring the golden flecks in his fixed appraisal. Somewhere in the background the phone rang twice before it was picked up, while the mantel clock ticked off the passing silence in precise measure.

"Yes, I was pregnant during the divorce proceedings," she declared, bristling when calculation hardened into accusation.

"And you didn't think that was important enough to tell me?"

"What difference would it have made?"

Nick swore, springing to his feet so suddenly that Kathryn couldn't help but back away a step. "I'd *never* have agreed to the divorce, Kate. Never! I'd have fought you tooth and nail."

"Because of a second baby you wouldn't even be around to see born?" The servants' ears had to be burning, but she didn't care who heard her raised voice at this point. She'd wanted to remain calm, but there was no

60

way she'd let Nick ride his noble high horse on this one. "You were a part-time husband and father, Nick, more absentee than real! You weren't there for Jason and me. How could I expect any different with Jeremy?"

"Blast it, Kate! I was working my tail off in every flea-bitten, vermin-infested third-world country there was to make enough money to keep you in the mighty Sinclair fashion. I couldn't make those bucks at a local station. I had to pay my dues abroad and was well on my way to the top when you decided to pull the plug on me and bail out!"

"*You* were more important than the money, Nick, but you were too bullheaded and proud to see that." Kathryn crossed her arms in front of her, as if that might protect her from the condemning blast aimed at her. "I won't take the blame for this!"

How dare he even try to make *her* the villain. Reinforced with indignation, she abandoned all semblance of defense for a direct offensive. "You're not going to hurt me again, and you're sure as the devil not going to hurt my boys! I've worked hard to rebuild our lives without you. I don't need you now, Nick," she ground out defiantly, "and neither do they!"

"I didn't mean to hurt you, Kate."

"Well you did, whether you meant to or not!"

"Excuse me, miss."

Kathryn momentarily gave up her warlike stance and nodded for her housekeeper to enter the room. "What is it, Ruth Ann?" Most likely it was Paul calling to make certain everything was fine. That was a laugh and a half!

"I hate to interrupt at a time like this, but it's...it's my son-in-law on the phone, ma'am. Maggie's water broke and she went into premature labor. She's in the hospital. They took the baby by cesarean and both my daughter and her new little girl are fine, but...well, someone's got to care for little Tommy till his mama comes home. Then the mother and babe'll need someone. What am I to do, this bein' your busy time?"

Kathryn sank into a wing chair to regroup. First Nick, now this! Ruth Ann had asked for the month of February off when her daughter was due, not December, Kathryn's busiest time of year.

"You'll go and take care of little Tommy and your daughter and granddaughter when they come home, of course. There's no other choice." Her thoughts raced ahead. "I'll call for a temporary tomorrow, although getting someone on a weekend might be a problem."

"Bless you, ma'am, but I don't need to go until Monday. My son-in-law's folks are there for the weekend."

Kathryn returned the grateful squeeze Ruth Ann gave her. "Go tell him you'll be there Monday then."

How on earth would she find a housekeeper, much less a nanny, during the holiday season when there was a run on temps for parties and vacations?

"The boys will be no problem," Nick put in after Ruth Ann rushed back to the telephone in the kitchen with her good news. "I'm not working yet. It'll give us a chance to get to know each other."

Kathryn's attention shifted back to her more immediate problem, wondering if she'd heard right. Nick take care of the house and the boys? The idea almost made her laugh.

"Sorry, Nick, but you're just not Mr. Mom material. They can't live on cold cereal and corn chips. Besides, I need a housekeeper as well, and you never were one to know which end of a broom to hold."

"Did it occur to you that you're not the only one who's changed, Kate?"

"Honestly, Nick!" This idea was more ludicrous than the notion that she'd have him back, yet he was dead serious.

"You hold the top of the broom," he went on smugly. "But I prefer the vacuum. It's quicker and more thorough."

Kathryn grimaced.

"C'mon, Kate. Give it a shot. You need a housekeeper *slash* baby-sitter, not to mention time to find that townhouse you insist on. I need to get to know my children. It makes perfectly good sense."

Her head pounded so painfully, Kathryn could barely shake it.

"Move out to a hotel and give me until Monday to break the news of your arrival to the boys, then I'll *think* about it. This is going to be a big shock, Nick." She held up a blurred finger to silence his objection. "It's only fair…to them and to me. Just until Monday. That's all I ask."

"I move out until Monday and you'll give us another chance?"

"Not *us*," Kathryn corrected sharply. "And I said I'd *think* about you and the boys." She'd have followed him with her gaze as he sauntered past her chair, but her neck would give no quarter. He was close, however. Every nerve in her body sensed it. And he was annoyed.

"Tell you what." Nick's voice dropped to a cajoling note as soft as the skirt she clutched at the touch of his hands on her bare shoulders. "I'll move out until Monday and you give us—me and the boys—until your housekeeper comes back to prove I'm fit for their custody."

Custody! Despite the nauseating discomfort it caused, Kate bolted upright and pulled away from the soothing massage Nick had initiated on her tight neck and shoulder muscles.

"Custody!" she blustered with do-or-die belligerence.

"Only in case things don't work out between us."

She had to get a pill or a shotgun, Kathryn thought, blinking to clear her pain-glazed vision. With the gun she could take out either the headache or its source; the latter, though drastic, was gaining favor by the minute. She wasn't ordinarily a violent sort, but at the moment she could blow away the smug expression on Nick's face without batting an eye.

He definitely had the advantage, but he didn't have to flaunt it.

"Done." The first skirmish was his. *She who runs away lives to fight another day.* Although the way her head was aching, she doubted the validity of the old saying.

"But I warn you, Nick Egan, seeing is believing. I intend to watch your every move. I expect this house to be kept in its current state of...keep ability," she said, her well-versed vocabulary failing her. "I expect balanced meals, cooked and served at the appointed hours—I'll make a schedule—and laundry will be kept up. That includes ironing cottons and rayons. The first sign of your fouling up and you're out of here, until I can find suitable lodging for the boys and myself. Those are the stipulations of the offer, take it or leave it."

"Done!"

"You...you'll abide by those stipulations?"

Nick was under no real obligation to grant her any consideration where the occupation of the house was concerned. Besides, he couldn't replace Ruth Ann in a million years, even if he tried. She knew he'd back off. Now she was certain to get the time she needed. He'd fail and she'd have the house on her own until she could make other arrangements. Her shock turned to a satisfaction that nearly took the edge off the driving pulse in her temples.

"To the letter," Nick agreed. "Shall we have Paul draw up some papers? I get the impression he'd do it for free."

"He would, but that won't be necessary. You were many things, Nick, but you weren't a liar."

Kathryn was so caught up in her triumph that she held her ground when Nick closed the distance between them. It wasn't until she felt the pressure of his hands on her arms that she realized his intention was more than a handshake. By then it was too late.

"Then let's seal it with…"

The kiss started, not with the fierce hunger of their earlier kiss, but with a tender, almost grateful brush of her lips. It so threw Kathryn that her mouth was still parted in surprise when Nick drew away and stiffened, exhaling as if to release all the tension built up in the coiled muscles of his stance.

He'd had the advantage, not only of surprise, but of her vulnerability, yet he'd let it go. Actually, he'd thrown it away, for she could see from his expression that he hadn't wanted to release her. He looked like a starving, caged animal, anguished and desperate, torn between food and an open cage door.

For one bizarre moment she yearned to set him free from whatever it was he wrestled with, yet she dared not unleash the beast. Kathryn pressed her fingers to her temple as if to clear the confusion pounding in her brain, when another realization came to her, one more urgent.

Oh no, not now!

With a moan churned from the depths of her stomach, she seized a beautiful oriental bowl and lost the pittance she'd consumed at supper. Nick was instantly at her side, keeping her from slumping to the floor as the nausea stirred by the unrelenting headache overtook her. Above the roar in her ears, she heard his voice.

"Somebody bring water, towels, and the lady's headache medicine!"

As she struggled to regain her footing, Nick swept her legs out from under her and carried her to the sofa. Ever so gently he laid her down, his arm remaining behind her head to supplement the pillow.

"Please go, Nick. I'll be fine."

In the periphery of her vision, a concerned David appeared with a glass of water. "Here, give her this."

Nick lifted her head so that she could swallow the medicine and water without choking. Beside them, she heard her assistant's lament.

"Good night, Kathryn, did you have to use the Indonesian piece? It's irreplaceable!"

She managed a semblance of a smile. To laugh at David's attempt at levity would be too painful. Somehow she'd always known that when choices boiled down to concern for her or a priceless collector's item, her attentive coworker would choose the latter first.

"How long has she been having headaches like this?" Nick glared at David. Gently he eased her back against the pillow.

"I'm fine. Just *go*, Nick."

David was too young and impetuous to be daunted by a man half again his size. "About a year now, I think. Yours is the worst I've seen to date though."

"Thanks, March."

"Marsh, with a *sh*," David corrected.

"I'm fine. Just *go*, Nick." She sounded like a broken record, but that was all she had the strength left to say.

"I believe Kathryn's trying to tell you that her headaches are stress related and she is currently suffering from a major overload."

Bless David's heart! Kathryn hated to let her assistant fight her battle, but she was out for the moment.

"I put your coat on the receiving sofa in the foyer. Your voices sort of carried across the hall to the salon," David explained without apology. "We heard you were leaving tonight. Quite civilized of you."

She would've loved to see Nick's face about now but couldn't bear to admit the lamplight, from which her eyelids shaded her pained vision. Some men took offense at David's prissy take-charge manner, while others didn't quite know how to handle it. Nick fell somewhere in between.

"All right, Mar*sh*. Something tells me she's safe with you."

"As a babe with its nurse," David responded, unoffended. Kathryn knew he'd grown used to men's incorrect conclusion that his less-than-macho voice and manner were indicative of a more-than-effeminate nature. "And considering all the packing we need to do, I'm going to have to take the guest room tonight anyway."

She couldn't help herself. Kathryn opened her eyes in time to catch Nick's expression sharpen, then fade beneath a smooth facade. "More like a sister with little brother in tow," she amended quickly.

"Oh, I'm comforted now."

Nick's tone belied his comment. Kate prepared for him to vent more of his explosive emotion, but instead he bent over and brushed her forehead with his lips.

"See you then, Kate. I'll call."

Unable to believe the confrontation was over, at least for the present, she held her breath as he retreated from the room and up the steps two at a time, not unlike Jason was given to do. As his footfall faded down the hall on the opposite side of the upstairs landing, Kathryn exhaled wearily and tried to wipe away the lingering warmth of the brief contact. For two cents she'd crash right there on the sofa, except that it would have to go back to the showroom early tomorrow. With any luck, she could sleep in a little before going to get the boys. A full-blown migraine usually knocked the stuffing out of her the following day and this was a granddaddy.

"Oh, David, *how* am I going to handle this?"

"I'll handle the store, and I'm sure Aunt Kitty will help. She's in there most of the time anyway." Her assistant's mind was already back on the business at hand. "I don't think she's as thrilled with early retirement as Uncle Austin is."

David followed her gaze, which was still fixed on the stairway where Nick had retreated. "Oh, you mean volcano man!"

"No, I mean the kids." Kathryn closed her eyes. "A

father they don't even know suddenly comes back from the dead and takes over? They're going to be devastated by all this...just devastated!"

It didn't take two days for Kathryn to realize that she had the monopoly in the household on the devastation linked to Nick's unexpected arrival. The boys hadn't come down to earth since she'd taken great pains to break the news that their real father had not been killed as first thought, but was alive, well, and coming to live with them for a while.

She'd been dumbfounded and a bit hurt at their elation. The hardest part was keeping them quiet about it, especially when she didn't completely understand the reason for the secrecy. Jeremy wanted to tell every one of his friends. As for Jason, he was certain he'd make the minor league soccer team now. Going over his back-logged homework had been tedious for both of them, despite Kathryn's pointing out that his father was an honor student *and* sports star.

One would think Nick Egan was a hero rather than a father who'd placed his career ahead of family. She'd been the one who'd been there for them, sacrificed for them, loved them with all her being while Nick had let his lust for the ultimate interview get him captured by terrorists, or at least that's what CNN reported on the Monday news. Even then, the facts were sketchy.

Nick and his crew had been used as hostages to be

exchanged for some imprisoned left-wing fanatic held by the state department, but the government would not or could not deal. Their release came after the local government over ran the terrorist compound and set the news crew and other hostages free. Video footage used during the under-the-table negotiations with the fanatical group had shown Nick being entertained in the lap of Eastern luxury at a golf club by his captors, hardly the hole-in-the-wall prison he'd claimed.

Although the general did have an irrational gleam in his eyes, as if torture might be as entertaining as golf, Kathryn admitted, her dour speculation tuning out her mother's indignant lecture over a static-riddled phone line. If only Jeremy hadn't answered the ship-to-shore call from the Caribbean and spilled the beans before she had the chance to break the news to Stella Sinclair first! When Kathryn heard her youngest blurt out that his real daddy was alive and coming to live with them, she wished Ruth Ann were there to intervene and tell her mother that she wasn't in. Although they meant well, Paul, David, and Kitty had already drained her of reassurances that she was and would continue to be fine.

Avoiding an issue, however, wasn't Kathryn's style, especially with her mother. She *had* learned that much since her failed marriage, to which Stella Sinclair had contributed a monumental share of discord. While she meant well, the woman was an endless supply of advice and criticism, particularly where Nick was concerned.

"I can get a flight out of Mexico when we arrive at

Cancún." Her mother's voice crackled in her ear.

Flight out of Cancún? Kathryn nearly choked at the thought. "Don't be absurd, Mother! I am perfectly capable of handling this situation. I already told you, Nick will fall flat on his face and have to move out. Kitty and David are backing me up at the store until I can find suitable help."

The last thing she needed was her mother butting heads with Nick and making an already bad situation worse. Hopefully, by the time the holiday season cruise was over and her mother joined them for Christmas Day, Kathryn would've found a place for her and the children and all would be settled. Paul had already contacted a real estate friend who was making inquiries for her.

"You know I'd do it for you, dear," Stella insisted. "You always had a weak spot where that man was concerned."

Nick was always *that man* to her mother. To Nick, she was Stella the Hun. At times Kathryn felt more the referee than daughter and wife.

"Believe me, Mother, I haven't come this far without Nick only to take him back. I doubt he'll last the week. You just enjoy your cruise."

Although if he didn't arrive soon, she was going to fire him right off the bat. He was an hour overdue and the boys were beside themselves. They'd been staring out the front window for the last two hours, just in case he arrived early. Not only had they taken pains to make certain their shirts and trousers matched—a first Kathryn thought she'd never see—but Jeremy had even put a bow on Buttons, the new kitten he'd brought home from the Andersons.

Kathryn grimaced, but not at the continued warnings echoing in her ear. So help her, if Nick disappointed those children in any way, she'd never forgive him. He claimed to have changed, but that remained to be seen.

Driven by desperation, she found herself praying for the first time since she'd finally believed Nick was dead. She and God hadn't parted on the best of terms. She blamed him for letting Nick die instead of making him see she'd really wanted him, not a divorce. She'd said things in hurt and anger that shamed her to remember. Yes, the church taught that God forgave, but she wasn't asking any favor for herself. She was asking that Nick's alleged change was real for the sake of her two children—two innocents caught in a tangled web spun by her feeble attempts to make things right, according to *her* will, not God's. Hopefully, God wouldn't hold a grudge. If he was all-knowing, then he knew how sorry she was, how she wished she could have done things over.

"He's here! Mom, he's here!"

At the heralding chorus of the boys, a pair of headlights flashed through the Palladian window over the front door confirming the approach of a vehicle. Instantly her chest tightened like the little fists resting on the back of the sofa, where Jason and Jeremy strained to see who was getting out of the vehicle.

"Look, Mother, I have to go. Nick's here." The groan on the other end of the line made Kathryn grin, despite herself. "I'll give him your regards." Her grin widened. "And you have a wonderful time. Don't worry about us. I can handle Nick Egan."

At that moment the sound of an accelerating car and the sweep of headlights around the living room wall highlighted two fallen faces at the window. It was only someone turning around, something far from unusual situated as the home was at the end of the cul-de-sac. Her heart constricted as the two boys dropped back onto the sofa in disappointment.

"I have to go now, Mother. Good-bye."

As she hung up, Jeremy slid down from the sofa and scooped up the calico kitten in his arms. "He *is* coming, Buttons. You'll see."

"Of course he is!" Kathryn forced a brightness to her tone. "You know how bad rush hour traffic is."

"Yeah!" Jason jumped up, her suggestion catching on. "I bet he's hung up on the Beltway. Maybe there's an accident!"

"Not Dad!" Jeremy's eyes were wide and swimming with sudden tears. "I don't even know him yet! He can't die again!"

"Of course not, love." Kathryn turned to her youngest. She gathered him and the kitten in the circle of her arms. "It's just that your daddy isn't used to this traffic and the roads have changed dramatically since he lived here. He might have made a wrong turn..."

"I'm going up to our room and see what the traffic report on the radio says," Jason declared, avoiding the open arm Kathryn extended to him.

"Me too!" With renewed spirit, Jeremy wriggled out of Kathryn's embrace and darted for the stairs after his older brother. "We can see farther down the street from the bedroom window anyway."

Her brow furrowed, Kathryn watched the mini-stampede up the stairwell and tried not to view their enthusiasm with too green an eye. All the boys had talked about was their father, making it clear that she had failed to fill the void left by Nick in their lives. Although she had her doubts, she sincerely hoped for the boys' sake that Nick would fulfill their expectations, at least to the degree of fulfilling visitation rights. Jeremy and Jason deserved that much.

Once again the phone rang in the hall, startling Kathryn from her thoughts. Maybe that was Nick. She picked up the line the same time as the boys, who'd obviously seized upon the same conclusion upstairs. It wasn't Nick, however, but Paul Radisson.

"Mom, it's for you!"

"Ruth Ann is now flying blissfully toward Cleveland, content with two fuzzy navels in her belly," the attorney informed her cheerily. "You know, I don't personally deliver just any client's maid to an airport in the midst of rush hour."

"I know, Paul. I owe you one."

There was a hesitation on the other end. "I could drop by on the way home, if you'd like. You sound a bit tightly strung."

"I'm not exactly on the way to Bethesda, Paul."

"Ah, well, you know me and directions."

"You're being sweet, but I have everything under control," Kathryn assured him, "except Nick. He's late."

"Well, I'm not trying to defend the rascal, but traffic is bumper to bumper. All I can see ahead are streams of red lights. We're barely moving."

"Mom!"

Immediately Kathryn looked out the front window again but saw no sign of approaching headlights.

"Mom, can you come upstairs quick?"

"Uh, look, Paul. I'm being paged. Thanks for helping out."

"I'll call you if Jim finds anything in your price range."

"Mom!"

"Right," Kathryn acknowledged hastily. "Now don't worry, I'm fine! Bye now."

As she replaced the receiver in its cradle, Jeremy appeared at the landing on the steps. "It's an emergency, Mom! Hurry, *please!*"

Kathryn was seized by the sight of her youngest's ashen face.

"Jason?" She started up the steps two at a time. She couldn't imagine what had happened. She hadn't heard a thing.

"No, *Buttons!*" Jeremy answered breathlessly as she passed him.

Upon entering the boys' room, Kathryn immediately saw the nature of the emergency. In their excitement to keep an eye out for their father's approach, they'd opened the window, which overlooked the street below as well as the roof of the enclosed breezeway connecting the house to the garage. At the chance to explore new territory, the ever-curious Buttons had run out on the snow-covered roof and now meowed pitifully near the garage end.

"Should I call 911?" Jeremy's voice trembled with genuine fear for his pet's safety.

Kathryn eyed the distance to the wailing Buttons thoughtfully. "No, if we call her, Buttons should be able to come back. After all, she walked out there."

It was a logical statement. Buttons, however, defied logic. After fifteen minutes of coaxing and calling, the kitten still clung, quivering and howling, to the peak of the roof as if frozen there.

"I wish Dad would get here."

"Yeah, I bet Dad would be out on that roof in no time and have Buttons back." Jason's attitude smacked of chauvinistic superiority.

Except that Nick was *not* here. He was late. Nothing new about that. Kathryn measured the distance to the cat again. It didn't seem so far. If she straddled the peak and inched along on hands and knees…

"I'll get it." And strangle its scrawny, adventurous neck when she got her hands on it, Kathryn vowed lamely to herself.

"I could do it." Jason's expression was clearly dubious concerning her going out.

"No, *I* will!"

Kathryn was not about to let her sons risk getting hurt.

"Then you can call 911 if I get stuck. They'll come for humans," she quipped as she stepped through the window and planted one slippered foot in the crusty snow blanket.

"You *could* wait for Dad."

"We all could freeze by then, Jason."

After testing the foothold with her weight and finding it substantial enough, Kathryn leaned forward on her hands and knees, one on either side of the ridge, and crawled the rest of the way outside. Ahead of her, Buttons, distracted by her company on the precarious perch, ceased to yowl and eyed Kathryn with wariness.

"That's right, kitty," Kathryn promised in a voice only the animal could hear. "If I go, you go with me."

With kitty only a body's length away, it seemed a cinch for Kathryn to ease her way forward, collect the cowardly furball in her sweater, and slip back to the window. The forward half of her journey was a success, although Buttons did not act as though being stuffed in a cardigan was preferable to freezing to death in the night air.

Just as Kathryn reached for the kitten, it backed farther away, pressing against the steep adjoining garage roofline. At the same time a pair of bright headlights swung into the driveway, illuminating the roof and spooking both Kathryn and Buttons. The kitten jumped straight up in the air and, upon striking the icy crust, began to slide down the front slope.

"Buttons!"

"Mom!"

Kathryn registered a small pang of satisfaction that at least she shared equal ground with the errant kitten as she lunged after it. Miraculously, she caught it by its front paw, but in doing so, her weight pitched dangerously to her right. Kathryn heard a scream and realized it was her own. With her left hand and leg still hooked on the icy ridge, she lay frozen, too frightened to move and barely able to breathe.

"For the love of Pete, Kate!" Nick's voice sounded from below.

"No, Nick," Kate countered. "For the love of Buttons!" The moment the spontaneous words were out, she felt even more the idiot.

"Dad, don't let Mommy fall!"

Part of her was thankful the boys echoed her sentiments and another mortified to be caught in such an absurd situation.

"Don't move, Kate. I'll be right up!"

As if I could! Kathryn closed her eyes to the bright headlights still focused on her. Somehow Buttons managed to hook her other three paws onto Kathryn's arm and, at the kitten's sudden brave tug, Kathryn let it go so it could secure a better hold as well. With the children's encouragement, Buttons not only managed to climb over her, but from the hooplas of welcome at the window, had finished a leisurely jaunt back into the house.

"I'm coming out, Kate. Just hold on!"

"This is a great shot!"

A burst of light more intense than that of the car lights went off, forcing Kathryn's eyes open in blind surprise. To her dismay, she saw Nick was not alone. A second car with 'a video crew had come up into the yard. Her nightmare was being taped live! She could see the headlines now: Super Mom Falls off Roof and Dies, but Hero's Home for the Kids.

"Put those blasted cameras away or I'll make you eat them! You're blinding us both!"

Nick's voice thundered close, but when he addressed Kathryn, it gentled.

"I'm going to anchor your foot to the ridge with my body, Kate. Then I'm going to pull you up by the waist. Got that?"

The lights went out, even the car's. Kathryn made a noise of acknowledgment. Maybe she would be better off to simply plunge headlong into the front shrubs and break her neck. Then she wouldn't have to deal with what the press would make of this fiasco.

Why hadn't she let Jeremy call 911? Why had she ever let him keep the kitten to start with?

Her ankle was twisted awkwardly under Nick's weight, but Kathryn bore the discomfort in silence. It was a small price to pay for the reassuring feeling that, regardless of her wounded pride, she was going to be all right. At the first groping brush of Nick's fingers at her waist, she caught her breath. He missed. The second time he tried, he shoved them beneath her belt and hooked it.

"Come to papa," Nick grunted, dragging her ever so slowly, yet steadily, back to the ridge of the roof.

Renewed by Nick's command of the situation, Kathryn tried to help by pushing herself along as well, but her frozen hands only slipped on the snow-blanketed surface. After what seemed an eternity, she was back on the ridgepole and beneath Nick Egan.

"I guess you could say I have you right where I want you, kid." Nick's breath fogged near her ear. "Well, *almost.*"

"Nick, how can you joke at a time like this?"

"Right!" he answered, not the least repentant. "Let's get you inside. You're shivering enough to dislocate all your bones."

"I never was a snow bunny."

"Okay, we're going to inch back together. It may look a bit obscene, but I assure you, my only intention is to get you safely inside."

Kathryn chuckled, more of a hysterical jerk than a laugh. Nothing could embarrass her any more than she'd already been. Besides, the mental picture Nick conjured of the two of them writhing along the roofline was comical. If it were someone else, she'd be roaring with amusement.

"Golly, Mom, *you* were brave!" Jeremy gushed, sparing Kathryn one arm while clutching a now contented

Buttons in the other. "You didn't cry or nothin'!"

"Bet you're glad Dad is as strong as he is, huh," Jason chimed in.

"I didn't cry or *anything*," Kathryn corrected automatically. "And yes, I am glad your father is strong." She ventured a sheepish glance at Nick. His cheeks and nose were a bright winter red, while the rest of his face was tinged with the purple cast of outrage.

"What the...the blue-blazing devil," he censored stiltedly for the little ears present, "possessed you to climb out on that roof? Thank God you weren't killed!"

Four

"Buttons was in trouble."

She should have bitten her tongue for putting the entire blame on the kitten, but Kathryn couldn't admit to Nick that she'd done it to prove herself to the boys, that the mention of his name had goaded her into such a ludicrous, not to mention perilous, situation. She crossed her arms as though that might stay the trembling that would not quit. Whether the result of fear or cold, even her teeth rattled.

"Close up the window, boys, before Buttons gets in trouble again," Nick advised gruffly. "I'm going to get your mom something to warm her up."

Kathryn shook her head. "Oh no, I'm fine. I…"

Nick's arm about her shoulder robbed her of the remainder of her protest. "Hey, it's part of the job. So I'm going to work right away." She couldn't help but wonder if his grin was malicious or just teasing. "One hot chocolate coming up. I make a mean one, if you recall."

He stepped back to let Kathryn precede him through the door, saving the hot flush that warmed her cold-stung cheeks from detection. It was a low blow and she did indeed remember. She'd had a cold and Nick brought her a steaming concoction that, along with his tender attentions, made her forget her aches and pains for a heavenly while before she drifted off to sleep, nestled in his embrace. She'd certainly had no complaints to speak of when Nick *was* around. He simply hadn't been around enough.

"I…I'm going to change into dry clothing."

"Do you mind if I fix myself something? You scared the daylights out of me, Kate."

Kathryn stopped short as Nick leaned against the textured-papered wall, his arm blocking her entrance into the master bedroom.

He studied her. "I hope you aren't given to such folly often."

Only since you came back. That's what she was on the verge of saying, but she bit off the words with a flippant, "No, not often."

Was that sweat on his brow? He really *was* shaken!

"And help yourself to whatever you want," she offered, still taken aback. So the blustering bear was hiding marshmallow emotion. "It's the least I owe you for my gallant rescue."

"Not even a kiss?"

The comment had come from the end of the hall.

Kathryn spun around and stared. A man she'd never seen before stood there, camera raised.

"Come on, Ms. Sinclair! We couldn't get a good shot of you on the roof. The least you can do is give us a smooch for our story. What a homecoming finale!"

"Who invited you in, Harrison?" Nick's question came out in a low growl.

The reporter shrugged. "The front door was open. You knew we were following you for a homecoming story. Ah, come on, Nick." The man took a retreating step toward the stairwell as Nick started toward him. "We cut the lights. Don't cut our shot!"

Kathryn was sure there were times in the past that Nick had been as pushy as their intruder. Right now, though, after the television interviews she'd watched all day on CNN while the boys were at school, she figured Nick's patience was frayed to the limit. "Oh, for heaven's sake." Kathryn grabbed Nick's arm, turning him toward her. She'd do anything to get the press out of her home. "If it means *that* much! Here!"

Raising on tiptoe, she moved to plant a chaste kiss where an annoyed muscle twitched at the juncture of Nick's jaw. Except that Nick's jaw was no longer where it had been. His lips were. They met her own in fierce possession, setting off camera flashes as well as more intimate bursts of light amid her senses. There was anger that she'd risked her life so carelessly, then gratitude that she hadn't been hurt, followed by apology for the intrusion of their privacy—all the things Nick Egan would find hard to say came across with breath-stealing physical eloquence.

"Wow, what a kiss!"

"Yuck!" Jeremy added hastily to his older brother's opinion.

"That's all I want, Kate," Nick whispered huskily for her ear only as he slowly drew away.

No longer the least bit chilled, Kathryn fled from the "for now" that he mouthed silently and turned into another brilliant flash. Mercifully, it blinded her to the sweet spell Nick cast upon her. She forced authority into her voice as she addressed the reporter, although there was no question as to who was *really* in control at the moment.

"Now, will you *please* go and close the front door behind you? You're letting out the heat." Kathryn summoned her most maternal look of disapproval for the cameraman at the top of the steps, as well as for the crew. The icy rush of wintry air seemed to sweep from the foyer below. Yet she shriveled inside, hastening in a lame retreat.

By the time Kathryn had taken a shower and changed into peach-colored fleece sweatpants and top, she'd mastered her unsettled nerves with a healthy dose of reason. Yes, Nick had been protective of her, even turning against his own kind, but they'd both just been through a harrowing experience. An adrenaline rush could explain his testiness away, even his kiss, for that matter. Nick might even believe he wanted her and the boys, but Kathryn knew how short term his attentiveness could be. The past was proof positive.

Even before her feet touched the first step in the stairwell, she sensed, rather than saw, that something was different. There was a foreign, woody scent drifting through the house, decidedly masculine compared to the potpourri Ruth Ann frequently put out. As she walked into the family room, she saw the source.

There, diligently tending the beginnings of a fire on the pristine firebrick of the restored hearth, was Nick Egan. Aside from the light filtering in from the hall lamp, the only other source of illumination was the bright flames being fed with sticks evidently gathered from the winter debris in the backyard. Cast off to the side were the electric logs Kathryn used for aesthetic purposes. She'd meant to replace them with new gas-fired logs, but time had slipped away.

The snapping and hiss of the burning wood muffled her approach, leaving Kathryn free to study the sweater-clad intruder unobserved. Although Nick's hair was brown, the flames gave it a golden glow that complemented his sun-bronzed skin. He might have been one of those glamorous ski instructors at Lake Tahoe with his eyes crinkled from exposure to the bright sun in a way that would age a woman, but only added character to a man.

His photogenic good looks were part of his success before a television camera. He'd turned down a chance at pro football for a career in journalism, although his sports popularity had given him the break he needed. With a clear baritone voice and a charisma that was somewhat boyish yet all man, Nick had gone straight to the top. In no time at all, he worked his way from local sportscaster to a leading foreign news correspondent.

Not that his brawn and good looks were solely accountable for his success. He'd graduated in the top ten in his class at the local college and, as his first employer had remarked to her one time, the boy might know his sports inside and out, but he also had an uncanny knack for bringing out the human interest story, regardless of the news he covered. Nick could see beyond the obvious.

Except in his own home.

She pushed the thought away, easing into one of the plump recliners that had replaced the more formal Queen Anne wingbacks from her show. She'd felt like the cobbler's child who'd gone shoeless. For all her education and popularity among her own circle of friends, she'd been intimidated into becoming a wallflower by Nick and his media acquaintances, always listening, but never quite a part.

"Here we go, Dad! Mr. Anderson said help ourselves to all we wanted!" Jason announced, bursting into the room through one of the double French doors that opened onto a small back patio. He was pulling something, a red wagon it turned out, loaded with firewood. At the rear, his dark hair as vibrant in the firelight as his cherry red cheeks, was Jeremy, steadying the precarious pile with Buttons clinging to the top. Of course the hood of his jacket was thrown back and ignored with childlike recklessness.

"Look, Mom! We got a *real* fire," he said gleefully upon spying Kathryn. "Dad started it."

"So I see."

She hadn't used the fireplace since it had been rebuilt. For one reason, fires were messy. For another, candles were the extent of her fire-starting capability. The electric fire had done well enough until now.

Nick had been there less than an hour and already the house was infused with his masculine presence. And yet…the mauves and blues of her furnishings and decor pitted against stark white walls adorned with oriental prints were somehow cozier, warmer, she conceded reluctantly. Something about a fire must bring out the primitive in them all.

"The chocolate's in the microwave in the kitchen." Nick pushed himself to his feet. "I'll get it for you."

Kathryn jumped up, abandoning the comfortable cradle of the easy chair. "No, go on with the fire. I can handle that."

"It's my job, remember?"

"But you're off duty after supper. Tonight I thought you'd just get settled in the guest room…unless you want to go there now."

"Aw, no!"

"Mom!" Jason protested in unison with his younger brother. "Can't we stay together?"

"I can sleep on the floor in my sleeping bag and Dad can have my bed," Jeremy volunteered. "He's never spent the night with us, *never!*"

All three males looked at Kathryn expectantly—big Nick, his smaller image, and her own image in Jeremy. There wasn't much choice, not without appearing cold and selfish. Nonetheless, she couldn't resist exacting a pinch of flesh in her surrender.

"Like I said, *three* kids."

"Man!" Jason whooped, taking time to slap five with Jeremy before giving Nick his turn. "It's gonna be great, Dad. You can tell us about life in the jungle and all the places you've been."

"Yeah, Mom always takes us to places we have to dress up for." Jeremy's face was a mirror of his thoughts. Above his wrinkled nose his eyes grew wide, but he quickly covered himself. "They're fun, but I bet where you've been is really cool...for *men* like us."

Another victory for Nick! In the time it took her to shower and change, a macho alliance had been formed that excluded her. Kathryn's feelings were mixed, glad for the boys, sorry for her. She hid her feelings and hugged Jeremy for trying to give her equal measure.

"Believe me, Jeremy, it was anything but cool," Nick spoke up, catching her eye with a grateful yet disturbingly haunted look. Suddenly, it was gone as quickly as it had appeared. He dashed out of the room to fetch the promised treat.

Now *there* was a change. Nick usually barged in and

took charge, permission or no. It was his nature, not insolence. He simply was used to being the center of attention. It never occurred to him that it should be any other way. Avoiding a subject involving himself would never have crossed his mind.

"That's right," Kathryn joined in, intrigued by this new side to her husband. Soon to be *ex*-husband, she reminded herself sternly. "The jungle is a hot place, and I'm sure it wasn't exactly pleasant at the terrorist stronghold all the time, despite what they showed on television."

The account Nick gave during his television interview with the press, after the propagandist footage of him lazing about in luxury, had held her riveted with simultaneous interest and dismay. It hadn't all been bad. He'd made that clear. But when it was bad, it had been horrible. Too horrible, she thought, recalling the scars about his wrists and ankles, now hidden by winter attire. So help her, she'd felt the pain in his voice as he calmly reported the conditions of the prison and the seesaw treatment of its victims.

When his interviewer asked if he'd ever wished for death, the answer surprised her as much as the peace that seemed to settle on her husband's face as he shook his head in denial. His love for his family and eventually his faith had kept him going. That was what Nick had said, right there on public television. All she could think was she was glad God had been more help to him than he had her during those awful days following Nick's disappearance. She stopped her speculation before it

91

dragged her down even further.

"Still, I'm sure your father has some interesting stories to share with you two."

Touched by the short, grateful smile Nick gave her for clearing the way for a more pleasant subject, she kissed Jason on the head and smiled inwardly at the color that rose to the young boy's cheeks. She'd have to remember, at least for the next few weeks, that a mother's attention wasn't welcome. Her eldest seemed intent on proving to his father he was all man. He'd already made some strides in that direction with Kathryn, like refusing her good-bye kiss when she dropped him off at school.

She rose and met Nick returning with the steaming drink at the door. "I have some new window layouts to work on, so I'm going to leave you men to your fire and tale telling. Would you like me to fix hot chocolate for you guys first?"

"Naw, Dad's going to fix it over the fire."

"We're going to cook hot dogs, too!"

"But you just had supper!" Not that they'd eaten much of the potpie Ruth Ann had left for them, Kathryn recalled. They'd been too excited. Not wanting to be a spoilsport, she gave her blessing.

"I don't suppose a hot dog for a bedtime snack can hurt this one time. Just don't expect to stay up all night talking. You have school tomorrow."

"Yes, Mother!" Nick saluted her sternly, devilment lighting his gaze and erasing the bleakness the mention of his captivity had put there. "Thank you, Mother."

God, just don't let him hurt them! Kathryn forced a chipper smile and buried her concern.

"You're welcome, *son.*"

Nick watched as she turned and walked into the adjoining library, flipping on the desk light with a switch. Kathryn still had the greatest retreat he'd ever witnessed and he'd seen his share of them. She moved like a model but with a grace more inherent than schooled. As much as that pride with which she carried herself irritated him at times, it was what first attracted him to her.

Kathryn had been a challenge, out of reach for the son of a local farmer. Her father was a well-known diplomat in the inner circles of D.C. society. She'd lived in countries he'd only read about. They were as different as day and night. On a dare from his buddies, he'd taken the plunge and asked her to be his date for the homecoming at the college where he was working on a master's in journalism in the after hours of his sportscasting career. To his surprise, the Washington debutante had another side, one that enjoyed the *lowbrow* activities of his circle at the time.

One date and Nick knew right then that Kathryn Sinclair was the woman he wanted to grow old with. He still did. A shower of sparks stirred by Jason's tossing a log on the fire interrupted his quiet contemplation.

"Hey now, not too much too fast." He ruffled his

eldest boy's hair. "We'll put it out."

Not too much too fast. That was the tact he had to use if he was to get his wife and children back.

Nick watched as Jeremy carefully put a smaller log on the fire and then turned delighted eyes, the same blue as his mother's, at him. Nodding in approval, Nick opened his arms to receive the spontaneous hug his youngest son gave him.

"I'm so glad you're here, Dad!"

"So am I, sport."

Nick embraced the child in return, purposely tempering his strength lest he do harm in his fervor. He was hungry—no, *starved*—for this intimacy. Only memories of Kathryn and Jason had kept him company—kept him sane in an insane environment—memories and the faith that he'd be delivered to make more of them. Now that his family was here in the flesh, the long denial of their company gnawed at him to be satiated. The boys, thank God, seemed as anxious for his attention as he was to give it. Their mother, understandably, was another matter.

No, he couldn't rush Kathryn or he'd put out that flicker of an old flame he'd detected behind the strong declaration of independence and indifference she tried to enforce. There was a glimmer of the magic they'd once shared tonight when he'd stolen more of a kiss than she'd intended to give. He'd felt it more than seen it and wanted to grab at it like a lifeline. Speculation about Jason's growing up had not been the main motivation that kept him alive and sane during his years of captivity.

It was the prospect of returning to Kathryn, of making up for all the time they'd lost, and of being the husband that the Scripture he'd studied in his captivity challenged a man to be.

Six and a half years had given Nick plenty of opportunity to reassess his priorities and see where he'd failed in his marriage. God, his wife, and his children were at the top of the list now. His missionary companion had told him God could turn the bad things brought about by Satan to good results. Nick believed that. He'd been abducted before he signed away the love of his life. He'd been given time to evaluate his life and then a chance to make it right.

The maid's dropping out of the picture so conveniently was the pièce de résistance, the final card dealt by God, which won him the chance to prove to Kate that he was through with public life on the road. The old Nick would have thought it fate or luck, but the man he was today knew better. Their marriage had been put on hold to keep him from making the biggest mistake of his life, giving Kate the divorce.

No, he wasn't going to let her slip through his fingers again. He couldn't. Somehow, with God's help, he'd win her back. Without that help, he didn't stand a chance—not with his quick temper, which still slipped through before he saw it coming, or with a testosterone surge leading him into temptation to rush the reconciliation. As his godly friend had once explained to him, marriage was a love triangle with man and woman at the bottom and God at the pinnacle. To grow closer together, they would also grow closer to their heavenly Father and vice versa.

Therein lay Nick's hope.

Five

APPROACHING HER HOME—*NICK'S HOME*—ON EGAN COURT, Kathryn wondered how it could appear so warm and inviting when inside it held a potential time bomb. The candles in the window cast a warm glow that threatened to undermine the icy barrier she'd prepared for another evening with her husband...*ex*-husband. She frowned. What, exactly, *was* he? Their divorce hadn't been finalized, but he hadn't been a real husband to her for a long time. She clenched her jaw at the memory of their last year together. Whatever the reality was, it was better for her to keep Nick very firmly in the *ex* category. That was much safer.

As she sat there the garage door went up, giving away the fact that she was anticipated.

Despite the profuse warmth supplied by the car heater and her cashmere coat as she drove into the shelter, avoiding the two bicycles overturned on their sides, she shivered. Whether it was the prospect of the emotional war with Nick or the fact that she'd spent all day in the cold warehouse arranging the shipping of the latest orders, she couldn't say. *Both,* most likely. She shut off the engine, gathered up her briefcase and purse, and got out.

Nick met her at the door in casual slacks, a sweater, and an apron.

"You're late!" he chided, a grin spreading on his clean-shaven face. "But we took a vote and held dinner for you."

Kathryn had to admit, the apron was a novel look and not the least bit effeminate, at least on Nick. He took her briefcase before she thought to avoid it. By the time she'd unbuttoned her coat, he was taking that as well.

"You're just a housekeeper and nanny, Nick, not a doorman too. I've managed quite well without someone to take my things at the door."

"Right! Sorry."

His awkward grimace was as heart-tugging and bone-melting as the sleepy-headed, sheepish look he'd given her that morning when she called the boys to get up for school. The three of them had been sprawled on the floor, one child tucked under each of their father's arms. She was answered with three boyish yawns, one shadowed by sandy brown bristle, and all accompanied by stretches and male grunts of protest.

"You'll get the hang of it. It's just your first day." Grateful that her back was turned, Kathryn struggled to make room in the closet for her coat, dumbfounded by her own words. As if she really expected Nick not to fall flat on his face! What on earth was she thinking? She turned back to face him.

"And Ruth Ann never holds dinner for me when I'm late. The boys have a schedule and I don't believe in disrupting it because my life is so…um, unpredictable."

The last word she wanted to use was *disrupted*. Her life was far from it. Work simply required her to be late from time to time, just like any head of the household's employment.

"What if I'd been even later? The boys need to eat at six o'clock; it's…it's simply better for them."

Nick preceded her into the kitchen. "Oh, I'm sure you'd have called," he said over his shoulder. "That's the usual domestic procedure, isn't it?"

How dare he insinuate she should have called! "I can't believe we are having this conversation!" Hot on his heels, Kathryn nearly collided with him when he stopped and pivoted.

"You're right. I've no reason to complain. I've been slaving over housework and a stove all day to provide a decent meal for you."

Kathryn met his gaze for a moment, unable to tell if he was teasing her or serious. Nick was a master at confounding her. Besides, it was a stretch for even her imagination to put Nick and a stove in the same setting.

"Right! I can just imagine the scene—" She broke off, following the exaggerated sweep of his arm to the dining room, where the table was set, complete with lighted candles. Sitting proudly at either side of the fine mahogany piece were Jeremy and Jason, faces scrubbed and eyes bright.

"Fancy, huh, Mom?"

"Indeed!" Kathryn cut Nick some slack. "I'm impressed...so far."

She allowed him to seat her, distracted by the undivided attention of her children. Heaven only knew what they'd cooked up. Peanut butter and jelly under glass?

"And now, madame, with your permission, I will serve the meal."

The boys giggled at their father's sharp heel click and turn. Even Kathryn felt the corners of her lips tug, in spite of her wariness. If only she felt as sure of herself as she had when she'd told Kitty Whitehall that she'd made Nick's place clear in the scheme of things and that she had the matter in hand.

"Dad said it takes more of a man to wear an apron than a football jersey," Jeremy whispered to her.

Jason grinned. "That's 'cause if anybody laughs at him, he can still knock their socks off."

"But he wouldn't because it takes more of a man to walk away from a fight than it does to participate in one," Kathryn pointed out to her bellicose eldest.

Some pots rattled loudly in the kitchen. Grateful Nick hadn't used the glass cookware, Kathryn gave in to a wicked thought. "Unless it's a battle with dishes. Sounds like a full-blown war in there."

The boys joined her in a laugh. Score one for Mom, she thought, rallying against the testosterone kinship.

"And here we go, *madame et messieurs!* Coq au vin on a bed of wild rice."

"Souped-up chicken!" Jeremy's face beamed.

"On seasoned maggots."

"Jason!"

Kathryn shuddered, giving the older boy a reproving look. She didn't have to guess where he'd gotten *that* idea.

"S'okay, Mom. They've been boiled. Clean protein. Dad's eaten 'em."

"That's not dinner conversation, Jason. It's campfire talk and just between us guys."

Jason sobered at Nick's quiet reprimand. "Sorry, Dad. I forgot."

Her insides wrung more at the thought of Nick having been subjected to such a meal than the general distastefulness of the subject. Kathryn took a sip of sparkling cider from the glass sitting in front of her plate. Her hand shook as she put it down. Thank heaven she hadn't known he was a prisoner in some desolate rebel encampment, suffering whatever her vivid imagination could come up with. At least she'd been spared that.

"It wasn't quite that bad, Kate. Do I look like I've had a diet of vermin and insects?"

Nick turned around, modeling his well-defined torso for her with his hands locked behind his head in a muscle-magazine pose.

"Well, if you had, you may have started a new fitness

fad," she murmured with a forced lightness.

Their gazes locked and Kathryn felt as though for one brief moment they were one, drowning in the intense emotions neither of them was willing to admit to and both of them feared. Nick was the first to pull away, leaving her somewhat taken aback at his retreat. He truly didn't want to go there, Kathryn realized. She should feel relief, but she didn't.

"Homework, Jason," she blurted out, shifting from the current quandary to a lesser one. "Did you have any tonight?"

"Done. Dad said he'd play soccer with us till it got dark if we did our homework right after school."

"Yeah, bribes work," Jeremy observed with an all-wise lift of his brow.

"You mean if Ruth Ann played soccer with you, you'd have kept all your homework up?"

"Yeah, right!"

The idea seemed to tickle both boys. They didn't have to tell her it was the prospect of playing ball with their *dad* that did the trick.

Nick returned from the kitchen with a side dish of fresh green beans, lightly garnished with toasted almonds, and a basket of steaming rolls.

"The rolls may be hit and miss." Nick placed them on the table. "The bottom layer got well done when I was trying to keep everything warm. Not that that's a problem, now that I know how things work dinner-wise," he added, cutting off Kathryn's objection before she even thought it. "And now..."

With another brandish, he turned his apron around so the ties were in front, approached the place set opposite her, and, flipping his set of "tails," sat down. "I hope you don't mind the help eating with you. The boys said Ruth Ann always did when there weren't guests for dinner."

"No, you're quite welcome."

Whether he was at the table or in the kitchen didn't matter. Nick was the kind of man who made his presence felt wherever he was. Besides, if they got along well enough, perhaps he'd realize that the life she'd made for the boys was the best after all. This Mr. Mom role would surely wear thin soon and he'd be jumping at the next opportunity to sniff out a hot news story. Kathryn wondered if he was even fooling himself in believing this was what he wanted to do. He certainly was giving it his best effort. She tasted the chicken. It was delicious.

"Mind if we say grace?"

Caught with a mouthful, Kathryn shook her head and swallowed with a guilty flush. Grace wasn't new to the boys. They'd been taught it at an early age and it was always said at formal suppers and special occasions. The daily habit had sort of gone by the wayside—as had attending church regularly—when she embarked on her new life without Nick.

She couldn't help but feel God had somehow robbed her of the closure needed in their relationship by allowing Nick to die and leaving her with a shroud of guilt to wear as his widow. Maybe that's why she drifted away from him and his people—that and the endless stream of well-intended questions: So how does it feel to be back with the wife and kids at last? Are you and Kathryn planning a second honeymoon? I hear there's trouble on the home front. Is it true?

Nick took each of the boys' hands and lowered his head. "Heavenly Father, we thank you for this food and the hands that prepared it. We thank you too for each precious person gathered at your table. May we each be filled with your Spirit and learn to love with the mercy and forgiveness of Christ. Amen."

Mercy and forgiveness. The words lingered on her mind even as Kathryn offered to help Jeremy cut up his serving. Part of a plea, or just some canned phrase? She cut a little harder, causing the knife to squeak against the china. Easing up, she finished and concentrated on her own food. When had she become so cynical?

"Was it worth waiting for, guys?"

Two high fives answered Nick.

Kathryn nodded. "Like I said, I'm impressed. Did you learn to cook while you were gone?"

"Yeah. You know, the basic survival skills. I've come a long way. By the way, do you often miss supper with the boys? Not complaining," Nick insisted with a facade of sheer innocence. "Just curious about your work."

"On occasion, especially during holiday season."

"I think you're gone too much," Jeremy observed uninvited. "You were only home for dinner once last week."

Leave it to a kid to contradict one every time. Kathryn gave her youngest a patronizing smile. "That's because this *is* my busy season, sweetie. It just seems like I'm away a lot right now."

"You know, that reminds me, Mom." Jason leaned forward on his elbows in sudden earnest.

Instinct stiffened Kathryn's posture. "Of what, Jason?"

"Well…" The boy glanced sideways at Nick, then back to her. "Now that Dad's here, he says he could pick me up from soccer practice after school."

She met Nick's inscrutable gaze across the table.

"Have we been conspiring?"

"I told Jason that if he kept up his grades and all his schoolwork that I didn't mind picking him up after practice. If that's conspiring, we're guilty, I guess."

"And did Jason tell you that I'd already told him I didn't want him playing, that he could get hurt playing with those bigger boys?"

"This isn't European soccer, Kathryn. It's a tame sport…rarely any serious injuries that couldn't happen on a daily jog. The boy's pretty fast on his feet."

"Well, it certainly seems like someone is always getting hurt in sports, no matter what the game."

"That's it, Mom. It just *seems* like it, like it just *seems* like you're gone all the time…right?"

"Oh, for heaven's sake, Nick—*Jason!*" Kathryn was flustered at the way her own argument had been used against her. Nick would never be able to deny Jason as

105

his son. She reined in her annoyance and stood firm.

"Bribes do work," Jeremy echoed to no one in particular.

"And what do *you* have to say about this?" Kathryn turned to Jeremy, snagging her youngest's undivided attention.

Not the least intimidated, the boy shrugged. "I get to watch 'em practice and play and help Jason here at home."

He who runs away lives to fight another day... or something like that. Kathryn nodded, taking it all in. "I see."

And she did. It was very clear that she was becoming the heavy while Nick walked around with hero's laurels draped about his broad shoulders.

"Since your dad is willing to pick you up, Jason, I'll agree, but with one stipulation. If you get so much as a nosebleed or I find you're falling behind in school again, you'll quit."

"All right!"

The high five he gave his dad underscored her surrender with a loud clap. Better to lose a battle than the war. The adage was valid. She knew it. Yet, as she returned to her cooling meal with less than an appetite, she certainly didn't *feel* it.

"I tell you, Paul," Kathryn confessed later on the telephone in the library, where she'd retired to go over the inventory order sheets David had prepared. "Nick is a pied piper, the way he has the boys under his spell. To them he's a hero. *I'm* the bad guy all of a sudden."

She stared blankly at the list of items, not really seeing them. Her eyes stung with the hurt she felt. She'd always been there for Jason and Jeremy, and in less than twenty-four hours their loyalties had shifted. Paul's assurances on the other end of the line that this was a temporary situation were of little comfort. Poor guy had just called to ask her to dinner, not to get dumped on like this.

"He's manipulating them! They'll give their hearts to him and then, when he takes off for Bosnia or some other God-forsaken place..." Her voice trembled. "I've been left behind. I *know*."

This was not like her, she admonished herself as Paul tried to console her. Never once had she come apart in front of anyone, even when she'd heard the news that Nick was dead. This despair was always saved for the lonely hours of darkness preceding the dawn. Her confession to Paul Radisson was only making him more hostile toward Nick, which only made her situation worse. Kathryn reached for a tissue on the edge of the desk when a movement in the periphery of her vision drew her gaze to the open library door.

Nick stood there, jaw clenched. The black look in his eyes told her he'd been there for a while. Kathryn shrank inside but forced a brightness to her voice.

"Anyway, Paul, I'd love to go to dinner tomorrow. Six-thirty is great. Bye now."

She placed the handset on the receiver as Nick entered the room.

"I popped some popcorn for the boys and thought you might want some."

He put the bowl on the desk in front of her, his gaze full of accusation.

"I won't be home for supper tomorrow. Paul has some clients who are interested in having their new office complex decorated. We'll be meeting over dinner."

Let him be mad. Kathryn raised her chin. *It's what he gets for eavesdropping.*

"I want to make one thing clear, Kate, right now."

"Yes?"

"I am not *manipulating* my sons." Nick leaned forward on the desk, knuckles white with tension. "I am trying to make up for some very precious lost time. I dreamed about the time I'd spend with Jason, and now I have another son I didn't even know about!"

Kathryn refused the guilt that nudged her. "That's very noble, Nick, but they are children and believe in happily-ever-afters. I'm the one who will be left with the explanations when you get your fill of home life and go back to your calling. I don't want to see them hurt like—"

"Like you?"

Kathryn ignored her instinct to run and squared her shoulders. "Yes, like me." She recognized her mistake the moment Nick reached for her, cupping her chin gently with the palm of his hand.

"I never meant to hurt or disappoint you, Kate, and

108

I give you my solemn word, I will not make the same mistakes with our sons that I made with you."

Though a desk stood between them, Nick's touch welded their souls together as much as the lock of their gazes. It might have been a breath away, for all the difference the leather and cherry piece made. Kate saw the depth of an anguish all too familiar, drawing her into it despite herself. The raw emotion tore at the foundation of her resistance. All her instincts bade her to go to him, hold him, love the pain away.

Then Nick cleared his throat and backed away. The anguish was gone, masked but not forgotten. "You've done a great job with the boys, Kate. They're fine lads."

The compliment caught her by surprise. "I'm proud of them."

"And I'm proud of you." Turning, Nick pulled a curtain back, staring at the lights of the development. "I didn't like the idea that you'd cut up the folks' farm at first, but it's growing on me. It was the smart thing to do, financially, anyway."

Not quite sure why, Kathryn moved to the window as well. "At least I got the house fixed up the way we'd planned."

Nick chuckled, not quite with humor. "More than I'd planned. But I like it," he added quickly. "You thought of nearly everything."

"Nearly?"

"Well, I kind of miss my trophy room. Guess you tossed all those out?"

Guilt undermined her answer. "There was a matter of space, Nick, and with the boys—"

"I know. You had to look to the future, not dwell on the past."

"Yes." Kathryn nodded. He really meant it! The old Nick would have ranted and raved about his precious trophies being thrown out. He'd been so proud of them.

"Besides, we have to make room for the boys' trophies." Fatherly pride became Nick. The idea of Jason and Jeremy filling a room with trophies lit up his face like a Christmas tree.

"Dad, the show's started!"

Nick inclined his head toward the door. "Why don't you join us?"

"I've got work to do, Nick." But it was tempting.

"Dad!"

"Coming, guys!"

He took Kathryn's hand and, raising it to his lips, brushed her knuckles gently. "If you insist on dwelling on the past, try to remember, there were good times too."

With that he left. Kathryn listened to his reception in the family room. The boys argued over who was going to sit next to their dad. She was about to turn away when she heard Jeremy ask for her.

"Your mom has work to do."

"She always has work to do," her youngest complained.

"Sometimes we parents don't have any choice," she

heard Nick reply. "We work extra hard because we love you and want you to have the best of everything, even if it means we can't spend as much time with you as we wish."

Kathryn closed the door and returned to her desk. While she focused on the page in front of her, it might as well have been in Greek for all the attention it garnered. Her mind still echoed Nick's explanation to the boys over and over.

It wasn't the same thing, she told herself, desperate for the peace of mind lost to her since Nick's arrival. It *wasn't*, she argued against the quiet voice that raised the question again. It took sheer willpower to ignore it and concentrate on the work before her. The order had to go out tomorrow. Doubt could torture her later.

Six

"OKAY, MR. EGAN. I TOOK CARE OF THE DIRTY DISHES FROM last night you hid in the recycle bin and put the casserole from the gourmet shop in the oven for tonight's supper. It's set on auto. All's you gotta do is put out the salad in the fridge and the rolls."

Nick looked up from the letter Arnie Grossman's publishing house had sent him, an offer for the book he intended to write about his imprisonment. It took him a moment to surface from the legalese of the document and refocus on the young woman standing before him.

Laine was a barely postadolescent temp from Maid Services. She cocked her head expectantly, her one-sided ponytail bouncing. When she spoke, her words were chewed as ferociously as the man-sized wad of gum always in her mouth.

"So what's next, boss?"

"I don't know. Just straighten up, and if something looks dirty or cluttered, clean it or put it away. Pretend it's your house and you're expecting company. What would or wouldn't you want them to see? Then take care of it."

The house looked fine to him, but then it always had, even when it had been his bachelor pad. Nick had never worked out the fine line between cluttered and the lived-in look. Women made a science out of it. No, he thought, taking a second glance at the maid as she left the room with a shrug, they'd made a *profession* of it. Some better than others, he mused, wondering where the service had swept up this gal. Neon, no matter how tight the fit or shapely the body, just didn't trigger his attention, except on warning signs. If a real leopard had spots of neon it would starve to death, unable to sneak up on anything short of a blind bat. And those dark blue fingernails, even with glitter, made him think of an old horror movie.

He didn't know if he was becoming more mature or just picky, but business was the priority of his day while the boys were in school, not a moon-eyed youngster impressed with a television personality. First thing to do was forward this offer, which included a ghost writer, to John Waters, a former colleague turned literary agent. In the meantime, Nick needed to see what he could do on his own. He wasn't convinced anyone else could write his story. How would they know what it felt like to be forgotten, to be thought dead for over six years; even sometimes, in the midst of the living hell he'd been in, wishing he *were* dead.

He'd even thought God had forgotten him, until he witnessed the unwavering faith of the Columbian priest imprisoned with him. No matter how bad things got, Papa Rico was never without something for which to thank God. Nick learned many things from the missionary, not the least of which was that God never abandoned any of his lost sheep, no matter how misguided they were.

For every complaint Nick had with God's plan, Papa Rico found a way to make it a blessing. Day after day, night after night, it was always the same. Then sometime, somewhere along the way, Nick began to listen, to believe. God had not spared his life in the explosion to torment him in his capture. He'd answered Nick's prayer for another chance at his life with Kate and his son. When the days seemed to stretch ahead of them for an eternity, Papa Rico would remind Nick that God had not brought him this far only to let him die. Nick knew now that God had not brought him home just to take Kathryn away from him, either.

Nick curled his hand around the telephone receiver as if it were Paul Radisson's neck, anger tightening his fingers until they were bloodless. Kathryn's plaintive conversation with the attorney would not leave him be. He'd prayed for patience and God had afforded him just enough to get himself out of the immediate danger of pushing her too far.

The front door chime drew him from his contemplation of the night before. The tension in his jaw slackened at the distraction. He shoved away from the desk and started for the hall. The chimes rang again. What kind of visitors did housewives get during the day? Vacuum cleaner salesmen?

A peek out the peephole revealed no one. At the most, it was a dwarf salesman. Nick slid back the dead bolt and opened the door wide. A car was parked in the driveway where a friendly, attractive woman behind the wheel was waving brightly. A loud sniff drew Nick's perusal from her to the little boy in front of him, bundled in a bright royal-blue-and-red hooded jacket. Big blue eyes peered out of a ruddy-cheeked face, his buttonlike features pulled slightly out of proportion by the taut drawstring. *Jeremy?*

"Jeremy?" Nick said in surprise.

"Hi, Dad. Boy, you sure talk on the phone a lot!"

"What gives—" Nick tucked in his feet to avoid being trampled by the charging boy who pushed past him.

"Hi! You must be Nick!"

Confused, Nick swung his attention back to the woman calling through the car window.

"I'm Karrie Anderson, your neighbor around the corner. Excuse me for not getting out, but I have aerobics in twenty minutes and I don't want to dazzle you with this leotard-clad figure!" The perky blonde shoved a forelock full of tight curls off her face and grinned at her joke. "Anyway, the school called and said Jeremy was running a bit of a fever. They couldn't get you or Kathryn and I'm the emergency backup."

"That's funny. The phone hasn't rung. But thanks for picking him up."

Karrie waved and shifted the car into gear. "No problem. Catch you later!"

Her words faded, the rising electric window sealing them in.

Realizing the chill he was letting in, Nick pulled the front door closed and turned to the stairs where Jeremy had headed. He hadn't counted on this. Second day home alone and he was busted by a six-year-old!

A feverish one. Concern deepening the line of his brow, Nick headed up the steps two at a time to where Laine was running the sweeper in the hall like a Fury on a battlefield. He stopped short of tripping over the hose and gingerly stepped over it. As he reached for the boys' room door, Jeremy yanked it open. Shed of his heavy coat, he looked three sizes smaller. Damp dark hair clinging to his head, he gave Nick a panicked, ashen look and dashed past him, hurtling the vacuum hose toward the bathroom.

He didn't make it. Leaning against the open door, the child lost his lunch and, from the duration of his retching, last night's dinner as well. He stood statue still until the convulsions stopped and he turned toward Nick.

"I don't feel so good, Dad."

"Ooh, gross!"

A featherlike tickle threatened the back of Nick's

throat, the ensuing gag reflex demanding more attention than the distracted young housekeeper. He swallowed hard, knowing full well that if he gave it the slightest thought, there would be two messes for him to clean up. Maybe more. He glanced hopefully at Laine only to see her as white as Jeremy was and Nick felt.

It's just mind over matter. That's what Kate told him time after time when she'd cleaned up after Jason. Except in Jeremy's case, it looked like more matter than Nick's mind could handle. It was all over the front of his clothes, in his shoes. Somewhat at a loss himself, the boy pulled a hand towel off the rack and started dabbing ineffectively at his shirt.

"I'm not cleaning *that* up. I'll get sick too."

Nick didn't answer Laine. He hoped Papa Rico's assurance that the Lord would give no man more than he could handle was right. *Lord have mercy!* He summoned a deep breath away from the damage control area and plunged into the job at hand. He'd faced worse conditions than this during his imprisonment.

"Come on, sport." Nick helped Jeremy out of his clothes. "Think you can step in the shower so I can hose you down?"

Jeremy was warm, Nick noticed, stopping long enough to feel the boy's forehead. It was clammy cold compared to the child's bare chest. Did kids go into shock from throwing up?

"Better sit down on the mat," he added, tugging at Jeremy's pants.

Jeremy grabbed Nick's hands and looked beyond to where Laine was moving her gear into the master bedroom.

"Not in front of *her!*"

"Right."

Nick reached up and closed the bathroom door, all too aware that he was shutting himself in with the mess, fumes and all. He'd nearly forgotten the girl in his concern over the boy's temperature.

"You'd better sit down. Don't want you slipping and falling," he said, imitating the forced brightness he'd heard in Kate's voice when she'd tended to Jason. *Or passing out.*

"You feel dizzy, sport?"

Jeremy shook his head, then looked around. "Who's doing the cleaning?" Instead of answering, Nick pulled bath towels off the rack and made a bed of them in the tub, in case the boy should fall. If Jeremy did faint, what would he do? Call 911?

"Laine, get me the portable phone!" he called over his shoulder.

"Who's Laine?"

"The housekeeper," Nick answered shortly. "Laine!"

"I hear ya! I'm looking for it!"

With a short release of breath, Nick turned on the water.

Jeremy shrieked as the cold water struck his small naked body, and he scrambled out of the tub and into Nick's arms, trembling. Swallowing an oath, not to mention his startled heart, Nick adjusted the water flow.

"Sorry, sport."

"S…sss…s'okay, D…Dad!"

Water soaking his clothes, Nick reached into the linen closet for more towels. He wrapped the boy in one, keeping him pressed against his chest for additional warmth, then tested the running water again. It was at least body temperature now. But where in the world was—

A knock on the door answered his question as to Laine's whereabouts before he could finish it.

"Just put it on the counter and close the door."

"Yes, sir."

Once the door closed and he was assured that Jeremy's modesty was not compromised, Nick dropped the heavy bath towel and knelt down, easing the boy into the tub.

"Who is she, Dad?"

"I'll explain later, sport. Right now I want to get you cleaned off and into warm clothes."

Jeremy cleaned up faster than the bathroom. In no time at all Nick was tugging a warm fleece shirt over his dark head, allowing time for the towels he'd scattered everywhere to soak up the mess they'd left behind the closed bathroom door. The boy tugged on a pair of skid-proof sock slippers while Nick felt his forehead again. It was still warm.

"Can you take pills?"

Jeremy wrinkled his nose. "Mom gives us cherry-flavored acetoniphen when we're sick."

"Acetaminophen," Nick corrected, more for his own benefit than his son's. "Know where it is?"

"In the bathroom cabinet."

After a trip downstairs to fetch a spoon and sorting through an incredible number of medicines for children for all manner of symptoms, Nick read the label and gave the boy the recommended amount. Tasting the remnant on the spoon afterward, he mimicked his youngest's wrinkle of disdain. "I'd rather take a pill!"

Jeremy climbed off the bed to look under it for Buttons. Since the vacuum cleaner had come out, Nick hadn't seen hide nor hair of the kitten.

"You're gonna catch my germs," he told Nick matter-of-factly. "Miss Ward says we shouldn't use silverware after someone else without washing it, because—"

"Yeah, I know!" Nick cut in, somewhat irritable over a child's justifiably correcting him. "I'll clean out my mouth with mouthwash when I clean the bathroom. Okay?"

Nodding, the boy sat back on his knees. "No Buttons under here." He sighed. "Maybe the housekeeper has seen him. What's her name?"

Jeremy was his mother's child in more ways than physical coloring. He had her tenacity to hang on to a subject Nick would just as soon let be. "Wanna wrap up in a blanket in the family room and watch TV? I'm sure Buttons will venture out of hiding once the vacuum noise ceases."

"That's cool!" Jeremy climbed to his feet and gathered up his pillow under his arm. "Buttons sure is a scaredy-cat."

"So I gathered," Nick said, grateful for the shift in the conversation.

"So is *she* taking Ruth Ann's place till she gets back?" Jeremy tossed a nod toward the master bedroom where Laine running the sweeper.

"Actually, she's helping me. I told your mom that I'd take care of you guys and the house while she worked, and Laine is helping me."

Nick swallowed a pang of guilt as he trailed Jeremy down to the living room. And that was exactly what he was doing, he reasoned. He *was* taking care of the home front. Nothing had been said specifically about his not getting help to do it.

"But let's just keep this a secret between us, eh, sport?"

"Why?"

Waiting for Jeremy to get settled on the sofa, Nick tucked an afghan around him.

"Because I love your mom and I don't want her worrying about someone else coming in the house—you know, a stranger. Women are funny about that sort of thing. Ever notice that?"

The boy nodded, his wide-eyed expression leaving Nick to think the child merely wanted to please him. Nick ruffled Jeremy's dark hair and straightened. "We guys have to stick together, right?"

"Right! 'Sides, you don't want Mom to get jealous."

A kick in the stomach wouldn't have left Nick any more dumbfounded. Now where'd the kid get a notion like that?

"No, sport, that's *not* the reason. I told you I love your mom and promised her I'd take care of things. I'm getting help because I don't know how to do everything around here. I'm still learning."

"Dad, even *I* can tell you which end of the broom to hold!"

That did it. Obviously Kate hadn't kept her opinions about him completely to herself. A thread of patience snapped, stinging Nick with its recoil.

"Good, because I just might need your help." He forced lightness into his voice. "But in the meantime, let's keep this a secret between us."

"It's not lying, is it?"

"No, it's just not telling everything we know. Besides, *all's* fair in love and war, and this is love! I want your mom to stay my wife and I'm going to do whatever I have to do to keep her." Nick put out his hand tentatively. "Deal?"

Jeremy's small hand fit in his like a nesting cup. "Deal! Just between us men!"

"You got it, partner."

"Will you put on the cartoon network now?"

Nick pretended to zip his lips and grinned a little too wide when his son imitated him, as if the relief could overshadow the twinge of guilt he felt. Thank heaven

123

that crisis was over. As he tuned the television, he glanced toward the stairs where the next one awaited. Since Laine had made it clear that she didn't clean after sick kids, it was up to him. Maybe a woman's hormones changed after childbirth, enabling her to withstand the distasteful side of child care. Or maybe it *was* mind over matter. He told his stomach that's all it was, but from the way his insides tightened, he wasn't certain it was convinced.

By the time the worst was behind him, Nick had little appetite for the hot Italian casserole steaming on the kitchen table. He curled his lip in distaste. From what he'd seen, Jeremy had had something with similar ingredients for lunch. But even if that hadn't been the case, plain exhaustion could account for the fact that he had little interest in a meal.

What a day he'd had! First Jeremy coming home sick; then how was he to know the washer wouldn't hold all the towels it took to wipe up afterward? He'd thought the washer was going to explode when it went into the spin cycle and started walking across the utility room floor, pulling the drain hose loose in the process. Now the entire floor behind and under the appliances was squeaky clean, including the dryer vent leading outside. One mess just seemed to lead to another.

Laine was certainly no help, as it was her time to leave, despite the fact that he was ankle deep in water and wrestling a jarring machine twice his size to keep it in its place. One would have thought the maid service had convinced her she'd turn into a pumpkin if she stayed a minute past four! At least she'd had the presence of mind to reach over his shoulder and push the blasted button, turning it off. Although another six inches and the cord would have pulled out of the socket.

When Kathryn walked in from work later at six, however, it was worth the travail just to see that look of total surprise overtake her face once again. He'd just called the boys to dinner, Jason from upstairs and Jeremy from the family room. Power dressed in a becoming pantsuit, she was a welcome, not to mention comely, sight, even if a few strands of her hair had escaped the bow at the base of her neck. His attention was tapped for a moment as he recalled just how sensitive she was there, until she spoke.

"Well! You've done it again, Egan. I'm impressed."

"So am I." Nick reached out to tuck a lock of her dark hair behind her ear. "You look no worse for wear for your day in the working world. Welcome home."

Kathryn felt a blush spring to her cheeks at the gesture, leaving her at a loss to deal with the compliment. The natural follow-up would be for Nick to weave his fingers into her hair, cupping the back of her head and giving her a welcome-home kiss. Her wandering thought shocked her so much she stepped away abruptly, grateful for the distraction of Jason's descent from upstairs. It resembled what an elephant falling head over heels down the stairs might sound like.

His face brightened when he saw her. "Hi, Mom! I got my homework finished, so is it okay if I stay up and watch the football game with Dad tonight?"

Disappointment took the enthusiasm out of the hug she returned to her eldest son. She checked her instinct to retaliate with a no for his obvious motivation. "I'll decide *after* I see your homework."

"It's only fair, Mom. Jeremy got to come home early and spend the day with Dad."

"Jeremy came home early?" she echoed, turning to where Nick was divesting Jeremy of a protesting kitten. "The school didn't call me."

"They called a Karrie Anderson," Nick explained. "After no one answered the phone here. Seems Buttons likes to play with the handset in your room by the bed. I don't know how long it had been off the hook when I found it."

"I was sick and heaved ho all over the bathroom!"

"That he did." A half smile tugged at Nick's lips.

"And *you* cleaned up?" Kathryn checked the pager attached to her purse and groaned. A small blinking red light signaled time for a battery change. It seemed she had just changed it! Equally unbelievable was Nick's admission. He had never taken care of that sort of kid thing when Jason was a baby.

"That I did, but I'd just as soon not dwell on it."

"Thank God for Karrie! My pager must not have picked up the school call. They're to call home first, then my office, then Karrie."

126

Leaning over, she bussed Jeremy on the forehead, lingering long enough to note he had no noticeable temperature. "Did you take anything, honey?"

"Dad gave me the fever medicine and hosed me down in the shower."

"Good for him…and you!" His eyes were over bright and his color paler than usual, she thought, brow knitted in concern.

"What time does Paul pick you up?"

The reminder of her dinner date swept all other matters from her mind. If there was any innuendo in Nick's innocent question, Kathryn missed it. Instead, she glanced at her watch in dismay.

"Half an hour. I'm out of here."

"Dad, can we watch TV while we eat?" Jeremy asked. "We can hear it if we turn it up, and my favorite show is on."

"Everything is your favorite show." Jason punched his brother in the arm.

"S'not!"

"Snot comes outta your nose, squirt!"

"For Pete's sake, Jason, we are trying to eat here! Jeremy, you can turn on the TV after we say grace." Kathryn had to laugh as Nick's taut voice faded in her wake.

That wasn't like Nick either. Crudity didn't exactly offend him when he was with the boys, whether adult or children. But he *had* lightened a shade just talking about Jeremy's ordeal.

Poor dear, she thought, hurriedly stripping off her suit and discarding thoughts of Nick Egan with it. She wanted a quick shower to wash away the warehouse dust. Then she'd don a simple knit dress, her pearl earrings, and low-heeled pumps.

After turning on the water, Kathryn finished undressing and, donning a shower cap, ducked into the glass stall. Her mind raced as she hurriedly scrubbed with a citrus-scented body wash. Knowing Paul, he'd be running a little late, having to come from the other side of the capital, so there was no need to work herself into a lather.

Smiling at her own wimpy humor, Kathryn turned until her skin was rinsed and squeaky clean. Then, stepping out of the shower, she reached for a towel, only to discover the rack on the door was empty. So were the other racks. Dripping on the soft, thick cotton rug, she crossed the room to the linen closet. To her dismay, it was also void of towels, unless she wanted to dry off with washcloths. What on earth? And her bathrobe— she looked on the empty hook behind the door where it usually hung. Where was her terry cloth bathrobe?

"Nick, did you do laundry?"

She stopped, shivering. Now that was a strange question to be asking Nick Egan! Cracking open the bathroom door, she called for Nick again in a louder voice. The only answer that came from downstairs was a commercial about some super bicycle with wings on the wheels.

"Nick!"

"Fly with wind on your Hermes wheels today!"

Looking about, Kathryn pulled the cotton throw off the rocker by the window and wrapped it around her. A hurried trip across the hall revealed the main bathroom had been stripped of towels too. The man had used every towel in the house to clean up after Jeremy?

"Nick!"

"There's nowhere to hide, Valstar! My turboblaster will..."

With an exasperated sigh, Kathryn started down the stairs. She should have expected something like this!

"Nick, there are no towels to be found in either bathroom!"

At the sight of her standing, dripping wet save what was covered by the homey printed throw, Jeremy put the TV on mute with the remote. The three males at the kitchen table all looked at Kathryn as if she'd grown horns.

"You sick, Mom?" Jason ventured, the first to thaw.

"I need a towel." Kathryn leveled a scathing look at Nick. "Don't tell me you used every towel in the house to clean up after Jeremy!"

The slight curl of his mouth as he looked her over from shower cap to wriggling toes was not the reaction she wanted. Remorse or panic at the trouble he'd put her through would have been more like it.

"No, I only used the towels in the main bathroom for that. I used the ones in your bathroom when the washing machine flooded the floor."

"The washing machine? You flooded the floor?" The cold of the kitchen tile seemed to have seeped from her feet to her brain. She sounded like a parrot, mimicking him.

"The hose slipped off. No big deal." Nick jumped to his feet. "But there's nice dry towels in the dryer. I'll get a couple."

"Ah," Kathryn said, relieved that something was still working.

As Nick disappeared into the adjoining laundry room, the doorbell rang.

"I'll get it." Jason nearly overturned his chair as he bolted past Kathryn into the hall.

Before Jason reached it, the door swung open and Paul stuck his head inside. Very much at home, the family friend usually let himself in that way rather than bother Ruth Ann.

"Anybody home?"

"It's Mr. Radisson," Jason announced belatedly.

Unable to decide which way to run, Kathryn grinned, frozen to the spot.

"Paul! You're early."

The attorney straightened and removed his hat. "So I see…but I don't think that's appropriate for the Hartford House, Kathryn. Not to say it's not becoming."

"Here we go, hot out of the dryer!"

Kathryn turned into the warm wrap Nick secured around her with his arms.

"Th—thank you." Her face was as hot from embarrassment as her feet were cold.

"Need help?" Nick whispered into her ear.

"Thank you, no! You've done *more* than enough!"

Drawing as much of her dignity as she could muster with nothing but a bath towel and a cotton throw between her and the riveted appraisal of her companions, Kathryn marched to the stairwell and up the steps with a toss of her plastic-crowned head.

"I won't be long, Paul. Make yourself at home."

Seven

HARTFORD HOUSE HAD BEEN THE PERFECT SETTING TO RELAX after leaving the insane asylum on Egan Court. Feeling her muscles at long last ease, Kathryn rode beside Paul, hypnotized by the smattering of late night traffic ahead. They'd met another couple over dinner and spent the remainder of the evening in the lounge, talking about a new commercial building in Bethesda that the couple was financing. Before she could even suggest the Emporium's decorating service, Paul volunteered the pitch for her. Tomorrow she had an early appointment with Mrs. Malchow to take a look at the job in order to work up a proposal on decor and furnishings.

Kathryn had to admit that another of Paul's assets, besides being a sharp legal counsel and a supportive friend, was the fact that many of his clients had become hers by association. Nick's friends were vagabonds for the most part, living out of a suitcase.

Next to her Paul hummed with the soft music from a local classical radio station. It was a lyrical love song, one of her favorites. Not once had he said that he'd warned her that her *deal* with Nick was going to be difficult. Considering he'd found her standing in the hall, dripping wet and straight out of the shower, wrapped in a cotton throw, she considered him to be a true gentleman.

When Paul turned his car into the drive at Egan Court, the house was asleep, its windows dark and shaded. Only one of the two coach lanterns lighted the flagstone walk to the front door. When Paul took her in his arms on the front stoop for a good-night kiss, Kathryn was surprised to find she was suddenly ill at ease. It wasn't as if he hadn't kissed her before. He had and she'd enjoyed his attention. Except then she'd thought Nick was dead. Now he was anything but.

"Something wrong?"

It shouldn't make a difference. She and Nick were as much as divorced. It was simply a matter of signing papers.

"Let me guess. Nick."

"There is *nothing* between us!" Kathryn declared, as much to herself as to her companion. She grasped Paul's face between her hands. "I'm being paranoid. Too much work, not enough play."

She initiated the kiss, anxious to make up for her foolish confusion. Paul needed no further encouragement. In a twinkling, it was he who was the aggressor, hungry and possessive. Kathryn tried overriding her instinctive reflex to retreat, and endured rather than participated. She thought the world of Paul. He'd been her savior when Nick had disappeared. He'd rescued her tonight and given her refuge from the emotional roller coaster of her home. When the overhead light came on, startling them both, it only served to bewilder her more.

"Looks like *daddy's* waiting up for you, little girl."

Paul's wry remark cut through Kathryn's confusion like a sharp blade. Nick was waiting up for her? Incredulity steeled to indignation. She stepped closer to Paul.

"I'm not a little girl."

With that, she returned Paul's kiss with the force of her emotion, determined that Nick's obvious ploy to ruin their good night would not work. It was time Nick learned she was her own woman, not his. Her satisfaction, however, was short-lived. Paul's response crushed the last of her breath from her. When he kissed her with an uncommon fierceness, Kathryn realized her folly too late. Shame rearing boldly, Kathryn stepped away abruptly when he released her. It was only with the greatest restraint that she resisted the urge to wipe her mouth. What on earth was she doing?

"Well, *that* should set our peeping tom back on his heels." Paul reached out to cup the curve of her cheek with his hand. "I know it did me."

"Well...let's hope he learned a lesson."

135

She turned and fumbled with the lock, only to discover the door was already open. When it opened farther of its own accord, Nick stood there, wearing nothing but a pair of sweatpants and a guileless grin. He didn't even have the conscience to hide the fact that he'd been spying on them!

"You two kids have a good time?"

"Wonderful." Paul smiled and folded his arms.

Kathryn felt like stamping her foot. "I'm not under curfew, Nick Egan! You needn't wait up for me."

With a face that would put an angel to shame, Nick met her accusing gaze. "I noticed the lantern on the walk had gone out earlier, so when I heard the car pull up, I turned on the overhead light so you could see your way to the door. I'll change the bulb tomorrow."

He yawned with a halfhearted stab at covering his mouth. "And I didn't wait up, Kate. I've been doing laundry so you don't have to run around the house wearing nothing but a little cotton thingy. Though you do look good in fringe."

"You are pitifully obvious, Egan!" Paul's mouth thinned with displeasure.

"Me?" Nick scratched his chest, looking for all the world like a perplexed bear. "I've got nothing to hide."

"For heaven's sake, you two, take your chest beating outside if you must, but close the door! It's freezing and I'm going to bed!"

Leaving the men in her wake, Kathryn had started for the steps when she felt an all-too-familiar twitch in her shoulder and groaned. She hadn't been home five minutes and already her muscles were having spasms. Curse Nick Egan and his meddling!

She made a side trip to the kitchen to get a muscle relaxer, in case a full-blown tension headache was developing, but was distracted by the sight of five large balls of something on the kitchen table. Kathryn picked up one, studying it. *Lint?* She sniffed it, detecting the scent of laundry detergent. It was clean lint at least. Upon hearing Nick's barefooted steps approaching, she dropped it and wiped her hand on her skirt.

"Lover boy's gone. Ah, you see the fruits of my labor."

"They're balls of clothes dust, Nick." Kathryn was in no mood to play games. Still, she had to wonder. "Why did you save lint balls?"

"There's one for every load I put in the dryer," he answered, unruffled by her disdain. He picked up the largest and turned it with a sense of pride. "And *this* baby I collected from the dryer vent hose." He sniffed it. "Least it's clean dust."

Oh no, she was thinking like him! Kathryn popped the pill in her mouth and swallowed it with a chug of water before she remembered she was going to take it upstairs *in case* she got a headache. Aggravated, she slammed the glass down and marched past him.

"Well, I'm not having your trophies on the mantel or the kitchen table, big boy. Trash them."

"Naw," he called after her. "I'm saving them to throw

in the fire. They're kinda neat the way they just go *pooff*. Dust bombs!"

Dust bombs. Kathryn held back a renegade chuckle until she was out of earshot. Leave it to Nick to make a game out of laundry! When would he ever grow up?

Between the Malchow project and the holiday business, the rest of the week passed in a blur. Jeremy was home for just one day before bouncing back to his usual energized self. When Kathryn came home on time, there were good, if not extravagant, meals prepared for the family and the house was as spotless as Ruth Ann usually kept it. Although Kathryn was often too tired to participate much in the dinner conversation, she enjoyed listening to the boys tell Nick about their days.

She found herself regretting having to give up watching television or making s'mores on the hearth fire afterward in order to work on the new proposal. Her only consolation—that the boys were enjoying the father they'd never had—was not consoling at all. She knew it wouldn't last. *She* wouldn't get hurt. It was her boys who would suffer. They didn't know Nick like she did.

"Don't you want to be part of the family?" Jeremy charged one evening. "You *always* have to work."

"I have to finish this, honey. I don't have a choice."

It broke her heart to see her youngest drag his feet out of the library where she'd set up her office, his chocolate-and-marshmallow-smeared face downcast.

Was it really work that kept her away or fear of being taken in? Kathryn closed her eyes against the nagging thought, as if that might sort out the confusion.

"Don't worry about it, Kate. You do what you have to do."

Startled, she looked up to see the primary source of her inner turmoil standing in the doorway with a small tray of fixings for s'mores. "I've been there and know how it feels to be torn between supporting the family you love and being with them. The boys and I will be fine, but if you need to talk about it, I'm here."

Nick's tone was sympathetic and sincere enough, but Kathryn felt as if she'd been axed between the eyes. How dare he insinuate that she was becoming what he'd been, an absentee parent! She buried her face on folded arms. Was her quandary the same as Nick's had been when he'd been the breadwinner of the family, or was Nick just playing with her mind? What she needed was a good rest, she decided, willing away fatigue with a second wind and returning to the color scheme at hand, which was far less troubling.

Friday evening the Emporium was open late. Saturday, Kathryn presented her ideas to the Malchows. Impressed with her prompt response and creative suggestions, they insisted on taking her and Paul out to dinner, so that when she fell into bed after an early Saturday evening, she slept straight through until noon on Sunday.

In somewhat of a stuffy stupor from battling the latest

bug her youngest brought home, she was sipping black coffee at the kitchen table while catching up with her mail when the front door burst open.

Jason bolted through with Jeremy hot on his heels and headed for the stairwell.

"Whoa, whoa, wait!" she called out, halting the dynamic duo and causing a minicollision. "What's the rush?"

"Dad's gonna play soccer with us soon as we change!"

"And me too!" Jeremy beamed, his face flushed pink from the rush.

Behind them Nick came in, decked out in a topcoat and suit. He closed the door behind him. The latest cover of *GQ* should look so good, she mused grudgingly.

"So the sleeping beauty awakens." His eyes, as he shrugged off his coat, were twinkling. "Okay, guys, coats here; you know the rules."

The boys, small replicas of their dad, deposited the coats, formerly left on the landing in their wake, on hangers and handed them to Nick, who hung them on the high closet rod. It had been so long since Jason had worn his dress suit, it looked like he'd borrowed Jeremy's.

"It *was* a treat," she admitted, retreating from the motherly pit of despair that her babies were not only growing up, but away from her. "I don't usually get to sleep in on weekends. Ruth Ann is usually off."

Despite their expensive suits and ties, Jason and

Jeremy were still all boy. The youngest one's shirt was untucked and Jason's trousers hung on his hips by a breath, rather than by the belt he usually put on with them.

"So, did you guys go out for breakfast on the town, or what?"

"We went to church, then brunch." Nick tucked the coats inside and closed the closet door.

Suddenly, Jeremy dug into his pants and pulled out a folded paper. "I colored this for you, Mom!"

"Can I change clothes now?" Jason asked his father, bouncing up and down.

"Go for it." Nick glanced at Kathryn's coffee cup. "Any left in the pot?"

"He's the progidal son," Jeremy told her. "He ran away from home and was bad, but when he came back and said he was sorry, his dad was so glad to see him that he just hugged him instead of punishing him."

Nick's question about the coffee was no more than white noise in the background of Jeremy's excited words: *"He just hugged him instead of punishing him."* It took a moment for Kathryn to find her voice. It was somewhere in her throat, blocked by a sharp blade of emotion that appeared from nowhere.

"Well, I bet he was glad."

Jeremy nodded. "They had a feast and everything!"

She rose from the table before she lost control altogether. It felt as if a tide of tears was about to wash over her, and she couldn't break down in front of Nick and

Jeremy. How could she explain it when she didn't understand herself?

"I'm going to put it on my dresser mirror." She forced brightness she was far from feeling into the statement.

Nick looked up from pouring the last of the coffee in the carafe at the waver in her voice, but whatever he thought, he thankfully kept it to himself.

"An' I gotta change these duds!"

"Duds?" She followed her son to the steps.

Jeremy stopped at the landing, hands on hips. "I'm a dude, Mom, and we dudes wear duds!"

Kathryn chuckled. "Oh, I see."

It was all she could do not to mimic Jeremy's helter-skelter scramble up the stairs, she was so anxious for the privacy of the master bedroom. She didn't know what she felt or why, but even as she settled on the edge of the bed, she knew she couldn't outrun it. Her nose started to run and she grabbed a tissue from the box. By the time she finished blowing it, tears sprang out of nowhere, along with the invisible garrote about her neck.

Was it guilt? The last time she'd set foot in the family church was for the children's vacation Bible school program last summer. Regular attendance had stopped after Nick's alleged death. She'd been so angry at God for denying her the chance to set things right with Nick, both legally and spiritually. Then there were always the questions, the looks—no matter how sincere, they'd been unbearable.

Or was the source of her dismay the timely message lovingly colored on the page in her hand? Her eyes studied the picture. It was almost as though—she swallowed more tears—as though God was reaching out to her in spite of her absence. Or was *she* missing *him*?

I can't go back there now! she argued in silent anguish. *God, you know I can't face all those people with Nick living here. I need time.*

Sniffling, she had put the coloring on her dresser when another thought assailed her from some sermon or devotional of the past. *"And ye shall be led by a child."* Was that what God was trying to tell her through Jeremy, that she should welcome Nick home after all the hurt he'd caused? Kathryn wasn't paranoid enough to believe Nick had managed to choose the Sunday school lesson most appropriate to his cause of the moment. God was trying to speak to her and she knew it. Deep in her heart, she knew it.

Please, God, not now. She closed her eyes and sat down on the edge of the bed. Stacking the pillows behind her, she lay back, her arm over her eyes to keep the sunlight from assaulting them through the French doors that opened onto the backyard balcony.

Anger, guilt, shame, frustration…they were a whirlpool of clouds in her mind.

She didn't need all these second thoughts now. Kathryn quelled them before the resulting battery building in her chest assaulted her. That's just what they were, second thoughts. Anybody knew that when in doubt, go with the first answer rather than dwell on the question and wonder. Her first instinct was to get out while the going was good. Nick was good for the boys so far. If he continued like this, all the better. Her sons deserved it. As for their marriage, she didn't want any man: not Nick, not Paul, not anyone. She'd worked hard to gain control of her life.

Blowing her nose again, she bolted upright. And she wasn't going to do it by weeping in self-pity and remorse up in her room! She always got weepy when she was toying with some virus or cold. Today was the only day she'd have free to spend with her kids, and Nick was not going to hog them. By heaven, she'd just begun to fight!

She met Nick in the hall. He'd changed to a jogging suit, looking like a cover model for some fitness magazine. When he brandished a smile at her, she couldn't help but respond in kind.

"So what's the game plan today? Soccer? Football?"

Nick snorted. "I'm not playing football with you. You cheat!"

Kathryn grinned, recalling the powder-puff match against the guys. It was years ago. They'd been so young and recklessly in love. She was to block Nick from charging the lady quarterback. Squared off, face-to-face, she'd flirted outrageously with him, blowing him soft kisses through the chin guard on her helmet and winking provocatively. The heavy mascara and liner of the day made her eyes look twice as big and naughty. The play started, but the strapping young lineman missed it.

The ball was nowhere near Kathryn, but she was his tackle. They'd kissed through the helmets and giggled at the futility of their effort.

"I can't help it if the big boy can't keep his mind on the game," she rallied with exaggerated innocence.

"*Mom's* playing?" Jason exclaimed as Kathryn and Nick descended the steps together.

Kathryn couldn't decide whether it was shock or horror that contorted her eldest's face.

"I'm going to try," she countered, feigning outrage.

"Well, you can be on Jeremy's team."

"Yay, Mom!" Jeremy piped up, jumping up and down until Kathryn thought he'd lose his baggy trousers.

Warmed by Jeremy's ready acceptance, Kathryn impulsively hugged him.

"Mom! Team players don't hug!"

Taken aback by the reprimand, she mimicked a high five instead.

"There, is that better?"

The weather was mild for winter. Somewhere in the fifties, all trace of last week's snow was gone, leaving the ground to the barren browns and grays of December. Makeshift goals were set up at either end of the yard and the soccer ball was placed on a midline. Jason was actually very good at controlling the ball as opposed to his younger brother, who too often ran past it in his excitement, forcing him to turn and backtrack.

Kathryn was goalie, which was a good thing because

she could use her hands. It seemed no matter how carefully she kicked the ball to Jeremy, it never went where she intended it to go. It was just as well because their opponents had no idea where it was going either, giving the little guy a slight advantage. Although she moved back and forth, shouting for Jeremy to go ahead, the experienced team had no trouble taking the ball away from the little guy. They did find, however, that getting it past Mama was another story.

Of course, she knew Nick was holding back, not making a play for the goal himself. There were a couple of times he'd even run past the ball, enabling Jeremy to snatch it from him.

"We're out here to practice soccer, not win a trophy," Nick told Jason when he protested. "You work on controlling the ball and passing it to me. We'll worry about the goals later."

For Kathryn, however, there was blood at stake. After all, moms can be fun too. She gave it her all, determined not to let Jeremy down after he'd graciously accepted her as his partner. Catching, kicking, throwing her body in its path, she took more than one smack of catapulting leather, but no goals had been made. As she climbed to her feet from intercepting a mean kick driven by Jason straight between the two bushes being used as goalposts, Jeremy ran up and hugged her.

"I thought you said teammates didn't hug," she teased as he danced away, thrilled with her block.

"S'okay when the goalie is their mom!"

She caught Nick's eye and they both laughed. Although they were a good five yards apart, the union of their spirits might just as well have sprung from a close physical embrace. There were many things in which they did not share a common interest, but the boys…who else could appreciate them with her like this? Her smile faded with a wistful sigh.

Certainly not Paul, she thought, disheartened. Boarding school was his idea of a proper upbringing. Kathryn couldn't imagine parting with Jason and Jeremy for the better part of a year. She didn't see them like an everyday mom, but they had quality time together and that was what was important.

"Heads up!" Nick warned, drawing her attention to Jason, who'd cut the ball away from Jeremy and was heading straight for her.

Like a train forging ahead at full steam, the determined eight-year-old came on, head slightly bent so that he could watch her and the ball at the same time. Just before he reached her, however, he gave the ball a side kick, forcing Kathryn to shift her ready position. As she shuffled to the side, her foot caught on a fallen branch and turned. At that moment, Jason went for the kill, kicking the ball as hard as he could.

All she saw was a white-and-black blur coming at her face as she plummeted down. She broke her fall with her hands, which left the spinning ball free to smash into her nose. Suddenly everything was a bright white blast of pain. She didn't feel her wrists jamming into the dirt or her hip jarring against it, only the explosion where her nose had been. Surely there was nothing left but a gaping hole of pain.

"Mom!"

"Kate?"

The voices echoed in the swirl of agony encompassing her senses, but she was more concerned with where she was. Still in midair? Did she need to brace herself? It felt as if she were floating, which was totally absurd.

No, she was being lifted by the shoulders. Blinking in the bright sunlight, she saw the shadow of Nick's head and heard the concern in his voice.

"Kate, are you all right?"

He cupped her chin with his hand and shook her face gently. Her nose was there, she realized, increasing in size and discomfort with each movement. Jason's face swam in front of her, stricken. In the background, she could hear Jeremy's trembling echo of his father's question. There was no sense in alarming them any more than they were.

"I'm fine, I think." Those were the words she mouthed, but they certainly didn't sound coherent.

"I'll get some towels!" A scurry of footsteps digging into soft earth signaled Jason's exit.

She was floating now, upward, in Nick's arms. They were warm and his body inviting as she cradled her head against his shoulder. "Think I hurt m...nose," she mumbled into the soft fleece of his jacket. There was a faint scent of cologne, or was it the fresh scent of all outdoors?

148

She sniffed and nearly choked.

Wiping her nose with the back of her hand, she saw blood.

"What...?"

"You have a bloody nose, Kate. You'll be all right," Nick told her before raising his voice in command. "Jeremy, open the door."

"You look like me the day Jason slammed the door in my face and the knob hit my nose, Mom!"

How on earth could a collision with a soccer ball hurt so much? Her nose felt as if it were broken and throbbing big as the ball that hit it. She couldn't breathe through it and dared not blow it until she had tissue.

As if in answer to her quandary, a hand towel was shoved in her face. "Here, Mom, catch the blood with this."

Kathryn dabbed the towel gently to her face as Nick lowered her down on the family room sofa. His arms had been so warm and protective that the ensuing cold outside them made her shudder. He quickly remedied that by tucking the afghan her mother had made snugly around her.

"Are you dizzy, Kate? Do you feel like you're going to be sick to your stomach or faint?"

Something in Nick's tone struck Kate funny, a panic perhaps that he might be faced with another cleanup like Jeremy's. She laughed and then winced when it hurt.

"I just feel like my nose is going to grow until it falls off!"

"Just keep your head tilted back. I'll get some ice and some water to wash you off."

Kathryn felt the pillows shift beneath her head and opened one eye to see a white-faced Jason trying to fix them for her.

"Just relax, Mom. We're here."

His gruff assurance almost made her smile. It was heart melting. He might idolize his dad, but he still loved her. To Kathryn's horror, unbidden tears welled and spilled down her cheeks.

"Does it hurt, Mom?"

She had to raise her head to see the little boy who folded her hand in his cold dirty ones. "A little. I think blows to the nose tend to make your eyes water and nose bleed."

After what seemed an eternity with her two boys squirming uncomfortably at her side, Nick came back. Ever so gently, he wiped her face and neck with a cold cloth.

"Do you really think Jason should be playing this game?" Her voice sounded muffled, as if balls of cotton had been stuffed up her nose.

"Kate, this was a freak accident. Even so, very few boys get through life without a bloody nose or two. It's a step toward manhood."

"Guess I'll be able to chew tobacco and spit with the best of 'em then."

Nick had no idea that his smile was more soothing than all his tender ministrations. It was mesmerizing. At that particular moment, Kathryn felt as if she could bask in it forever. When was the last time she'd had someone to lean on?

But you don't want someone to lean on. You want to be in charge.

Oh, shut up!

"I brought you a clean sweatshirt to replace that bloody one. How about sitting up a little?"

It was natural to obey Nick. After all, the voices arguing in the back of her mind certainly made no sense. Nick's leg pressed against her side as he helped her take off her pullover. The touch served to further reassure her there was no danger here. By the time the cool air against her bare skin registered what was happening, he was already helping her get her arms in the oversized clean replacement. He paid no more attention to her than if she'd been one of the boys.

"There we go." Nick eased her back against the pillows. Quickly he bussed her on the forehead, then tilted her head back before she could muster an objection. "Now keep your head tilted like this for a while and I'll put this ice pack on it."

"Am I going to look like that old song-and-dance guy with the big nose?"

Nick laughed. "No, it'll just feel like his schnoz. You know, when a coach says to throw oneself into the game, I don't think he means it quite so literally."

"I think I turned my ankle."

Her nose had caused so much commotion, she'd

not even registered the dull ache in her foot. She poked it out from under the afghan so Nick could examine it.

"It'll probably swell a little. Nothing seems broken." He ran his fingers gently up both sides of her foot, but the report of her senses was as though he'd brushed her from head to toe with them, conjuring responses that had no business coming to life here and now.

Kathryn winced, but she was far from feeling pain. She had to do something to short-circuit the reaction filling her being with an uncommon desire to go into his arms again. There was a powder keg of emotions and feelings inside ready to blow, and she was at a loss to control it! Through the slit of a half-closed eyelid, she watched as Nick cleaned up the bloodied towel, shirt, and water. Panic welled within at the decided direction of her unbridled thoughts. And he mustn't know. *He simply mustn't!*

152

Eight

THE FRONT DOOR CHIME AWAKENED KATHRYN WITH A START.
The bag of frozen peas Nick had fetched for her from the
freezer in lieu of ice was now soggy and fell off her face
as she bolted upright in confusion. In the hall, Nick
crossed the entrance to the family room on his way to
answer the bell.

"Is this the Eg—hey, I know you," someone
exclaimed in the cracking forerunner of a mature male
voice. "You're the guy on the news, the one caught by the
revolutionaries or somebody. So you're *that* Egan."

Kathryn glanced toward the windows in alarm. It
was dark outside and she hadn't done a thing for supper.
Like Ruth Ann, Nick was supposed to have weekends off
and he'd already done breakfast with the boys. She
swung her legs over the side of the couch and sat up
before her senses came to full alert. The sudden rush of

blood to her brain made her wince, for real this time. It all came back to her quickly—the soccer game, getting hit in the face with the ball. Tentatively, she touched her nose. Oh, good grief. Did it look as swollen as it felt?

"I ordered in pizza for supper," Nick said, poking his head in the door. "Didn't think you were up to cooking."

"Thanks." She didn't even want to eat, much less cook.

"All right, gang, the food's here!" Nick's shout even made her nose hurt and triggered regret that she'd not had an intercom system wired in when the house was redone. Communicating from floor to floor of the sprawling house was far from easy. With the poinging sounds and bells of the boys' video games running upstairs, shouting was a necessity. Even she had developed a drill sergeant's blast for those hearing-impaired occasions, during which she always used her children's full names. *Jason Avery Egan! Jeremy Brent Egan!* Use of all three of the boys' names meant serious business.

"Yo, Jase! Yo, Jer! Front and center! *Now!*"

The resulting chorus of acknowledgment and ensuing stampede down the steps revealed to Kathryn that shorter versions were just as effective, given their father's commanding voice. Nick was their hero. He could get them to jump over the moon. He could do no wrong in their eyes, while she, on the other hand, played the heavy, no matter how she tried to soften her demands with bribes of extra television or a rare trip for supper to a fast food place with the latest promotional toy. That hurt…even more than her nose.

Kathryn got up and went into the downstairs powder room to see if she looked as bad as she felt. She did. Her eyes and nose were welded together by one giant bruise. She'd seen losers in boxing matches come out looking better. Ever so gently she touched her nose, feeling the bridge and flexible gristle below it. It didn't appear to be broken, or at least it wasn't shifted to one side or the other. It was just big and puffy with an unbecoming red-black-and-blue color scheme.

How on earth could she go to work tomorrow looking like this? Sunglasses would only cover so much, if she could even stand the pressure of them on her face. Disheartened, she went into the kitchen, but dinner was not set up there or in the dining room. A quick peek told her Nick and the boys had been busy with paper plates, napkins, sodas, and accessories in the family room while she took inventory of her injury.

There, stacked on a low eighteenth-century dropleaf table, was the main course in all its cholesterol-laden profusion.

What if the heat and grease turn the color of the wood? Her protest died on her lips, though, when she saw that they'd covered the impeccably polished top with newspaper. It fell short on ambience but was effective.

When Nick helped Jeremy light a candle in a blown-glass globe from the dining room, she had to laugh. She'd paid over a hundred dollars for the handcrafted glass in Williamsburg to grace gourmet extravaganzas, and now it presided over carryout pizza.

155

"You guys are something else."

"Feeling better, are we?"

"If you call carrying an aching melon that feels like it's pulling the front of your face off better." Kathryn gave a good-natured shrug.

She sat on the sofa, noticing for the first time the pleasant fire Nick had built in the hearth while she slept. It looked so right...soot-blackened firebrick and all. Candlelight, firelight, and...

Kathryn looked on the TV screen to see what Jeremy was tuning into. Disney, she recognized. The perfect family evening right out of a fifties television show, except Ma Cleaver looked as if she'd been on the losing end of a round in a heavyweight boxing match.

After saying grace, Nick handed the boys plates and told them to dig in. Which they did. With gusto. The perfect picture of adoring children and beloved father—

"Can I get you a soda?" Nick intruded on her thoughts.

"That would be great, thanks. Oh, and another pill. That last one has worn off."

Earlier, just as she'd drifted off to a pain-free nether land, Nick insisted she take something for the swelling and discomfort that was sure to follow. It was the best thing they could do, considering that even if her nose had been fractured, no one could do anything about it until the swelling went down. Nick had suffered enough football injuries to know that much. Besides, this was definitely better than sitting for hours in the hospital

emergency room, only to be told to come back later fo
an accurate diagnosis.

"This is just like that dinner theater you took us to,
Jeremy ventured, his mouth full of pizza. "Fancy, huh?"

"Yeah, except we don't have to dress up and the
food is better here," Jason put in.

"An' the show is cartoon instead of real people dancing around and singing like dummies."

Kathryn let the criticism slide without comment.
She'd thought the boys should be well rounded in their
cultural education and that a musical at a local dinner
theater might contribute toward that end. Their father's
sons, they lost all interest when the singing started. They
made fun of the dancing. She finally had to call them out
for playing hockey with spoons and an olive after the
olive landed in Paul's lap.

"Fresh ice pack for the lady and a cold soda." Nick
placed the drink in front of her on the table they'd pulled
in front of the sofa and handed her the medicine for the
swelling and pain. "Now you just sit back and enjoy the
show, madame. Moi and les boys are at your disposal."

"Sorry I cut your soccer game short." Kathryn tried
to ignore Nick as he dropped down comfortably next to
her on the plump sofa. She supposed if he wanted to be
within arm's reach of the food that was the only seat left
On either side of the table, the boys sat on the floor i
oriental fashion on the oversized pillows they used t
make themselves comfortable while watching televisio

"Gee, Kate, it's *our* story," Nick quipped when t

screen introduced the Disney classic *Lady and the Tramp*.

"Right!"

"Did you and Dad have dogs once upon a time?" Jeremy's eyes were wide.

Kathryn didn't like pets in the house. The kitten, Buttons, who was sitting under the drop-leaf table in desperate hopes that a tidbit or two might be dropped, was the first exception she'd made to the rule. After all, the kitten had already moved in, kit and caboodle, by the time Kathryn was approached with the decision.

"Nah." The twinkle in Nick's eye was aimed at Kathryn. "*I* was a tramp, a guy from the poor side of town, and your mom was a classy lady."

"Did Mom run away from home and you help her get back?"

"Dad's just pulling your leg, squirt! Sheesh, you believe anything!"

"Do not!" Jeremy's chin jutted out as he glared at his older brother.

"Do too!"

"Do not!"

"Do—"

"Just watch the movie, guys, and eat before your pizza gets cold," Nick reminded them.

"*You* started it!" Kathryn reminded him. She settled against the back, letting his comparison slide. Her parents had not approved of Nick. He was a farm boy and a jock, not likely to fit in the Sinclair social circles. At least he'd proved them wrong there. Nick was at home

wherever he went. Maybe too much so, she mused, considering that his real home was the place he seldom stayed more than a few days.

Without realizing it, she picked up a piece of the pizza and took a cautious bite. She hadn't been hungry until she saw it, steaming before her, wickedly caloric. It was hard to recall the last time she'd sent out for fast food, what with Ruth Ann being such a good and diligent cook and Kathryn insisting on healthy meals.

While Nick and the boys watched the show, she was content to watch them. If she didn't know better, it would appear that this was the perfect family, the parents seated together, the children at their feet, watching a wholesome show. *This* is what she'd always wanted.

At the moment, it would be so easy to simply give in and take Nick back, but she couldn't. She'd trusted her heart to him once and he'd neglected it. This was just a fairy tale for now. When reality hit in the form of a great job offer, it would be over.

No, Disney didn't show what happened with the rich girl and the poor boy after the honeymoon was over. She'd learned the hard way that there was no happily ever-after. She wouldn't be taken in. She couldn't. She only prayed God would help her keep the boys from knowing the same hurt and sense of abandonment she'd suffered. But if he'd heard her prayer, he certainly wasn't showing it. The boys were going to be devastated, and there was nothing she could do to stop it. Nothing...

Later, Kathryn was sitting and staring into the fire

when Nick came downstairs after tucking the boys in. They'd insisted she be content with a good-night kiss and rest while their dad put them down. She was hardly aware of Nick's return until he sat down beside her and handed her a fresh pack of crushed ice, the last of her frozen peas having outlived their usefulness.

"Well, it's been an entire week and I don't think you have anything to complain about, do you? Unless you count the black eyes and the big nose."

Kathryn couldn't resist smiling. "You have truly amazed me, Nick." She tried to think of something witty to add, but his gentle caress of her cheek robbed her of any coherent thought.

"It's not been that hard. You've done a wonderful job with the boys, Kate. I want to thank you for giving me a chance to get to know them."

How easy it would be to melt before the warmth kindling in his earnest gaze, or to lean against the arm he casually placed on the back of the sofa.

"And thanks for tonight."

"Tonight?" She had to draw herself from the spell before it was too late. There'd be no more moonlight kisses cooling in the warmth of the sun for her.

Nick inclined his head. "For humoring us. I doubt the show was that riveting, what with the discomfort of your nose and all."

"Not at all. I enjoyed it too."

Nick gave a wistful smile and studied her face—her lips in particular.

Kathryn's breath caught in her throat, wedged by her tripping pulse. He was going to kiss her, and if he did, she feared she wouldn't be strong enough to fight this invisible force drawing them ever closer, despite reason. Part of her urged retreat while another whispered surrender. Amenities were over. What held the moment frozen in time was raw emotion.

She moistened her lips at the feel of his breath, no more than a heartbeat away. His arm, which had rested innocently on the sofa back, now circled behind her, his fingers slipping up into the silk of her hair. It was easy to revel in their heady massage, to sway against them, to bare her throat to the risk of a thousand hot kisses.

"Ah, Kate," he sighed, backing away with a disconsolate expression. "If only we had spaghetti."

It took a moment for his meaning to sink in. The recollection of the two animated dogs nibbling at opposite ends of a strand of pasta until their lips met was like a dousing of ice water on Kathryn's heightened senses. Before she could think of retaliation, Nick climbed to his feet and stretched lazily.

"But I guess I blew my chance for spaghetti, didn't I?"

"Years ago." Her response was cool, stung as she was by the cruel play with her emotions. Gathering her glass from the table, she retreated to the kitchen with what dignity she could muster. Nick hadn't changed. Life was a game for him. He reveled in playing the master. Except this time, the pawn had a will of her own. So help her, it wouldn't happen again!

Soccer practice began that week. True to his word, Nick saw that Jason made the practice and did his homework before any other recreation, managing still to have a hot meal on the table by the time Kathryn arrived home. Upon questioning him as to where he acquired his culinary skill, when frozen dinners had been his specialty before, he shrugged and pointed out to her that if one could read, one could cook.

Dinner conversation revolved around the practice and events of the day. She had to admit, Nick possessed a knack for getting the boys to talk. She'd heard more in a few days about what they were doing in school and their latest interests than she had since she'd first put them on a school bus. Perhaps it was his reporter instinct or maybe Nick had really found his calling as a father. For the boys' sake, she hoped it was the latter.

"Did it ever occur to you, Kathryn, that Nick's experience in the prison may have actually changed him for the better?" David Marsh replied after she'd complained about the growing hero worship in the Egan home. "Besides, you said yourself that you needed a stronger hand with Jason."

"Jason has an older playmate, that's all."

"What about the teacher's note?"

Jason's teacher had sent a message to Kathryn praising Jason's renewed interest in his schoolwork.

"She loves Nick too." Kathryn threw up her hands. "Everyone does! My neighbor thinks he's adorable. For all intents and purposes, save mine, he's a bloomin' saint."

"But to you, he's a devil in disguise." David bit the flap of a cardboard box he was unpacking and growled with a demonic gleam in his eye.

"Just what I need. Another joker!"

Kathryn flipped the Closed sign on the customer entrance. A rare lull in the late-afternoon business had given her and David a chance to set up some new displays. As she reached for her coat on the handsome Victorian rack behind her desk, she gave in to a sneeze. Despite her efforts to resist, Jeremy's germ had plagued her all day, which did nothing for the *sports* injury she'd taken so much teasing over.

"Bless you!"

"Thanks." She sniffed, rubbing her tender nose with a tissue. The swelling had gone down considerably and the bruise now had a yellowish cast. "The dust in here is awful. Good thing we got most of the unpacking done before the cleaning crew comes tonight."

David helped her into her wrap. "Want to hear what I think?"

"Do I have a choice?" She softened the question with a teasing smile, then broke off with another sneeze. She'd taken an antihistamine earlier, but it wasn't doing the trick.

"Not really." Her companion produced a tissue box for her convenience. "I think you're afraid of Nick."

"I'm afraid of him hurting the boys by growing close

to them and then leaving."

"*You're* afraid of getting hurt, Kathryn. You've kept your heart boxed and on a shelf for so long, you're afraid to set it free again. How many times have I heard you say that you wished you'd given him one more chance?"

"That was when I thought he was dead, David."

"So fate didn't accommodate you!"

Kathryn had to chuckle at David's shrug.

Seeing he had her attention, he went on. "Look ahead, Kathryn. Focusing on the past can make you bitter, like Lot's wife who insisted on looking back instead of forward. She turned to salt, and frankly, your attitude where Nick is concerned smacks of brine."

"I'm not bitter!" Kathryn argued against the seed of doubt so masterfully planted by her assistant. She'd heard of people being haunted by their past, but haunted by Scripture learned over the years? What on earth possessed David to use a biblical reference? He didn't actively practice his faith as far as she knew. Still, she admired him for his honesty and straightforwardness. That was why she felt comfortable talking to him about her personal life, although not at the moment. "I have reason to be wary."

A rattle at the locked front door drew Kathryn's attention to the street, now sparkling with seasonal lights. She was about to tell David to stand ready by the security alarm when she recognized Jeremy's face plastered against the glass show window. Surprised, Kathryn unlocked the door and admitted Nick and her sons.

"What is *this* about?" She was careful to close and

lock up behind them. The crime rate in the district was among the highest in the country, although the Emporium had never been burglarized nor any of its customers harassed.

"We guys were going out to celebrate and thought you'd like to come along. We're headed for the Burger Palace."

Kathryn turned to Jason, framing his joy-bright face in her hands. "You made the team!" She'd become so involved in work, she'd almost forgotten the big tryout was today. At his proud nod, she hugged him. There were a million things for her to think about and she had only one small mind. There were times she felt pea brained, and this was one of them.

"Well, congratulations! You've certainly worked hard to earn it."

"Our first game is next Friday." He fished a folded schedule out of his pocket.

"And there's more."

Distracted, Kathryn looked at Nick expectantly. "I am now employed with the local news team at *Metro Journal*. They called this morning for an interview and made me an offer I couldn't refuse."

"Are you sure this is what you want to do? After all, our local news isn't quite as fascinating and exciting as that in a foreign country." And surely Nick would be taking a cut in pay to work locally. The *Metro Journal* couldn't possibly afford to meet his global network wages. There had to be a catch.

"I told you before, I've had all of that sort of excitement I can stand. My priorities have changed. I want to be near my family."

"Case closed!" David Marsh announced behind them. At Kathryn's sharp look, he lifted the box he'd been unpacking. "*This* case is closed. That's it. I'm done for the day."

Leaving his desk, the rascal offered a congratulatory hand to Jason. "I've never been too interested in sports, but I'll certainly turn out to see my buddy here play." He glanced over at Jeremy, who'd immediately become fascinated by a carousel from Germany on display, and made sure to include him, too. "But *you'll* have to tell me when to cheer, deal?"

Jeremy shook his hand. "Deal!"

"So how about it, Kate? Are you up for burgers and fries?"

"I hear they have a passing fair salad bar," David informed her before extending congratulations to Nick as well. "And if you are as superb a news writer as I hear you are a housekeeper and nanny, you'll be running the show in no time! I'm always willing to admit when I've made a mistake in judgment, and that seems to be the case here. Good work, Mr. Egan."

"Call me Nick."

"Glad to!" Looking past Nick's broad shoulders, David scowled. "Isn't that Paul Radisson climbing out of that cab?"

Paul! Kathryn groaned silently. She'd forgotten she'd

promised during a hasty phone call this afternoon to go to dinner with him tonight. What was wrong with her brain?

"Oh, boys, Mom's taken too many antihistamines in all this dust today," she groaned in apology. "I forgot I told Mr. Paul that I'd go to dinner with him tonight. I did leave a message on our answering machine." She seized upon that sudden memory as though it were a lifeline to her sanity. She looked at Nick expectantly.

"I picked up the boys from school for soccer practice right after my interview."

That explained that, Kathryn thought, torn as to what to do. Jason was so excited. This was his big night, and he'd done so well in school to get this far.

"Paul!" Kathryn called out as David let him into the building. Outside a cab waited with blinking lights. "Paul, something has come up and I'm going to have to back out. Jason made the soccer team and this is his celebration night."

If her decision upset him, Paul didn't show it. He clapped Jason on the shoulder. "Way to go, son. Your mom told me your schoolwork is improving too."

"And Dad's got a new job so he can live with us all the time now," Jeremy volunteered.

Paul stared at Nick, eyebrows raised. "You took a *local* job?"

Nick's gaze was as firm as his tone. "I meant what I said about coming home to stay."

Clearly taken aback, Paul recovered from his shock

gracefully. "All the luck, then." A second glance at Kathryn, however, gave him another jolt. He stared, his mouth dropping open, then managed, "My word, what happened to your face?"

Kathryn gave him the canned account of the soccer incident. She'd explained it to so many people during the course of the past few days it was well rehearsed. Paul was no different from anyone else who'd asked her. It was clear from his expression that he had a hard time picturing her as a goalie, much less one lunging into the path of a soccer ball. But then, who'd have pictured her straddling a rooftop, either?

She gave a weary shrug. "Actually, it looks wonderful compared to what it looked like at first."

After a bit of fawning attention, the attorney smoothly shifted his tact regarding his plans for the evening. He was a formidable opponent in a courtroom where thinking on one's feet was a necessity.

"Then what do you say we *all* go out then? I've a bit of celebrating of my own to do. I just closed the deal on the Malchow building."

To her dismay, the decision was turned over to Kathryn by every eye in the room. Caught between the proverbial rock and a hard place, she took the path of least resistance. "Why not? David, why don't you come with us too?"

"And miss the symphony Christmas show at the center? Thanks, but no thanks. You all get going so I can lock up."

"Where to?" Paul asked. "I have a cab waiting."

Both boys chimed in at once in decided agreement and delight. "Burger Palace!"

Kathryn had booked Jason's birthday there one year. The king's colorful court of tunic- and leotard-clad clerks and a roaming jester and magician kept them thoroughly entertained. While Paul was a master of composure in a courtroom, this was clearly a far cry from what he expected. If Kathryn hadn't felt like the rope in a tug-of-war, she might have laughed at his discomfited expression.

"Quite a plunge from what I had in mind, but why not? It's been a while since I had a common burger and fries." He slipped his arm easily around Kathryn's waist. "You can ride with me, dear. We'll meet your gang there."

"There's room in the van for all of us." Nick's strained smile portrayed contained annoyance, as did the telltale tick of his jawline. "I think we can squeeze you in the back."

Looking like the slick cat that swallowed the goldfish, Paul waved the suggestion aside. "Thanks, but no. I've got a little surprise of my own to share with Kathryn on the way. We'll meet you there."

"Now *that's* an intriguing suggestion!" Caught in the middle, Kathryn was feeling more frayed by the moment. "We'll meet you guys later." Giving each of her sons a good-bye pinch on the cheek, she allowed Paul to usher her outside to the taxi and called her good-bye to

Nick over her shoulder, not daring to make eye contact. Yet she could feel the man's gaze on her, even if she didn't see it. Nick didn't like taking a second seat to anyone, and that's just what she'd done, made him second choice.

Well, he'll just have to live with it. She settled against the back of the seat while her companion gave the driver instructions. The tension between Nick and Paul had really thrown her off, Kathryn realized as she wondered for the first time why Paul hadn't driven over himself.

"Wescott Hills?" She looked at Paul, startled by the address she overheard. "That's your condo complex! Burger Palace is on *this* side of the beltway."

"We're just taking a little detour." The deep tan lines of Paul's face crinkled in mischief. "I found a place for you and the boys in my own building. The price is right, too."

Kathryn stared at him, speechless. She hadn't had time to look at the classifieds, so she knew she should be grateful. But all she felt was irritated. Why was everyone trying to take over her life?

He went on. "I knew you were in a pickle, and when I heard from the doorman that the Mesinos were moving, I asked the building manager to give you the first option. Kathryn, I can't bear the thought of you trapped in that house with Egan."

He meant well, she told herself. And if not for her strong suspicion that his motives were more selfish than considerate, his gesture would have been sweet.

"I appreciate this, Paul, but there's no point in our going to Wescott Hills. I don't want a condominium. I want a home in a neighborhood with kids the boys' ages."

"Just take a look—"

"I will *not* be late for Jason's celebration, Paul!" Sliding forward, she tapped on the cab window. "We've changed our minds. We're going straight to Marion Mall to the Burger Palace."

"Just in time," the driver remarked dourly. He shut off the turn signal and passed the beltway turnoff where cars had slowed to a crawl to access.

"Honestly, Kathryn—"

"Honestly *what?*" Her face grew warm with indignation. "What gives you the right to waltz in and spirit me away from my family for something like this without consulting me first?"

"I thought—"

"You *thought,* you didn't ask! I can do my own thinking, Paul, and make my own decisions."

"I never said you couldn't." Now it was Paul's face that showed signs of increasing heat. "Kathryn, you're a bright, intelligent, lovely woman who, for the moment, is in over her head in a sticky situation."

"I am in control of the situation!"

"Like you were the other night when I walked in and found you standing in the hall wearing nothing but a blanket?"

Kathryn took a sustaining breath. "That was sheer

happenstance. I can assure you, I have been fully clothed ever since."

At the same instant, both Kathryn and Paul cut their eyes toward the driver, whose ear was pressed against the sliding plastic window at full attention. Paul's solemn expression faltered first and Kathryn's followed. She could imagine what the man must be thinking.

"Regardless—" she folded her arms across her chest—"I'm doing just fine. Nick is just…well, he's Nick."

"That's what worries me. I don't want to see you hurt again. If you recall, I was there to pick up the pieces."

An acknowledging smile touched her lips. "You've always been there, I know. I'm sorry I blew up." Maybe David was right. Maybe she *was* turning bitter as salt, even with those who didn't deserve it. "Truce?"

"Truce." Paul pulled her into his arms and lowered his mouth to hers, but Kathryn turned away at the last moment.

Stiffly, he released her as the cab braked to turn into the parking lot, where a giant neon castle dominated the scene and Burger Palace banners waved from the parapets.

"Promise me one thing," he whispered, clearly loath to release her. "Say you'll go with me next weekend with the Malchows to their ski lodge."

"Oh, Paul, I don't think I can take off—"

"You said this afternoon that until more stock came

in, the only thing to do was work the showroom. David can do that." He pressed his forehead against hers. "You've been burning the candle at both ends; you need a break. Besides, they really like you, though I can't for the life of me figure why."

Kathryn let the tease slide. "I don't know, Paul, with Nick's coming back…"

"It's business, Kathryn! They own lots of investment property in the area. Look at it as the perfect opportunity, one you can't afford to miss…*especially* with Nick coming back."

"Six bucks even," the driver announced from the front seat.

Kathryn backed away, straightening her coat with annoyed tugs while Paul paid the fare. Ever the gentleman, he got out and opened the door and held it for her.

"I'll think about it." She glanced toward the flashing castle gate, wondering if Nick and the boys were already inside.

A burst of light from the vehicle parked abreast of them came on, drawing her attention to where Jason and Jeremy emerged, play fighting. Nick climbed out the other side and locked up, his face inscrutable despite the glare of the pole lights overhead.

"You go on with your family and enjoy. I'm heading back home," Paul told her as Jeremy seized her hand and began to tug anxiously.

She ought to be relieved that she wouldn't have to referee Nick and Paul, but it also bothered her that once

Paul didn't get his way, he was bailing out on an evening with the boys.

"Change of plans?" Nick called out, his long-legged stride easily catching him up with them.

"Yes, but you folks enjoy. Congratulations again, Jason boy!" Paul held out his hand to Jason. Hands shoved in his pockets, Jason grunted an acknowledgment as Paul turned from him to buss Kathryn unexpectedly on the cheek. The eldest of the Egan boys had never liked Paul, and now Kathryn was beginning to see why. Stuffy, her son called him. *Presumptuous* was actually the word that came to her mind.

As the cab pulled away and headed toward the mall exit light, Nick cuffed Jason on the back of the head playfully, but there was no nonsense in his voice. "Jason, the next time a gentleman offers you his hand, you take it. It's simply good manners. You want to be treated like a man, you act like one."

Jason nodded and then darted to the castle gate.

"Get us a table for four!" Nick waved him on; then stood back, waiting for Kathryn to precede him.

She rewarded him with an approving smile. At least they agreed on something. And a table for four sounded so nice, so warm and cozy. If she were honest, she had to admit that she'd rather be here with the boys than in some fancy restaurant with Paul and his clients. The revelation stunned her. Maybe her sons' tastes were rubbing off on her after all. She glanced down and smiled at Jeremy as he tugged on her hand. The boy's scowl surprised her, but not nearly as much as his words.

"Gee, Mom, does Mr. Paul kiss you a lot?"

Nine

"HEY, NOSY, THAT'S YOUR MOM'S BUSINESS. SHE'S A BIG GIRL."

Kathryn could have kissed Nick for his gallant defense...almost. There had to be a catch somewhere. He was never one to give up easily.

"Mom and Mr. Paul are just friends. Get real, Jeremy!" Jason's furrowed brow, however, indicated that he was not quite at ease with the idea himself.

"Besides—" Nick flashed her an irresistible grin— "that wasn't a real kiss. *This* is a real kiss!"

Before Kathryn realized what he was about, his arms closed around her and his mouth covered hers. What protest she might have made was frozen in shock—a shock that the warmth of Nick's lips slowly thawed, turning the strength in her knees to water.

"All right, Dad!" Jeremy's blue eyes were aglow with delight.

"That *was* a kiss," Jason admitted in gruff embarrassment.

Still dumbstruck, Kathryn staggered backward. As a reprimand formed on her lips, Nick gave her that incorrigible grin of his and pointed over her head.

"Mistletoe!"

Jeremy's attention was instantly diverted from matters of the heart by one of the king's jesters, who was doing hat tricks at a nearby table. Jason opted to give up Kathryn and Nick's company just as quickly after looking about to be certain none of his friends had witnessed their folly.

Maybe she *should* move into the condo Paul found as soon as possible so the boys wouldn't get mixed signals as to her and Nick's relationship, Kathryn thought, her legs still shaky from Nick's surprise attack. Heaven knew she didn't want to build them up for disappointment there, either. How could she make them understand that just because they did things together as a family, they were not a family. It was cruel to mislead the boys, even if Nick meant nothing by it. And he didn't. She *knew* that.

Kathryn said as much to Nick later, after the boys were in bed. The house was quiet and water was heating on the stove for a relaxing tea. Doubt and confusion pummeled her mind and her shoulders, making them ache from tension.

"I don't know, Kate. We've laid it on the table for them, that this is a temporary setup until Ruth Ann comes back. They just don't want to accept it, I guess."

blowup. It wasn't nearly as disconcerting as not knowing what to expect.

"No need to call Mrs. Anderson. I can do it. Her husband told me at soccer practice that she's out of sorts, drinking some kind of weight-loss stuff that didn't agree with her." He sniffed the steaming tea. "This isn't some of that brew, is it? Not that you need to lose weight."

The corner of his lip curled and humor dissipated the storm clouds. "What is the woman, obsessed or something? She doesn't look that big to me."

It *seemed* over…at least for now. Kathryn laughed nervously. "Karrie's a fitness fanatic. She's got to try every new trend, whether she needs to or not. Regardless, she should be fine by the time I go away. You've done enough."

"Now look!" Nick held up a warning finger. "You said you wanted to be friends. Well, I'm being one. Friends help out friends. I'll keep the kids. We'll camp in the family room all weekend. Deal?" He extended his hand across the table with an inquiring lift of his brow.

Why did she feel like she was inching over the edge of a cliff? Kathryn tentatively slipped her hand into his. "Okay, deal."

"Friends?"

"Friends." Wary unrest still nagged at the back of her mind.

Kathryn withdrew her hand from Nick's before it grew too comfortable there and concentrated on her tea. The muscle relaxer she'd taken earlier was starting to

Nick's smile looked forced. "Can't say I blame them. I certainly don't want to accept it either."

Determined to sidestep the land mine Nick laid before her, Kathryn remained silent, retrieving two cups from the cabinet. Then she sorted through the various types of tea bags she kept in a decorative tin, still at a loss for words to divert the direction of the conversation.

"You have to admit, of late we've had some golden times, the *four* of us."

She didn't need to be reminded of that. It only added to her quandary. "It's like a honeymoon. It won't last forever."

The bitterness in her reply astounded her. After six and a half years and all that had passed since Nick's disappearance and his world-shattering reappearance, one would think her emotions might have healed a bit.

Kathryn felt Nick's closeness behind her even before he lightly brought his hands to rest at her waist. Her self-analysis vanished with increasing awareness of the source of her quandary.

"We could try to make it that way, Katie girl."

She stiffened to fight the ripple of weakness he evoked by using his most intimate nickname. Memories of shared passion and joy flooded her mind, unbidden. Having prided herself on setting boundaries since her failed relationship with Nick, Kathryn steeled her mind-set. This could be a boardroom. He could be a client who was suggesting something that simply wouldn't work. She would change his mind.

Methodically, she ripped open two tea-bag envelopes and placed the bags in the cups before turning and stepping away, her manner aloof.

"We did, Nick." She forced her tone to be matter-of-fact. "Many times. It didn't work. You were always good in the starting lineup, but not for the entire game."

"I've had new training. Look at what I've done here so far. Any complaints?"

She poured the hot water into the cups and handed one to him. "It's just the starting half, Nick." Kathryn minced out the words as much for her own benefit as for her companion's. If he only knew how easy it would be to believe this would last, to listen to her feelings instead of her mind.

"So I guess we need to just take this one play at a time." His gaze held hers, searching…but for what? For a reassurance she couldn't give him?

She pushed away the sudden tears pricking her eyes. "This isn't a game, Nick; it's our lives. I…I truly hope you will continue to be the wonderful father you've been to the boys, but it's too late for us. Somehow we need to get that through to the boys."

Nick shoved away the cup of tea untouched. "*You* do, Kate, not me."

"Yes, I do…because *you* won't help. For their sake, it's imperative we remain friends, but that's all we are, Nick. Now and in the future."

Feeling backed in a corner, more by what Nick *didn't* say than by what he did, Kathryn braced herself with a

deep breath. She had to do something. She had to prov that his return meant nothing, that she was still in con trol of her life. Maybe not to Nick and the boys, but least to herself.

"Next weekend, I'll be going with Paul to Poconos for a retreat with the Malchows on busin We'll be leaving after Paul's annual office party."

"Was *that* his big surprise?"

"No. He'd found an apartment for me, but I w house for the boys. And the trip is strictly busin could get more work from the Malchows. They ov of property locally."

There was a long silence, one Kathryn fel pelled to fill. "I don't expect you to sit with the c I'm going to call Karrie Anderson to see if the b spend the weekend there."

"So was Paul's good-bye kiss *strictly busines*

"I believe you said that was my business."

Nick shrugged, but his expression told h not exactly indifferent to her reply. He Kathryn sipped her tea, waiting for the tellta gathering in the recesses of his gaze to ignite, He reconsidered the tea and carried it counter where he took a stool next to her.

"Okay, you're right, Kate. If this isn't g out for us, we at least have to be friends."

Once again, Kathryn waited with bate might blow up and walk out, but he neve Not without a catch. She almost pref

kick in. Until Nick showed up, she'd never been one to rely much on prescription medicine, having such a low tolerance for it.

"So what are your plans for next Wednesday evening, *friend?*"

"Wednesday?"

Kathryn's mind stumbled over the swift change of tactics Nick Egan was noted for. Get the person being interviewed relaxed, then zero in on the subject he or she may want to avoid. She scrambled for time to think. "Is this a trick question?"

"No, no trick. The newspaper staff is having a Christmas party and decided to make me the guest of honor, and I was wondering if you'd go with me. I haven't exactly had time to find a date the past week," he explained quickly. "All this housework and child chauffeuring…" Nick grabbed his head as though to tear out his hair, and raised the pitch of his voice. "It's driving me hormonal or something!"

Kathryn couldn't help but snicker. Unfortunately, it was with a mouthful of tea. She quickly covered her mouth to catch the spray but couldn't stop what went up her nose.

Nick went on. "I've even started to answer the phone with a grunted 'Yo!' from being around the boys and their buddies so much. And heaven knows, they don't appreciate my cookies."

"You—" Kathryn broke off with a strangled cough. Some of the tea had gone down her throat the wrong way. "You don't *bake!*"

"No, but I have to pick them out of scores of scrumptious-looking treats and brave the grocery store parking lot to get them. I'd rather parallel park during the Indy 500 any day. It's a lot safer! And don't get me started on the one-way rules of the school driveway and the power-incensed matrons in orange vests!"

"All right, Mr. Mom!"

"And how do you get home without eating half of the cookies and having to go back to get more?"

Nick could be adorable and funny when he chose to.

"I ration myself," Kathryn responded, trying to sober. "How can you expect the boys to be disciplined about their eating habits if you aren't?"

"Don't eat in front of them?"

The idea obviously never occurred to the man! Kathryn slid off the counter stool and carried her empty cup and saucer to the sink. "You're hopeless, Egan."

"So what about Wednesday evening? Will you go…as my friend, of course. Everyone is anxious to meet the great roof climber of Egan Court."

"Oh, great! I thought I'd lived that down." She'd lost count of the prank phone calls she'd received to rescue pets out on roofs and in trees after Nick's homecoming rescue made the news. The local fire department had even sent her a plaque of recognition as a joke.

"Besides, my boss's wife wants to talk to you about decorating ideas for the offices and lobby of the building, so you won't feel totally out of your element."

Out of her element was exactly how Kathryn felt around Nick's friends and colleagues. They had the most exciting lives and stories, compared to finding the perfect matching carpet for someone's ancient family heirloom. However, now she had nothing to prove to these people as far as being worthy of being the star reporter's wife. Her life was as exciting as she wanted it to be, even if a far cry from what most of Nick's cronies were accustomed to.

"I'll check my calendar, but I think I can make it." Kathryn knew she'd been set up for this, but somehow she didn't mind. Maybe it was the way Nick asked instead of simply expecting her to go; he'd softened her up with his humor, poking fun at himself.

She checked her watch and gasped when she saw the time. It was nearly eleven o'clock and she had an early meeting with the fabric suppliers in the morning. Besides, she was sleepy now from the medicine, relaxed, even if the state was medically induced. Nick could ask her to marry him right now and she'd think, why not? Well, not quite. Kathryn closed the dishwasher after putting in her dishes.

As she started out of the room toward the hall stairwell, she slapped Nick on the back.

"Good night, Mr. Mom. I'm out of here and morning will be here before you know it."

"Does that make you Ms. Mom?"

She chuckled again softly and waved away his light comment, making her getaway before she was snagged again for something she didn't see coming. *She who fights and runs away, lives to fight another day....*

Or at least, run away again.

Nick's grin faded as Kathryn climbed the steps to her room, their room, for the night. The suffocating mask of agreeability could come off now. He'd barely been able to keep track of the small talk regarding the Andersons and what great neighbors and friends they'd been. And, while he did want Kate to accompany him to the Christmas party and managed to garner a yes, his mind was hard put to the maneuver.

What he'd wanted to do was explode, to turn loose all this pent-up anger and frustration that the woman he loved was going away for a weekend with his former best friend, even if it was *strictly business*. Maybe that's what Kate thought it was, but Nick seriously doubted Paul Radisson saw it that way. He knew the man too well. What was God doing to him? Hadn't he suffered enough without this? He'd vowed to make up for all his past mistakes, but what if Kathryn didn't give him the chance to?

He contemplated the delicate teacup, knowing full well he could crush it in the palm of his hand, breaking it beyond repair. But in doing so, he'd cut himself. There was a time that wouldn't have stopped him. His life had been one where emotion and instinct led him...straight to imprisonment and a failed marriage. That's what following *his* will had gained him.

A multitude of doubts clouded Nick's mind until his head ached and the heart he'd opened to Christ screamed from the torture. So was he to meekly stand by and baby-sit while the woman he loved went away with another man? How could he endure it?

Hands clasped at his temples, Nick pleaded for an answer, but none came. At least none he could discern. God knew he was no priest. He was just a man, imperfect at that. God's will wasn't as clear to him as it had been to his Christian mentor. Sometimes it wasn't even clear to Papa Rico, but the little man of a great God had never failed to remind the imprisoned flock when they foundered in darkness and despair, not knowing what the morrow might bring, that they were not alone.

"We must not be like the Israelites in the desert, who enjoy the Lord's blessing, but the moment one lousy thing goes wrong, they turn from him. They think he is against them now. That is what the devil is for, no? The Lord, he would never leave them and he did not, even though they deserved to be left with their faithlessness. The Lord God will not leave us either. Never will he forsake us! Now, you gonna stay in the desert and complain, or are you going to the Promised Land like the Lord promised you can? Me, I go to the Promised Land."

Nick's problem was that there was a Promised Land on this side of heaven—the complete reunion with his wife. At the top of the steps, he turned away from the corridor leading to the master suite, away from the heaven he wanted most at the moment. He had to trust. He *had* to. God give him rest. Give him strength. Give him peace.

Nick knew God didn't always answer prayers in the manner and especially in the time frame man expected, but he always answered them. That was all that kept him going in the days that followed—that and a concerted effort to make the most out of the concessions God *did* hand him where Kathryn was concerned.

She went with him and the boys to Jason's practice game that weekend and not a complaint was made when they opted to make a day of the unseasonable spot of warm weather to picnic at the zoo later on bologna and peanut butter and jelly sandwiches. In fact, unless he was misreading her, she really enjoyed herself. That horizontal line of concern often creasing her forehead just above her eyes when she came home from work or brought work home with her vanished, stretched into nonexistence by laughter at his and the boys' antics.

While she declined to go to Sunday service with them, she offered no objection to going to see a local dinner theater's rendition of Dickens's *A Christmas Carol*, where he kept the boys' interest up by pointing out the amazing mechanics of the staging changes when the story started losing their attention. True, the good times were shared through the boys. Nick would've preferred to sit next to his wife with his arm about her shoulders and revel in her nearness, but, like it or not, he had to take this one day at a time, one play at a time, according to God's rules, not his.

The evening of the Christmas party, Kathryn was

truly a gift on his arm as they entered the club room at the yacht club. She wore the same ensemble she'd had on the night of his arrival—sleek, backless, and enough to rob any red-blooded man of his breath. She carried herself like a queen, but Nick had not missed the last-minute inspection she gave herself before they left home. There in the mirror, staring back at her regal image, he'd been amazed to see her eyes filled with self-doubt, like those of an unseasoned debutante making her first entrance into society.

What in the world did she have to be uncertain about? Surely a gathering like this didn't make her nervous. She'd taken on much more sophisticated crowds and been a virtual star.

And yet...Nick frowned, remembering. Kate had never seemed as up for his gatherings and parties as he had been. More often than not, she'd opted to stay home. He'd thought she was just being reclusive. But he'd seen firsthand how well she handled herself in a crowd at the party she'd held in their home.

Understanding dawned. Of course. In their home. On her turf. Kate was cool and confident in her own element. But in Nick's world, it was another story.

He watched her carefully that night as he introduced her to his new employers. Seeing the caution, the uncertainty in her expression, his heart constricted. Had she always been unsettled and intimidated by his colleagues and coworkers? Had his limelight blinded him to her insecurities as it had so many other things that had contributed to the near demise of their marriage?

Determined that she'd not have to face anyone here alone tonight, determined to *share* the moment with the woman he loved most, Nick broke away from the small group of fellow news writers who had smoothly spirited him away the moment his employer's wife asked Kathryn if she would take a look at the paper complex's antiquated decor.

"If I were you, Egan, I'd take a hard look at the development costs of your family estate...or any estate Radisson has had a hand in settling."

The mention of Paul Radisson stopped Nick in his tracks. Whether interest, instinct, or both lured him back to the conversation, which had started with a high government official's involvement in a real estate scandal, he didn't know. Regardless, it was taking a turn close to home.

"What are you saying?" He studied the burly senior investigative reporter of the *Metro Journal*. Lev Chandler had been in the business as long as Nick—they'd gone to school together. Lev had remained local purely by choice, not from lack of talent. If he smelled something rotten, chances were good there was something fishy somewhere.

Lev shrugged. "I'm saying there is a scam operation going on involving a Baltimore mortgage firm. They finance a developer who buys the farm at a nice price from ma and pa. Because it's such a good price and can save taxes hitting all at once, ma and pa are talked into agreeing to hold a note for a portion of the money… sometimes up to 50 percent. Of course, that note is secondary to the bank's mortgage."

"And the developer declares Chapter 11, the bank gets their share from the bankruptcy sale of the property, and ma and pa get nothing to show for their land, save a down payment," Nick finished dourly. It wasn't new. It was an old organized crime tactic. But that Paul Radisson might be involved in something like this was new indeed.

"Don't tell me." Nick fixed an intent look on Lev. "The list of the development corporation stockholders and those of the mortgage company share some of the same names."

"You got it."

"And Radisson is on both boards?"

"Now you have discovered the four corners of the bedsheet!" Lev Chandler finished his diet soda on the rocks and returned an unsmoked cigar to his mouth. He called it his pacifier because no one had seen him light it since he had a heart attack eight years ago. Until then, he'd been a walking smokestack with an inhuman tolerance for the worst food combinations Nick had ever seen ingested. A few years back Chandler could have easily posed as a poster child for heart and pulmonary disease. While still stocky, the man had trimmed down and changed to the point Nick almost hadn't recognized him. He wouldn't have, if it hadn't been for the ever-present cigar.

The thing that struck Nick most about his former acquaintance, however, was the change in his language, which had been unprintable and unfit for mixed company for as long as Nick could recall. Now, however, Lev's speech was as pristine as Katie's best cut crystal. The owner of the *Journal*, Syd Berman, said Lev "got religion" after his second heart attack.

Well, when a man is close to looking his Maker in the face, that's the last road open, Nick mused, knowing firsthand what that was all about. He glanced to where Kathryn was speaking with Ethel Berman. They were talking decorating, no doubt about it. Kate's face was more alive than all the glittering sequins adorning the female guests in the glow of the elaborate crystal chandeliers above. Far from being ill at ease any longer, she seemed to be right at home.

That was another mistake he'd made, expecting her to give up her passion so that he could pursue his. *Lord, there has to be a way to compromise, to fulfill our career passions and still be good spouses and parents.* Kate had done a great job alone, but together they could make a formidable team. He was sure of it.

Lev went on, "Just take a gander at the papers and see if your estate holds a second mortgage to Lands End Developers and the first is held by First Capital Mortgage Company. If you're holding paper for them, you might just find yourself bumped out of it in a bankruptcy auction further down the pike."

"Yeah, thanks for the tip. I'll get right on it." Nick

clenched his jaw. Paul Radisson was a shark. It was his business to be. Yet he couldn't believe the man would intentionally cheat Kate and the boys. Surely Paul's interest in Kate was sincere or she wouldn't be taken in by it. Not his Kate! She was gullible about a lot of things, but judging character wasn't one of them. The very idea that someone may have taken advantage of her made Nick's blood run hot.

"If you can work it in between soccer games and homework!"

Jarred from his thoughts, Nick turned to see the secretary, who'd been working with him since he'd accepted the new position, joining them. Marge Sigley's image matched the nineties grandmotherly advice she gave Nick when his exasperation with being a house dad pushed his patience. Her hair was short and stylish in a carefree cut, whitened by age and experience, but her eyes were as bright and energetic as the grandchildren she bragged about. No rocking chair for this grandma, who swore she only rocked on the dance floor.

"Marge, good to see you! You're looking great," he told her, complimenting the blue sequin-spotted pantsuit that flowed in a flattering manner over her petite figure. "Put my name on your dance card before it fills up."

"Flattery will get you everywhere." She stepped aside to bring her companion into the fold. "I brought someone over for you to meet...*again*, so she tells me. Do you remember Kit Cody from the EBS news team?

We've just bought some of her pictures."

A tall, broad-shouldered woman with sun-bleached hair swept up in a simple twist extended her hand to Nick. Her honey brown eyes full of enthusiasm struck a familiar, if unsettling, chord somewhere, but Nick returned her strong handshake while his mind raced. *Again?* Yes, he had met her, but where?

"Ms. Cody." *Ms.* was always a safe address.

"It's good to see you again, Nick. I had no idea when we wrapped up the shot in Pillar that you'd disappear on us the next day."

The new photographer! A stomach-churning panic sparked at the recognition of the newest member to the news team, a true rookie with stars in her eyes when it came to shooting star journalist Nick Egan. He'd forgotten the girl's name, but he hadn't forgotten that he'd awakened the morning before his capture in her room. She'd been shaking him cheerily with the announcement that they had a chopper to catch and urging him to get dressed quickly.

While memory failed him about that night before, it didn't take a genius to figure out what had happened. He'd just received the divorce papers to sign. The assignment was over. He'd had too much to drink and she'd been a sympathetic ear.

It was all Nick could do to withdraw his hand without acting as if the woman's touch had scalded him. God help him, this was all he needed for Kathryn to find out! He'd made a terrible mistake, one that had only added

to his list of transgressions where his marriage was concerned. Sure, it had been over, except for the finality of
his signature, but he'd not signed the blasted papers yet.
He couldn't bring himself to. Until then, he'd never been
unfaithful. Even so, he'd still loved Kate, although his
actions hadn't exactly proved it.

"So you're still in the business, Kit? Even with the
way we newshounds seem to be choice targets for every
nut that has a point to make?" He hoped his tone sounded
nothing more than polite.

"It's like you said that night, Nick; it's addictive. I'm
head of my own team now. We're moving out after the
holidays for Bosnia, but when I heard you were alive and
well, I just had to see for myself."

"Well, here I am, safe and home to *stay* this time.
Nothing cures addiction to news like capture and incar-
ceration by fanatics."

"I'd love to hear about it before I fly out again."

Nick stiffened as the girl put her hand on his arm.
Was her invitation as obvious to everyone else as it was
to him? At the same time, someone else claimed his
other arm gently. He turned to see Kathryn had joined
them.

"I don't mean to interrupt, Nick, but Mrs. Berman
wants everyone to take their seats for the meal."

"Absolutely, darling, but first, let me throw a bunch
of names at you, just to boggle your mind before we sit
down. Ladies and gentlemen, this is my *wife* Kathryn,
who has held down the fort like a seasoned trooper and

done a great job with our kids while I was away."

Slipping his hand casually behind Kathryn's back as though that contact alone kept him from going over the edge of panic, he made some hurried introductions.

"And this is Marge. She's been an immense help the past few days with homemaking advice...except she's not responsible for the pink-stained tie-dyed T-shirts. I put the red sweater in with them *before* I called her."

Actually the dingbat housekeeper for hire had done the deed, but Nick was the one left holding the bag. He'd called Marge to find out how to *undo* Laine's mistake.

Marge's giggle was infectious. "You should have heard him on the phone. He was in a panic!"

"Maybe you should take a stab at filling Erma Bombeck's void instead of the sports columns." Lev Chandler chuckled. "Oscar Madison with an apron!"

Nick ignored the jibe, turning to the last in the circle. "And this is Kit Cody, senior photographer for EBS. She's leaving on location after the New Year. Ms. Cody, this is my wife."

Kathryn glanced at him, then back at Kit as she shook the other woman's hand. He felt his heart pick up speed as he watched Kate's face; he could almost hear the wheels turning in his wife's beautiful head. Kit was attractive, confident, and clearly capable. Her bronzed skin, lack of makeup, and khaki silk jumpsuit all gave the impression of someone who was an outdoors person, the kind of woman who could be at home at a campsite without hesitation. The perfect sort for him—

for the Nick Egan he'd been so many years ago.

He barely stifled a groan at the thoughts that must be racing through Kate's mind.

"I've heard so much about you, Mrs. Egan."

"Oh?"

"The management would like at this time to ask the guests to please take their seats for dinner. Our staff will begin serving shortly."

As soon as the dinner announcement interrupted the canned background music, Nick seized upon it. He steered Kathryn away abruptly before she could ask the questions he was sure she wanted to ask after her appraisal of Kit Cody.

"We'd better get seated. After all, we're the guests of honor."

"You mean *you* are," Kathryn reminded him good-naturedly. "Nice to meet you all," she called back over her shoulder.

"I didn't mean to abandon you," he apologized. Leaving room for the Bermans next to the podium, where he was to give a small speech about being glad to be home and part of the *Metro Journal* staff, he pulled out her chair at the head table.

"Actually, I didn't feel abandoned at all. Ethel Berman is a delight. No skirting around price issues. She said she had a price in mind, and that after I looked at the building, if the budget could be worked with, great. Otherwise she'd just paint and freshen it up a bit."

"That sounds like her."

"She meant *she* would do it, Nick!" Kathryn's tone and expression were filled with more than a degree of admiration for the lady. "She's going to do this herself, with hired help, of course. I like her. She's a mover."

"That sounds like her too. The day I met her she was bagging trash for the janitor to take out."

"When have you had time to meet all these people with your harried house-husband schedule?"

Although her query was completely guileless, Nick's defenses heightened. There was no need for Kathryn to know he'd worked almost every morning the last week at the office while Laine put the house in order. He was going to tell her eventually, but not right now. He didn't want anything to spoil this evening. It could be his last shot at getting her alone and proving he'd changed, that she was foremost in his life now.

"I managed a few luncheon meetings when I braved the supermarket parking lot…or should I say, before I went to the market. My nerves are too shot afterward to discuss business."

"You know, you *are* a cute Mr. Mom."

And he wanted nothing to spoil her mood. He adored Kate when she felt playful, which appeared to be the case right then.

"Cute enough to dance with after dinner? A few of us are going over to the lounge. There's a combo playing."

"If you behave."

The truth was, Kathryn was having a good time. Some of the stories she'd heard from the people who had worked with Nick in the past and were there to honor and welcome him home reminded her of reasons she'd married him in the first place—his resilient ability to make the best of a bad situation; his sense of humor; the fact that he treated the lowest beggar on the street the same as some rajah or sultan, and had, on more than one occasion, shared precious rations with the needy. Nick loved people. He made a living out of watching and reporting on them. Being married to Nick was like being married to the world. The hard part was sharing him with it while she carried on like a trooper at home, a lone ranger.

That's what she had to keep in mind. All those times she'd felt so alone, so abandoned. If she didn't, the thought of dancing in Nick's arms was enough to turn her knees to jelly. As for the fact that she wasn't going home alone tonight…well, it was better her runaway thoughts not even go there.

Ten

NICK EGAN CUT A FINE FIGURE AT THE PODIUM AFTER A DINNER of petite steak Chesapeake and a scrumptious imperial crab. His new woolen-silk suit fit as though tailored to accommodate his broad shoulders and trim hips. Although her deed had been perfectly natural, Kathryn was embarrassed to admit to him that she'd ridded the house of everything that reminded her of her allegedly late husband, aside from mementos saved for the boys. Nonetheless, store-bought clothing was as handsome on him now as it had been the first time she saw him arrive in full dress for one of her parents' parties. Clothes, no matter how inexpensive, seemed to love Nick.

Just as he'd worked his charm on her parents' guests years ago, he now employed it for those who'd come to honor and welcome him back. Kathryn couldn't help but be impressed at the assembly of radio and television news celebrities, both local and national. All were as anxious as she to hear more about his capture, but he deftly dodged specifics with a finesse that would have left him utterly frustrated as an interviewer.

"So how long do you think you'll be happy on the home front before you get the itch to do foreign coverage again?" one of his colleagues asked.

"As long as I'm breathing," Nick answered. "My priorities have changed and, thank God, in time to enjoy them." He paused, locking gazes briefly with Kathryn before going on. "The foreign news network has been good to me, but it's time to let some of you younger guys take over. And gals." He nodded toward the table where the female photographer and her companions from EBS sat. "I want to see my kids grow up in person, not via satellite and video."

"So, are you and Ms. Sinclair going to make a go of it then?" Faye Ramsey, a local Washington social commentator, switched her gaze from Nick to Kathryn and back without so much as a blink of guilt for asking such a personal question. "If Washington is going to add an eligible bachelor to its ranks, I want to be the one to break the news."

"You'll be the first person I call, Faye. Promise." The uncomfortable titter of laughter following the woman's quip became a full-bodied roar with Nick's answer.

Masterful, Kathryn thought, relieved that another prickly issue was skimmed over. Her answer earlier to the same question from the very same female was that

Nick needed time to get to know his boys and she was giving it to him, but plans for divorce were still in the making. She wondered what would show up in the weekly society column.

"So there's still room for negotiation?" Ramsey countered with a wink, heavily accentuated by enough make-up to make Cleopatra pale in comparison.

Of course Kathryn *had* to be polite. She'd completely remodeled the Ramsey villa in Georgetown and the lady had sent many customers to the Emporium. Wishing she were as smooth as Nick, Kathryn stumbled over the word *amicable* and was grateful when Ethel Berman switched the subject with a warning look at her professionally curious guest.

When it came to Nick, whatever poise Kathryn had perfected from a life in the highest social circles and the best schooling simply flew out her mind's window like a startled bird. All she heard was the flutter of its retreating wings.

Or was that her heart? she wondered later as she danced in Nick's arms and clumsily stepped on his toes. Even her innate grace was a lost cause this close to the man.

"Sorry," she whispered hastily.

"I never felt a thing." His smile was slow and warm. "Everything is just perfect."

Heat spread to Kathryn's face, but it was not from embarrassment. Nick looked down at her as though she were the only woman in the world, his smile was as warm

203

as rays of the sun on a cloudless day. She could feel invisible, massaging fingers tearing down fragile defenses raised by reason.

In the big room where dinner had been served, she'd been much more confident than she was now in the cozy lounge, where a few of the special guests retired after the dinner for a more relaxed atmosphere. More Nick to the square foot, she mused helplessly, unable to deny his charismatic nature. She had to touch him, to move in his arms to his skillful step rather than wrestle like a schoolgirl at arm's length with a partner and dance forced upon her.

"It has been a perfect evening for you. I have to admit, I was proud of you and your speech."

"That wasn't what I was talking about, Katie girl."

Katie girl! A quiver of response robbed her of a suitable answer.

As if to demonstrate what he really meant, Nick pulled her closer while the band played a song about the magic of love. It felt right, perfectly natural, to allow it. She and Nick always had been suited to each other on the dance floor. Magic or no, *something* was overriding her common sense!

"I don't want the clock to strike twelve and have you disappear on me."

The tautness in his words kept Kathryn from meeting his gaze. The Nick she knew was invulnerable, and this was not like him. Her ready reply about life not being a fairy tale dissolved in an unexpected wave of compassion. She struggled against an urge to hold him even closer and assure him that she would always be there for him…

A rise of panic exploded like fireworks, its sparks showering her dream-dulled senses with sobering shards of hot ice. Instinct bade Kathryn to pull away and run, beyond the magnetic pull that was working its way toward her, despite reason. Thankfully the music came to an end, but not before Nick dipped her backward over his arm and leaned over her like some big-screen Romeo.

"I love you, Kate. With all my heart and soul, I love you."

A flash went off, breaking the unseen bond that held them there, suspended in spirit and time. Nick pulled her upright again, and with an unveiled look of hostility at Faye Ramsey, who stood in the doorway with a camera, he ushered Kathryn toward the table they were sharing with the Bermans and a few other select guests.

"Sorry about that," he growled under his breath, continuing with something about the annoying cost of fame.

His hand was bewitchment itself against the bare skin of her back. Kathryn stepped away from it. She needed to escape *this* Nick before she made a total fool of herself and did something she'd regret later.

"I gotta go to the bathroom."

The moment the clumsy words were out, Kathryn was mortified. A simple "I need to freshen my makeup" or "Excuse me for a few moments" would have sufficed, but no, she'd come up with a juvenile quote from one of her boys.

Trembling, at least inwardly, she headed for the ladies lounge in the lobby of the club. Her body was a riot of responses from their dance. The last shred of composure she possessed threatened to break. Yet once in the privacy of a small sanitizer-scented stall, a single runaway tear was all that marked her defeat. Without regard to her makeup, Kathryn wiped it away, but it had brought company.

Thankfully, Paul Radisson never made her feel like this. Her heart and emotions were safe from him. *With* him, Kathryn corrected herself. She unrolled some toilet tissue and blew her nose loudly. *With,* not *from.*

Even as she tried once again to convince herself, to dismiss semantics, Kathryn couldn't. The realization struck her like a demolition ball, knocking out of her mind for good all of her hopes regarding Paul as a possible husband for her and father to her children. She would never be more than friends with Paul. She'd been fooling herself—and him—to think otherwise.

The outside door to the lounge opened, allowing the combo's music in along with some women. Kathryn dabbed at her eyes, wrestling for composure.

"Get outta here! You slept with *the* Nick Egan!"

"No, I said he spent the night in my hotel room."

Grabbing her chest as if to remove the invisible knife that pierced it from out of nowhere, Kathryn froze.

She wasn't certain who the gawking female was, but she knew the voice of the other. Miss Nick-has-told-me-so-much-about-you!

"Same thing!"

Kit Cody responded with a full-throated laugh. "Not hardly."

"Don't tell me you two spent the evening *developing film!*"

Or worse. Putting down the cushioned commode lid, Kathryn sat down before her knees gave way, as befuddled by the photographer's answer as her companion was. She remained still, hoping that, since she was in the large, handicapped stall at the end of the pink marbled line of doors, the two women wouldn't know she was there.

Yes, she'd blamed Nick for many things, and there had been times that she'd thought he might have succumbed to any one of the attractive women he worked with, but deep down...Kathryn bit her lip to stop a renegade sob. How could she let Nick get to her like this?

The conversation lulled momentarily. A toilet flushed. Then another.

"Actually," the photographer said, picking up the riveting exchange again, "that's what we did, picked out some shots to send to the home office. I'd asked his opinion."

Kathryn held her breath while water ran in the sinks.

"C'mon!"

"We'd had a few drinks with the rest of the team at the hotel bar; then we went to my room, where I accidentally spilled some developer on Nick's trousers."

"And?"

"We rinsed the spot and hung them to dry over the fan while we had a few more drinks."

And? Kathryn dreaded the answer, but she needed to know.

"And I spent the rest of the bloody night listening to his divorce woes and how much he loved his wife and kid and how he regretted…"

The hand dryers came on and the words became muffled.

"And that's it," the woman finished.

The click of heels on the tiled floor stopped. Kathryn assumed they were checking their hair and makeup.

"He passed out across the bed, and I got the chair and a backache for my trouble. But I'll tell you…"

Two short hissing sounds preceded a drift of perfume, an expensive but strong scent Kathryn's mother used.

"If she does let him go, he won't be eligible for long. I'll stake a claim in a heartbeat!"

Music once again invaded the ladies lounge, signaling their departure.

"Yeah, you and dozens of other women!" Kit's companion laughed, muted by the close of the door behind them.

The emotion Kathryn had held at bay escaped, but this time with relief. At least her sinuses, which had been giving her a fit, were draining. With a halfhearted smile, Kathryn stepped out of hiding and took a seat in front of the mirrors to repair the damage done to her makeup.

Behind her, the door swooshed open again and Ethel Berman came in.

"There you are! Nick was worried you might not be well."

"Contact problems and a few allergies but nothing serious." Surely she could be forgiven a white lie in such extreme circumstances? "I thought a little cold water would ease the irritation, now that they're out."

The older woman waved her hand through the air in disdain. "This perfume isn't helping and neither is that smoke from the other side of the bar."

Having at least removed the mascara that was smeared under her eyes, Kathryn dabbed on some dusting powder to cover the redness while she waited until Ethel was ready to leave.

Upon rejoining the others, she was grateful for the dim lighting. One, because it hid her red eyes. Two, because Kit Cody and her friend had joined the group. Kathryn's answering smile of assurance when Nick asked if she was all right was genuine. Despite her misgivings about their future, she felt much better about his past.

"We're about ready to wrap it up here anyway," Nick said, "it being the middle of the week and early mornings on the slate for most of us. Folks, let me tell you. I'll never roll my eyes again when I hear a mother and housewife complain about being frazzled!"

"Don't tell me you're leaving, Nick! I'd hoped for a dance."

Kathryn turned to find Kit Cody looking past Nick, zeroing her attention in on Kathryn, as if asking for permission.

"I'm in no rush, Nick." Guilt over her eavesdropping warmed her neck. Did the Cody woman know?

"But I *am!* Sorry, Ms. Cody." Nick tightened his arm at Kathryn's waist. "Six A.M. will come earlier than it used to when you have to get two boys up and dressed for school."

"Definitely another time then."

"Sure thing."

Nick went through polite good-byes to his employers and their company as if he were expecting lightning to strike at any moment. A nag of suspicion eased in on Kathryn's former relief. Maybe those two women had known she was in the restroom.

Before she had time to dwell on it, however, the valet was opening the car door under the club's canopied entrance for her to climb in. Kathryn ventured a sideways glance at her companion as he pulled out into traffic for the drive home. What if Nick *had* had an affair with Ms. Outdoors? Why should it matter now, especially since the divorce proceedings were going to go through anyway? It simply *shouldn't* matter.

Yet it did, enough to invade her dreams with troubling scenes of Nick and Ms. Outdoors cuddled by a campfire readying it for the fish the boys were cleaning. Kathryn awoke, furious and distraught, when the two kissed. She wiped perspiration from her forehead, trying to separate dream from reality. Ms. Outdoors could probably turn out a gourmet meal from a greasy frying pan!

With an unladylike oath, Kathryn slung aside the bedcovers and pulled on her robe. The green glow of the alarm clock told her it was almost four in the morning as she paced past it like a discontented lioness in its cage. Running fingers through her hair, she fluffed it out as if to rid herself of the confounding quandary that robbed her of sleep. She was hungry. Maybe a little milk and cookies would help her salvage what was left of the night.

To her surprise, when she reached the staircase she saw that a light was on downstairs. Kathryn had made a hurried retreat to her room as soon as she, Nick, and the boys arrived home leaving him to put the kids to bed. Later, she thought she'd heard his footsteps in the hall heading to his room, but apparently she'd been mistaken.

Descending the steps, she strained over the railing to see into the family room, but it wasn't until she actually entered it that she saw Nick, still in last night's clothes and sprawled on the sofa. The lamp at his head was on full glow, but he was sleeping soundly. His jacket hung on a nearby chair along with a crumpled tie, while his sharply pressed dress shirt was open, as if he'd intended to strip it off and then got distracted.

By what? she wondered, moving closer so that she could see the book his hands were folded over. To her astonishment, it was a small, worn edition of the Bible. She'd never seen Nick with a Bible, much less reading one. Daring to step a little closer, Kathryn could see a passage highlighted on the well-worn page, just above where his fingers rested.

"The LORD *is my light and my salvation; whom shall I fear? The* LORD *is the strength of my life; of whom shall I be afraid?"*

Nick afraid? Kathryn drew away, feeling as though she'd intruded on something very private. Nick "Full Speed Ahead" Egan? She studied his face in sleep's repose, noticing a wake of a worry in the center of his brow. The furrow matched the one she'd been sporting of late, as if all the troubles of the world had hacked it with a single cohesive blow.

And the pain. That horrible, bitter anguish rising in the back of her throat was nearly choking her. In the old days, she'd have curled up against him and confessed her woes. He'd kiss away her tears and make her forget everything except the love they shared with his tender yet passionate attention, until she slept—safe, secure, and loved, in his arms. Chin quivering, Kathryn leaned over and brushed his forehead with her lips.

It was as much as she dared, considering her vulnerable state. Best to leave him be until morning. She reached for the afghan folded across the back of the sofa,

then spread it over the sleeping man with the same ten-
derness she reserved for her boys. Nick stirred but did
not awaken, even when she quietly turned off the light.

The words of the verse haunted her as she returned
to her room without the snack she'd gone after. With
confusion and misery churning within, she doubted she
could keep it down anyway. Kathryn blew her nose
again and climbed into bed, bracing against clawing
doubt and fear. It was *she* who was afraid—afraid of losing her boys, afraid of being hurt again, afraid of herself
and her feelings for Nick. A sob caught in her throat and
then erupted in the pillow where she buried her face.
Instinctively, she called out to the One she believed had
abandoned her. She needed his light, his salvation, his
strength.

Lord, help me, I'm so afraid!

On Friday school let out for the holiday break. Half the
houses in the neighborhood were running riot with kids
full of seasonal excitement and energy to be envied. At
least Kathryn envied that of the two boys with their
father downstairs dividing up a stash of Christmas cookies left over from the school party. Nick was one of the
room *mothers* who'd catered the affair.

Just what they needed, she thought upon hearing
Jason protest that Jeremy had more Christmas trees than
he did—more sugar! She warned Nick he'd have a devil
of a time getting them down off the walls for bed, but

Mr. Mom had to learn the hard way. *More than likely, he'll be on the walls with them.* A grin settled on her face at the thought.

Downstairs the doorbell rang. Kathryn sneezed and blew her nose as she heard Jeremy shout with far less enthusiasm. "It's just Mr. Paul."

"Mom, your *date's* here," Jason announced, imitating his brother's tone.

Date? Kathryn closed the fastener on her weekender bag. She'd gone to great lengths to explain to the boys that this was not a date, but a business trip following up the acceptance of her bid for the Malchows. She felt as though she had to go because she'd promised, even though now she could claim she was sick and back out, as Nick so innocently suggested.

Wishing she were wearing a flannel nightgown rather than a chic cocktail dress and headed for bed instead of Paul's office Christmas party and then the Poconos, Kathryn carried her suitcase downstairs. Mentally, she went over the contents one last time, focusing particularly on cold formulas and lozenges. She thought she had everything. If not, she was certain there were drugstores near the ski resort.

To her astonishment, Jeremy stood at the foot of the stairs with a tea towel folded over his arm. He bowed stiffly and held out his free hand. "Come this way, madame."

"What is this all about?"

Jeremy didn't answer. He just led her into the living

room where hot tea and shortbread cookies had been carefully laid out on the oriental rosewood coffee table.

Paul rose from the sofa, his gaze full of appreciation. "Red becomes you, Kathryn."

"Are you talking about my dress or my nose?" It was raw from blowing and felt twice its size.

"Both." Paul motioned to the table. "These gentlemen have put on quite a spread for our send-off. We're a little short for time, but I couldn't say no to such thoughtfulness."

Jeremy practically beamed under Paul's praise, while Jason took it with clear caution. Kathryn sat down next to Paul where her eldest son indicated, while Jeremy shoved a steaming cup of tea at her and another at Paul.

"Something to take the chill off." His childlike voice was infused with authority.

"It's a bit bitter," Paul admitted, after venturing a taste of the tea. "What kind is this?"

The boys answered at the same time.

"Chinese."

"Some earl or something."

Jason recovered first. "We mixed 'em together so they'd be special. Like wines." His voice was full of pride in their accomplishment. "It's a blush kind of tea."

"You're raising two connoisseurs, I see." Paul turned to Kathryn. "Who knows, this could be a new blend!"

"I never cease to be amazed." She was glad for the brief respite in the rush to get ready and the steaming warmth of the beverage. "You guys are so sweet."

Jason unfolded a napkin for Paul and Jeremy placed Kathryn's across her lap so that they might have cookies. Kathryn recognized them as those from their holiday party that had survived the ride home in a backpack intact. She thought back to Nick's soliloquy on braving the kamikaze parking lot to get them and smiled. Undoubtedly, he was in the family room watching television, which could be heard faintly over the Christmas music the boys were playing on the stereo.

Surely he'd not put the boys up to this! Somehow the idea was as disturbing as the fact that Nick never once voiced an opinion that she shouldn't go away with Paul, short of observing that her cold was a good reason to cancel. He didn't act thrilled with the idea, but the old Nick would have thrown it in her face at every opportunity. He didn't take losing well. Unless—a pang struck her deep in the stomach—unless he didn't feel he was losing anything.

Kathryn finished the last of her tea without really tasting it. She hadn't told Nick that she intended to break off what relationship she had with Paul. Whether or not there was a future for Nick and her as husband and wife, her evening at Nick's party had underscored the futility of anything serious with Paul. She hoped the relaxed setting, away from the chaos where Nick was involved, might be the best place to let Paul down. It was another reason she felt compelled to go now, to get it over with, to eliminate at least one problem in her life.

"Good to the last drop, huh?"

"My compliments to the chef…or tea mixer," she exclaimed, widening Jeremy's snaggletoothed grin even more.

"And the cookie hit the spot. Now I can make it until the dinner since I skipped lunch today," Paul chimed in.

His smile looked pasted on. Kathryn could tell by the way he glanced at his watch and chugged down the last of the tea that he was impatient to be on his way, rather than humoring two children. He was doing it for her sake, not theirs. At least Nick's arrival had cleared her mind on that account once and for all. Right now she was grateful for all favors, big and small.

Nick watched from his office window upstairs as Paul's car pulled away through the tree-lined drive. It felt as if his heart had been attached to it and was now being dragged behind, leaving nothing but anguish in its place. The old Nick would have never let her leave. If he'd changed for the better, why was he hurting so much? His nails bit into the flesh of his palms as he clenched his fist. It was like taking all the punches and not being able to hit back.

Or like going to a cross without a fight or so much as a harsh word, when one could call the heavenly hosts down to vent his fury.

Nick closed his eyes, recalling the mental and physical beatings they'd had to take from the terrorists, not daring to fight back lest the weaker prisoners receive even worse. Papa Rico reminded them to think of the cross, the long, painful walk to Calvary, fraught with torment and ridicule. The truth was, Nick would rather be struck physically than suffer what he felt now. Kathryn was gone, maybe slipping away and through his fingers for good.

A crash from the kitchen followed by a yelp and a collective gasp drew him from his desperate thoughts. "What are you guys doing down there, breaking up the house?"

"*We must be thankful for those blessings the Lord has given us!*" With Papa Rico's words echoing in his mind, Nick refocused with determination on the two *blessings* wreaking havoc in the kitchen. Taking the steps two at a time, he descended the stairs and headed into the kitchen, where Jason and Jeremy were sweeping up a shattered teacup.

Nick couldn't remember the name of the pricey china pattern. All he knew was that it had to be registered and none of the set had come from *his* side of the family.

"Accidents *will* happen, Dad!" Jason told Nick, heaving a shrug.

"Yeah." Jeremy shoved a dustpan under the broken china. "And this happened before I could catch it." He shook his head, his dark hair shimmering in the fluorescent light overhead. "One minute it was on the tray and the next, ker*blam!*"

In his enthusiasm, the youngest boy shoved the handle of the delicate teacup across the floor Nick had mopped that afternoon.

"Whoa, partner!" Nick spoke up. He took the broom away from Jeremy, who was smearing the tea over the linoleum with its bristles. "I'll take care of this."

"Like you took care of Mom going off with Paul Radisson?" Jason grumbled under his breath.

Nick stopped short. "What's that?"

"Me 'n' Jason thought you'd just pop him in the nose and tell Mom to go to her room! After all, you're the boss of the house, aren't you?"

Just kick me while I'm down, boys! Nick fortified himself with a deep breath.

"No, Jeremy, your mother and I run the house *together*. We share the responsibilities; and I don't go around popping people in the nose, no matter how much I dislike what they are doing."

"I thought you said all was fair in love and war."

Nick gathered up the broken china with a cluster of paper towels and disposed of it in the trash can. *Oh, what a tangled web we weave....*

"Well, not always. I mean, you don't do things to hurt people, like punch them in the nose. Your mom's trip was business. Besides, I can't tell her what to do. If she wants to stay with me..." He groped for the right words, well aware of the undivided attention fixed upon him. "Well, I just have to do my best and let God do the rest."

At the uncharacteristic silence, Nick glanced up from mopping the last of the spilled tea. Jason was solemn, as though lost in thought, while Jeremy looked as if he'd just swallowed a piece of china.

"What's wrong, Jer?"

"Will God get mad if he gets some help sometimes?" The wide blue of his son's eyes reminded Nick of Kathryn in one of her more gullible moments.

"Like when you got that girl to help us clean and cook," Jason suggested hastily. "It helps Mom think we can keep the house clean so she'll let you stay."

"Yeah, like that...sort of." Jeremy was less certain.

Nick glanced from one boy to the other, baffled by what he was detecting here. Were they afraid God was going to punish him for being deceitful, or was it something more?

"Or not telling Mom about the cup. We got plenty of 'em, and she'd just worry over it. She really gets hyper over some things." Jason looked away, avoiding Nick's direct gaze, and shoved his hands into his pockets.

So *that* was it. Nick smiled and ruffled his eldest son's head, then did the same to Jeremy. "I think no harm will be done if we save your mom some fretting by replacing the cup. God knows how mothers can be." He started away and then turned abruptly. "Unless she asks directly. No lying."

Both boys shook their heads as if the idea had never entered their minds.

"We'll just do our best and let God do the rest!"

Jason announced brightly. "And all our wishes will come true."

Before Nick could study his eldest son's expression further, the boy turned on his heels and headed up the stairs. "C'mon, dummy, I'll help you with your homework!"

Jeremy looked after Jason for a moment before putting his hands on his hips in grim disdain. "I don't know how God puts up with him! He's a *progidal* if I ever saw one!"

Nick laughed and hugged his youngest. Silently, he thanked the Lord for the unexpected blessing of a second son. "We *all* are at one time or other, Jer. Now let me get dinner going and you get to that project before Jason changes his mind."

"That's the friendliest I've ever seen Jason and Jeremy," Paul told her later as they drove through the Bethesda traffic toward the restaurant where his firm had booked the annual Christmas dinner party in a private room.

The plans were to stay for dinner until the first set of music started and then head up to the Poconos. The Malchows were already at the resort condo and would be waiting up for them so everyone could get an early start on the slopes the next morning.

Kathryn was tired just thinking of it. Of all the times to catch a cold! Instead of answering, she gave in to the sneeze she'd been holding at bay.

Paul reached over and patted her knee. "A little hot

tea and a cozy fire is what you need." He paused thoughtfully before going on. "You know, Kathryn, maybe Nick's coming home is turning out for the best where the boys are concerned. At least you've seen that he can handle them well, that they get along together."

Kathryn stiffened. *That* she did not want to hear.

"I'll never give him custody!"

"A shared custody was more what I had in mind."

The last bubble from the sinking ship of a future with Paul surfaced and popped.

"And what right have you got to an opinion where my children are concerned?"

Paul put on the blinker and watched for a break in the traffic before pulling into the parking lot of the restaurant. With ease, he slid his new Mercedes sports car into a space and cut the engine. "This isn't going the way I'd planned."

Instead of getting out of the car, he reached under his seat and drew out a small box, wrapped in seasonal red and green. "An early Christmas present." He handed it to her.

Silent, Kathryn studied the ring-sized box as though it contained a poisonous snake. Her mind was riddled with dread and despair. She'd selfishly allowed their relationship to go on too long and now…

It was a ring box marked with the logo of one of the capital's finest jewelers.

"Paul, I can't take this!" She handed it back to him without opening it.

This wasn't how *she'd* planned things either. She'd hoped to tell Paul that it was over between them a little more tactfully. But clearly that was not going to be the case.

"It's not going to work, you—you and I. I've taken advantage of our friendship and I'm so sorry, but friendship is all I can offer to you." Embarrassed and frustrated, she looked away, unable to meet his assessing gaze.

"It isn't what you think, Kathryn." Pursing his lips, he handed the box back to her. "But I thank you for saving me from making a total fool of myself."

The blood rush to Kathryn's face removed all doubt of who felt the fool. Hands shaking, she opened the ring box. There, sparkling in the overhead glow of the Victorian parking lot lanterns, was a fire opal. She recalled telling Paul that she'd asked her mother to look for one of a sunset orange hue when she visited Mexico.

She wished the cushy car seat would swallow her—that she was anywhere but here.

"Just a gift from one friend to another, okay?"

"Okay." Kathryn grimaced. "Paul, I hadn't meant to be selfish. You've been a lifesaver for me with all your help and advice. And I am terribly fond of you as a friend. I enjoy your company."

"But not on a twenty-four, seven basis—you know, a full-time relationship?"

Kathryn couldn't read his face. He was somber, no more, no less.

"No."

"So you're going back with Nick?"

"No!"

How could she explain something she didn't understand herself?

"I am still looking for a place to move to with the boys. I need time away from Nick, or any romantic interest, for that matter."

Paul took the ring from its case and slipped it on her finger. It was a perfect fit.

"I'm in no rush. The best things come to those who wait, or so they say."

"Paul, I can't make any promises." Kathryn was determined not to give her friend more false hope. "Frankly, my concern is more about you and the boys, rather than you and me."

"Guess that's where time can work for *all* of us. I'm not used to kids, but I'm learning. And Jason and Jeremy seem to be coming around where I'm concerned. I mean, look at tonight."

The car was getting cold now that the engine was shut off. Kathryn pulled her coat closer about her legs.

"No promises, Paul. I need a friend now, not a romantic interest."

"Then friendship it is!" With a wide smile, Paul extended his hand.

Thank you, God. Kathryn accepted it gratefully.

"Although I promise no mercy on the slopes tomorrow!"

She laughed, unleashing the tension that knotted

her stomach. "You'll be the one in need of mercy!" As Paul reached for the door release, she put her hand on his arm. "Thank you, Paul...for *everything.*"

Kathryn meant it. One relationship down, the dreaded confrontation over. Her relief, however, was lessened by the knowledge that getting Nick to take no for an answer would not be so easy, especially when there was a part of her that was hoping against hope that he wouldn't.

ul's housekeeper. I called when we first got to the
l and left a message on the answering machine
to call you and the Malchows. I figured she was
hower or something, and I only had one quarter."

u could have borrowed change."

thryn gave him a weary, half-lidded look. "I was
oncerned about Paul, poor thing. We got about a
ur out of Bethesda when he started feeling sick to
mach. By the time we decided to turn back, he
nt over with cramps. I had to drive him to the
ncy room." She paused and took a tentative sip of
tea. "Maybe it was the seafood salad appetizer,
h I had it too and didn't get sick."

o, you were *already* sick with that cold."

ing in the back of Nick's mind clicked, some-
ason said after the couple left about wishes com-
e.

know, I know. I shouldn't have left home in the
lace. Some company we'd make for the
ws!"

ddenly she gasped. "Oh, Nick! If Isabel didn't get
ssage to call you, she hasn't called the Malchows,
I was in such a dither to get Paul settled in when
to his house that it didn't cross my mind to ques-
bel about the calls."

l take care of it." Nick reached out to gently pat
. "Malchow called me a half hour ago, and I've
ying to find you or Radisson in every hospital
ncy room in the book ever since."

Eleven

THE SHRILL RING OF THE TELEPHONE INVADED NICK'S SLEEP.
He bolted upright in the guest room bed, disoriented for
a moment. The lighted digits of his clock radio revealed
it was 2:00 A.M.

Scowling, he fumbled for the phone and retrieved
the handset.

"Hello?"

"Hi, this is Herb Malchow. I'm sorry to bother you
at this hour, Mr. Egan, but can you tell me if Ms. Sinclair
and Mr. Radisson had a change of plans? We expected
them around midnight, but they haven't arrived. I'm
hoping there's no problem."

Dear heavenly Father! Nick cleared his throat, wide
awake now. "I haven't heard of any change of plans, Mr.
Malchow."

His mind raced ahead with possible explanations.

Maybe they'd had an accident. Kate was a responsible person, even if Radisson was sometimes lacking in that department. She'd have called if it was at all possible. Nick's chest constricted with his growing alarm. "Tell you what, sir. Let me make a few calls and see what I can find out. I'll get back to you when I know something."

"Fair enough. I'll do the same here, although I've already checked with the Maryland and Pennsylvania state police. No accidents have been reported and Paul's maid said they were not at his place."

"Right." Nick didn't know whether to be relieved or not. He didn't want to think about Kate alone in Radisson's apartment. "You give me a call if you hear from them."

"Got it. 'Night."

"Bye."

Dropping the handset back on the receiver, Nick slipped out of bed and headed for the bathroom. After dousing his face with cold water and toweling off, he still had no idea where to start—what with the state police and Paul's place already eliminated. Staring unfocused into the mirror, he caught a glimpse of a red cross on a box of Ninja Turtle Band-Aids on the shelf beside it.

Hospitals!

"Thank you, Jesus." He headed downstairs to start some coffee and make some phone calls.

No one by Kate's or Paul's names had been admitted to the first three hospitals he called. Frustration and concern mounting, he waited on hold for the emergency

---

room at the University of Geo[...]
flash of car headlights careene[...]
dows across the walls of the ha[...]
idling made him hang up, his h[...]
state into anticipation. When [...]
Kathryn was paying a taxi driv[...]
a yellow cab. Flipping on the ou[...]
storm door as she made her wa[...]

The moment she was ins[...]
arms, overcome with relief. Sh[...]

"Thank God, you're all ri[...]

Kathryn answered with a[...]
groaned. *All right* is up for del[...]

She sounded terrible. In[...]
forehead. It was burning hot a[...]

"Hot tea, cold medicine, [...]
lady!" he announced, allowing[...]
as he ushered her into the k[...]
happened? Where's Radisson?"

"He *was* at the hospital[...]
think." Kathryn's voice filtere[...]
"We were there for four hours[...]
safe to send him home with[...]
housekeeper's care."

"Why didn't you call me?"[...]

"Didn't Isabel call?"

"Who?" Nick poured the [...]
instant coffee over herbal tea t[...]
powers.

"I'm sorry, Nick."

Kathryn's voice trembled as she gathered her coat closer about her shoulders. Her red eyes were brimming with tears. The edge of Nick's exasperation fell away.

"Finish your tea." After a reassuring peck on her forehead, he took up the phone to call the Malchows.

"All's fair in love and war, Dad!" The boys' echo of his own words dogged Nick as he spoke to Mr. Malchow and extended Kathryn's regrets. Surely the boys had no part in this. The same gut instinct that made him famous for his ability to sniff out a good story seized at the suspicion with characteristic tenacity. Jeremy's guilt-stricken face came to mind. *"Will God get mad if he gets some help sometimes?"*

Nick glanced uneasily at Kathryn as she put down the empty teacup. The boys had insisted on having a tea party to send her and Paul off on their trip. In fact, Nick had felt a bit betrayed by the little guys and their gracious notion toward Radisson, especially when, to date, they'd made no attempt to hide their dislike of the guy. Paul's symptoms were disturbingly similar to those Karrie Anderson suffered after drinking that diet tea. And the kids had spent the evening of Nick's Christmas party at the Andersons' home. He groaned inwardly.

Heavenly Father, please don't let this be the case. If Kate even suspected foul play where the boys were concerned, the three geese at the Egan household were all cooked.

"I'm going to bed." Kathryn struggled to her feet.

She was exhausted as well as sick. Putting aside this new quandary for the moment, Nick went immediately to her side.

"Come on. Let's get you upstairs."

To his astonishment, Kathryn didn't resist when he accompanied her into the master bedroom. Aside from having him turn his back when her cocktail dress dropped around her ankles and she replaced it with a ruffled flannel gown, she almost seemed glad to have him there. And when he at last tucked her in and curled next to her atop the covers to warm her, she merely snuggled closer, as though she couldn't get close enough.

Nick felt guilty for taking advantage of both Kate's and Paul's misfortunes, but with his arm around the woman he loved, he couldn't help but count his blessings. He'd longed for this moment. Simply holding her was enough for now. It was God's fulfillment of a prayer he'd prayed many times during the long nights of his imprisonment.

Closing his eyes in quiet thanksgiving, Nick inhaled the perfume of her hair. For tonight his wife was his and he intended to enjoy her—her soft breath, the way she fit against him, her scent, her childlike trust. As for tomorrow, it would be soon enough to confront his sons with his suspicions.

Nick had forgotten what a good night's sleep was. With part of the thick quilted spread wrapped around him, and Kate bundled in his embrace, he lost track of

232

time in a world where it had no significance. Engulfed in healing slumber, he never heard the bedroom door open the following morning, but Jeremy's startled "Dad!" snatched him abruptly into wakefulness.

"What?" He bolted upright on the bed, startling Kate from her rest. Although it was too late, he put a raised finger to his lips to shush his youngest son, as well as the elder one who came running in at the commotion.

"Wh—what's wrong?" Kathryn mumbled, not quite alert.

"Nothing I can't take care of. You go back to sleep."

He stroked her hair off her forehead and planted a kiss there. Her fever had diminished as far as he could tell. Once he got the boys their breakfast, he'd bring up some more medicine and some toast and juice.

As he slipped off the bed and tucked his acquiescent patient in, he was all too aware of the two staring boys in the doorway. With an emphatic wave, he dispersed them and followed in their wake.

"You gonna have to get married now?" Jeremy whispered, tugging at Nick's sweatpants. He looked up at Nick, eyes brightly entertaining the possibility.

"Why do you say that, sport?"

"'Cause you and mom *slept* together."

"Get real, Jeremy! They got their clothes on!" Jason lightly shoved his brother. "Dad slept with us on the family room floor, but we ain't gonna marry him!"

There were times when silence was the best tactic, and this was one of them. Nick ushered the boys to their room, allowing the debate to continue.

"Well, Derek Parson's sister slept with a boy and they are going to have to get married!"

"Because they *didn't* have clothes on, dummy!"

"Buffalo breath!"

"Whoa." Nick hauled Jeremy back by the seat of his pajamas as the younger boy flew at his brother, fists drawn. Jerking his head toward the kids' room, he motioned Jason inside while he carried in Jeremy by the seat of his ninja flannels. He put the boy down and backed against the door, closing it.

"First—" he let them know by the tone of his voice that he meant business—"your mom is sick and I don't want any noise, much less any brawls! Second, you knock before you enter someone's room, got that?"

"But you weren't in your bed and we couldn't find you downstairs and—"

"Knock on a closed door before opening it," Nick insisted, cutting Jeremy off.

"Why's Mom home anyway?" Jason's face was a picture of innocence. "I thought she was going away with *Paul* for the weekend." Nick had to fight to hold back a grin at the way Jason said *Paul*, as though it were some disgusting disease rather than a man's name.

"Your mom is sick; too sick to go."

"*Mom's* sick?" Jeremy gasped, his eyes growing wider than his round little face. "But Mom didn't—"

"She's got a cold, stupid!"

Ignoring his eldest son's observation, Nick zeroed in

234

on Jeremy. "But Mom didn't *what*, Jeremy?"

Jason jumped in. "She didn't look sick."

Nick gave Jason a silencing look. "I was asking your brother."

As if the guilt of the entire world rested on his small shoulders, Jeremy shrugged under Nick's interrogating gaze.

"She didn't *look* sick," the little one echoed. "Mr. Radisson looked sick."

With a roll of his eyes, Jason flung himself back on the bed. The breath he expelled whistled through a pained grimace.

"Oh, he was sick too. They had to cancel their trip, but then you guys wouldn't know anything about that, would you?"

Jason shook his head, never looking at Nick or the brother who cut him a worried glance.

"Yep," Nick went on, plopping down on the bed beside the littlest. "Paul spent most of the night at the hospital. Your mom said he was *very* sick."

"Did they pump his stomach?" Jeremy's eyes were wide and worried.

"Don't know that, pal. But Mr. Paul definitely got very sick from something he ate last night." He paused for effect. "Or from something he drank, maybe?"

Jeremy's face was scrunched up, and his blue eyes told the story. They had that large, moist "Oh no, I didn't mean it" look commercial producers demand of kids who accidentally spill something so that the sponsor's product can clean it up.

"Jeremy, you look like you've seen a ghost." Nick lifted his son's dimpled chin.

"He always looks like that when he thinks of people getting sick."

Nick swung his gaze to Jason. "Son, maybe you ought to put on some boots today."

"Why? The snow's gone." Jason sat up with a bewildered glance out the window.

"Because the garbage is getting real deep in here, and it's bad enough coming from your mouths without you stepping in it too!"

Rising, Nick folded his arms and leveled a challenging look at each boy in turn.

"Now if you two have done something foolish, the least you can do is be men enough to admit your mistakes."

"It was Jeremy's idea about the diet tea. He…we didn't want Mom to go away with Mr. Paul."

"You figgered how to get him to drink it." Jeremy was not about to take the entire blame.

Nick felt a little sick with guilt that the boys had done such a thing, and even more so for finding it humorous. Not that he dared show the latter. This was serious. He supposed Paul could have been seriously harmed, although this was no worse a prank than the chocolate laxatives he and Paul had given a fellow schoolmate once to stop the guy from continually sponging food off them.

What was the verse about the sins of the fathers being visited upon their children?

"Well, it was a low-down dirty trick. Seems to me you boys owe Mr. Paul an apology, and you'd better hope he doesn't sue you. He's one sharp lawyer."

"Just so you don't tell Mom. I don't need my allowance, but we got to live with her!" Jason spoke up after some quiet analysis. "We didn't mean to hurt anyone."

"We only did it 'cause you love Mom and we want you to stay married! Besides, you said all's fair in love and war!"

"Yeah, she thinks you're doing all the cleaning and stuff and you're not." Jason rallied with an accusation of his own.

If someone had just struck him in the stomach with a bowling ball, Nick could not have been more staggered than he was by his children's defense of their actions. Shame, hot and immediate, swept over him.

Lord, forgive me.

How could he condemn the boys when he'd set the example of deceit? His charade had appeared harmless to him, but now he saw its ugly head for what it was.

"You're right, boys." With a half laugh, he went on. "Imagine, I'm supposed to be the father, the one who shows his family how to live right, and it takes you two to show me how wrong I've been."

He gathered Jeremy in his arms and reached for Jason. When the boys entered his embrace, Nick squeezed them. "I was wrong. We don't deceive people."

Left without a spiritual leg to stand on, Nick sat down, pulling the boys into his lap. "Guys, you know what we've been doing?"

"Lying?" Jeremy ventured.

"Yes...and worse. We've been praying for God to make things right with your mom, but then instead of letting him answer our prayers, we've been trying to do it ourselves. We've taken matters into our hands and out of his."

"You think God's mad at us too?"

Nick gave Jeremy a little hug and smiled in reassurance. "No, but I think he's disappointed in us. God doesn't think we believe in him enough to trust him."

Jason was not as quick to capitulate. "We were just trying to *help* him."

"Do you think the God who created us needs our help, Jase?"

The older boy lowered his head and shook it.

"So, are you gonna tell Mom?" Jeremy said in a small voice.

Nick thought a moment, arguing with himself. Truth was important, but telling Kathryn about the boys and the tea would do more damage than good. Besides, no serious harm had been done.

"Not this time," he said at last. "Instead, I'm going to get down on my knees and tell God that I know I was wrong and how sorry I am for trying to fix this myself instead of trusting him."

"Will he tell her?"

Not quite comfortable with his decision, Nick got down on his knees and pulled his youngest son to his side. God knew how Kathryn tended to blow things out of proportion. He *had* to understand their plight.

"Something tells me he won't because if we are really sorry and tell him so, he'll forgive us and help us try to do better and never disappoint him again. But from now on, no more tricks. I'm just going to do my best and let God show me how great and good he really is."

"Me too!" Jeremy dropped down beside Nick and folded his small hands eagerly. "You gonna say the words?"

"No, you have to speak to God yourself." Nick glanced at Jason. "Care to join us, son?"

Jason shrugged and scuffed the carpet with his bare foot. "I don't know what to say."

Nick's mind flew back to another time, a time not so long ago when he'd been the one awkward and uneasy about approaching God. He extended his hand to Jason, who took it and knelt beside him.

"Then I'll tell God what I feel aloud and, if and when you and Jeremy feel the same way, then you just say amen."

"I can say, 'Now I lay me down to sleep'!"

"That's a good prayer too, son," Nick assured Jeremy, "but sometimes the prayers we memorize just don't fit what we need to say. That's when we have to just talk to God like…well, like you would talk to me or to

239

any friend who loves you and in whom you can trust."

Jeremy nodded in understanding and returned to his ready prayer stance, hands folded, head bowed, forehead wrinkled in earnest.

As he and Jason followed suit, Nick offered one desperate dart of silent prayer. *Heavenly Father, help me to be a good example for my boys. I'm so new at this myself. Show me if I'm wrong. Guide me, give me the right words, I pray, in the name of your precious Son...*

Kathryn could hardly believe she'd slept through the entire weekend. Aside from waking up long enough for a little soup and crackers and to take her medicine, she'd hardly left the bed. Outside her door, she heard the men of the house running military operations against explosion debris and germ warfare—at least that's what the General called it, the general being Nick. He was so good with the boys, and they were adorable with their serious "Yes, sir!" She could picture salutes accompanied by sneakers clicking.

A call to the doctor on Monday resulted in strict orders for her to take it easy "to avoid a serious illness." Paul, already back on his feet and feeling chipper, sent her a lovely Christmas bouquet. He never did figure out what had upset his stomach but attributed it to some twenty-four-hour bug.

David Marsh called to tell her he'd sold the window display at the Emporium but not to worry. He already had an idea to replace it with the new stock that was arriving daily. No, they didn't need her. Kitty Whitehall was in her glory presiding over the floor and watching David's masterpiece come together. Besides, the student Kathryn had hired from the Institute of Art at Thanksgiving as a stock boy was showing promise as a salesperson as well, so she might as well take off the remainder of the holidays to recuperate and spend time with her family.

So she wasn't as indispensable as she'd thought. The idea stirred mixed feelings, with relief and dismay battling for first place. This cold was the final straw. She felt burned out, unable to get enough rest. Even when she curled up on the sofa and watched a movie with Nick and the kids, she kept inadvertently drifting off to sleep. It was as if she'd been on some grueling journey that had suddenly ended and, without deadline or goal, she'd given in to fatigue at last. Her go-at-all-costs stamina had gone, leaving her emotionally and physically wobbly.

She supposed her volatile emotions were just part of her sickness—and of the sentimentality of the season. Christmas was a time for family and celebration, not bed and separation. Her only relief was that she'd at least straightened out her relationship with Paul. Her relationship with Nick was quite a different tale.

"Here you go, Mom! Fresh from the pot!"

Drawn from the endless cycle of introspection that plagued her waking moments, Kathryn looked up to see Jason coming into the room with her lunch tray. On it was a bowl of piping hot chicken noodle soup. It wasn't homemade, but Kathryn couldn't have appreciated it more if it were. The boys were taking turns cooking lunch each day. Nick let them choose the menu and prepare it under his supervision.

"Umm, it smells delicious!" She settled herself carefully against the stacked pillows as Jason put the tray across her lap.

"It's the chef's favorite."

"I know." Kathryn chuckled. "What I didn't know is how well you men could make out without me! I'm being spoiled."

"You deserve it, Mom. You've carried the load of this house and us kids alone too long."

Kathryn came to attention, pricked by her eldest's choice of words. Or were they someone else's? Nick's perhaps?

"I made your favorite cracker snack too," Jason went on, pointing to the whole-grain wafers topped with cream cheese and olive slices. "Jeremy ate most of the red stuff."

"Well, it is a little short on pimiento." She cocked her head to the side. "So tell me, just how does your dad turn you guys into housekeepers in a few weeks when it's taken me years just to get you to put your dirty clothes in a hamper?"

"You never told us how important it was to operations." At the dubious lift of Kathryn's brow, he added sheepishly, "And he can't spend time with us if he has to use it all cooking and cleaning."

"Medicine time!"

"Speak of the devil," Kathryn quipped as Nick entered the room with a glass of water and her antibiotics. "I mean, *doctor.*"

"Doctor of medicine," Nick acknowledged, handing her the pills and water. "Doctor of housekeeping," he went on as she swallowed them. "And doctor of love."

Before Kathryn realized what he was about, he kissed her on the lips. It was a quick caress, but no less devastating than a long, passionate one. But for Jason's elated observation, the glass in her hand would've spilled its remaining water on the bed.

"He's the *man!*" Her son gave his dad a high five.

White flags of surrender fluttered in her mind as she watched Nick square off before their eldest.

"Now, soldier, the bathroom needs policing. No need to tell you the risk involved in germ warfare. Remember…"

"The stuff we can see is just there to divert us from the kind we can't see!"

"Well done, soldier! Your equipment is in a bucket under the sink. Remember, safety first."

"Safety first?" Kathryn questioned as Jason, dismissed by Nick's salute, darted out of the room. "*Equipment?*"

Nick turned, sober to a fault. "Rubber gloves, goggles, and knee guards for serious scrubbing. There's never enough protection for working around a toilet.

Sometimes those cleaning chemicals are worse than the germs, so we use a paper filter mask, disposable of course."

"He must look like he's cleaning up after nuclear fallout." Kathryn laughed. She was beginning to think Nick could make a game of everything. He was a pied piper. "Is that Jeremy running the sweeper?"

"No, he's on a search-and-destroy mission...dust mites. Once I showed him what one looked like magnified, he went to war. Of course, after I explained what they were and how they lived, I had to dissuade him from collecting dead skin in a bowl and setting it out as a trap for them." He grinned. "So how do you feel?"

Tingly from tummy to toes. She always felt that way when Nick smiled at her like that—half mischief and all man. Inadvertently, she licked her lips, which were still warm from his kiss. "Better, thank you. With all this TLC, I can't help but get well. Although I told Jason you three were spoiling me."

"Enjoy it while you can. I don't know how long it will be before I run out of ideas to motivate those guys." Nick sighed, glancing at her with unveiled admiration. "I don't know how you did it alone, but you've raised some great kids. I'm really proud of you, Kate, not just for that, but for what you've done with your career, too. Guess I was so caught up in mine, I never gave yours much thought."

How long had she waited to hear those words from him? She savored them in silence, hardly believing her ears. Nick was always handy with the polite how-was-your-day kind of question, but he usually started talking about his before she could answer. Not that she didn't enjoy hearing about his work and new ideas. She did. She just wished her life had been as interesting to him.

"Dad!"

The shriek from the opposite side of the house was followed by a telltale grinding noise invading the whine of the vacuum cleaner.

"Dad!" Jeremy cried out again.

Nick charged for the door as Jason, also called to arms by his brother's panicked shout, rushed past.

Kathryn started to move the bedside tray to the side so that she could get up; then the growling appliance motor shut off abruptly. Soup sloshed over the side, slowing her down as a small, incredulous voice squeaked in the ensuing silence.

"The vacuum cleaner swallowed my bedspread! I think it's dead, sir!"

Twelve

THE CENTRAL VACUUM SYSTEM DIDN'T DIE, BUT THE ROTARY-powered carpet beater had literally bitten off more than it could chew. A new beater was added to Kathryn's growing shopping list while the number of days left to find and purchase the items shrank. Although she missed Jason's first soccer game, she was able to make the second. Despite wearing her coat over a sweater to ward off the outside chill, she huddled next to Nick and watched the boys scramble in a sweating frenzy after the black-and-white ball. But when a goal was made, she pulled away from his warmth long enough to cheer.

"You're cheering for the wrong side, Mom!" Jeremy chastised her, clearly mortified.

"I know that," Kathryn shot back, feeling the heat rise in her face at being corrected by a six-year-old. Sports were always confusing to her. Give her a concert or opera any day. "I'm trying not to show favorites."

"Smooth recovery," Nick whispered, his breath tickling her ear.

"Thanks."

"Reminds me of the good old days."

"Except you were usually on the field."

"Wondering why my girl was bouncing up and down for the other team."

Kathryn delivered a good-natured elbow jab. "Stop it!"

As she fished out a tissue to dab her sore nose, the ball emerged from a pack of kicking, panting boys and shot straight toward the goal where Jason played blue defense. By the time he ran it down, the red players were surrounding him.

"Oh no, he's going to be black and blue!" She stood so that she could keep an eye on the familiar sandy brown hair he'd inherited from his dad.

Suddenly Jason emerged from the group, the ball at the command of his feet. As he ran toward the opposite end of the field, he looked around, apparently hoping for another blue player to pass the ball to. Meanwhile, the red players were moving out to meet him.

"Go, Jason! Kick that—" She sneezed, covering her nose with the tissue. When she looked again, the entire crowd around her was cheering. The blues had made the goal. *Jason* had made the goal—and she missed it!

Kathryn brushed a dark lock of hair that had fallen out from under her knit cap behind her ear and stared at Nick in exasperation. "I missed it!"

He pulled her back down beside him and hugged her. "But you were there in spirit!" Impulsively, he kissed her on the cheek. "You sports animal, you!"

"Yeah, Mom, you're a real sports animal!" Jeremy teased, kissing her from the other side. "Just don't come to any of *my* games, okay?"

"Awww..."

"Just kiddin'!" the boy piped up quickly. "We love you even if you are all mixed up."

Kathryn caught Nick's eye and the two of them burst into laughter at the same time. Lord knows, she *was* mixed up. She'd figured out what *not* to do, but what *to* do where she and Nick were concerned left her wary. She wanted this to go on forever, with Nick so attentive and loving and the boys and her so happy...

Her eyes widened. She *was* happy—happy to be here with Nick and their sons; happy to wake up with Nick curled around her, even if the layers of blankets separated them; happy when he stole even the most innocent of kisses. She couldn't remember the last time she felt so lighthearted, even if her head was still a bit stuffy with cold.

Later, after Jason and Jeremy went home with the Anderson boys so that Kathryn and Nick could do some overdue Christmas shopping, Kathryn giggled like a schoolgirl at Nick's equally childlike antics in the toy department. He had to try out every superpowered gizmo on display, particularly those the boys had put on their wish lists.

249

Always organized, Kathryn had photocopied the clumsily scrawled dream sheets, which were now in the mail to Santa. Jason and Jeremy didn't trust the phony Santas in the department stores, in spite of Kathryn's explanation that they were Santa's helpers since the jolly man himself couldn't be everywhere at once.

Usually she enlisted the help of the toy store managers to identify the items on the lists, but not this year. By the time Nick was through playing with the kids who were just as eager to try out the displays, he knew the names, specs, and background of every action figure, robot, and vehicle on the camouflage and outer-space aisles. Giving up on her engaging thirty-some-year-old *child*, she took a nostalgic stroll through the baby and toddler section she'd once known by heart to the pink rows of dolls and dollhouses. She always bought David Marsh's little sister an outfit for her fashion-doll collection.

As Kathryn looked around at the vast assortment of clothes and accessories, the little girl in her came out. The outfits were so beautiful and elegant. She recalled having a dollhouse and hot pink car, but now the all-American doll boasted more possessions than any royal princess, with even a magic coach drawn by white horses with shimmering manes and tails. She could get on the floor and play with the boys if they had some of this stuff, Kathryn thought wistfully. She loved Jason and Jeremy dearly and wouldn't trade them for the world, but still, a little girl would have been nice.

"There you are!"

Nick approached her with a loaded cart, but it wasn't the loot that caught her attention. Someone had painted his face with camouflage colors. A box of them was perched atop the other toys.

"Now, before you say anything, look!"

He took out a handkerchief, and with a couple of hard wipes, the paint came off. Well, most of it did. "See, easy cleanup."

"Nick, I told you the boys would have it all over the walls, the furniture—"

"But it wipes off! And when I get home, I'll wash this handkerchief and it will be white as a fresh spring mornin'." This last bit was delivered with a heavy Irish lilt.

"You've been watching too many commercials."

He raised his brow expectantly. Reaching up, Kathryn used a tissue to catch a smudge he'd missed. "Oh, all right! I can't fight all three of you!"

She picked up the magical coach and horses. "What do you think for a little girl?"

"Don't you think we'd better get one first, mama?" Sheer devilment danced in Nick's whiskey-colored gaze, and it was enough to warm Kathryn from the tip of her tender nose to her cold feet.

"It's for David's little sister."

"We could still work on a little girl of our own."

"Nick!" Kathryn sighed. "You don't know how to be serious!"

She stepped back against the display as Nick moved closer. He planted a hand on either side of her and lowered his head so that she couldn't escape his gaze. "I've never been more serious, Katie girl."

"Just because we've managed to survive living together for a few weeks does *not* mean we can do it for a lifetime." She kept her reprimand to a whisper, aware that people in the aisle were watching them.

"We can just do it one week at a time."

"Nick!"

"Okay, one day at a time."

"Nick!"

"Nine months?"

Exasperated and embarrassed, Kathryn pushed him away. As she grabbed the handle of the cart and started toward the front of the store, she heard him call after her.

"But darling, I *want* to have this baby!"

Her mouth dropped open, but she could think of no reply. All she wanted to do was get out of the eyesight of the people watching her. She'd kill him when—

"Let's get married tonight! Here, pick a ring, any ring!"

"They are going to call store security on you," Kathryn grated out under her breath, ignoring the package of gaudy toy rings he'd picked up and shoved at her.

"You said you loved me."

"*I* am going to call store security on you!" She shoved the cart into a checkout line.

"For Pete's sake, Kate, don't make me an unwed father!"

When Nick dropped to his knees beside her, Kathryn's fragile reserve melted in laughter. The man was certifiably loony! She should have known better than to be seen in public with him.

"My reputation is already ruined."

"Shusshhhhh!" She leaned over the cart, unable to say anything else.

"Forget one ring. I'll buy the whole pack!"

A cross between hysteria and humiliation robbed her of her breath. She knocked the rings aside, shaking her head.

"Look, there's one for each finger! Whaddaya say?"

"You…you're…crazy!" She dabbed a tissue at her eyes and then blew her nose.

"If you don't grab 'im, honey, *I* will!" the matronly looking woman in line ahead of them exclaimed. "Hey," she added, narrowing her eyes at Nick. "You're that news fella just out of some prison."

Nick walked over to the lady on his knees and extended his hand. "Nick Egan, ma'am. You know I've been dreaming about this woman for over six years?"

Kathryn looked at the customer, helpless to defend herself. She couldn't even manage a killing look—mainly because she'd laughed so hard she couldn't see.

"What's the matter with you?" The lady ahead of them clearly thought Kathryn had lost her mind, not Nick. He always came up smelling like a rose!

Taking a deep breath, she steadied herself. "I—I've never s-seen him in my life!"

253

It took an eternity for the clerk to check out their order. Kathryn finally managed to regain her composure, but she dared not look at Nick, lest she provoke some other ridiculous comment. When he insisted on paying for the toys, she held her tongue. Even when he bought the little princess assortment of rings, she looked the other way. By the time they reached the parking lot, she'd worked up enough steam to at least reprimand him with some semblance of authority.

"I have never been so embarrassed in my life!" she growled when he got into the car after loading the packages.

"You know, you're a knockout when you laugh. That is, until you started heaving and wheezing over the cart. I wasn't sure if you were going to accept one of the rings or cough up a hairball."

"Nick…" Kathryn caught an involuntary snicker before it undermined her effort at sobriety. "Oh, forget it. Let's get this stuff stashed away before the kids get home. I *will* be glad to have help putting it together."

"Wish we could give them some of it tonight." Nick glanced over at her and grinned. "I know, maybe one toy for each Christmas I've missed with them."

"Absolutely not! You are worse than any two kids."

Nick pulled out into traffic from the mall exit ramp and the conversation lulled, except for when Kathryn directed him through unfamiliar territory. The radio softly played Christmas music while packages rattled in the back with the promise of Christmas morning excitement. Overhead the night was clear, like a star-studded blanket over the hustle of humanity below. From a large bridge and overpass the city sparkled with man-made light, like a fairyland. All that was missing in this magic was snow.

While Nick hummed to the music, she ventured a glance his way. The past week had been one of the happiest she could remember in a long time. Nick was charm personified when he wanted to be. He was fun to be with and warm to snuggle against when she'd shivered with chills and fever. She'd even regretted getting better. He was the father her kids dreamed of, the caring doctor, the perfect house husband. Well, almost, she thought, recalling Jeremy's question as to how to get the ironing stains off his dress shirt.

"I love that quiet, wistful look of yours."

She started and met his eyes. His tender gaze told her he knew she'd been staring at him.

He went on, his tone as tender as his expression. "The way your lips curl just the slightest bit and your eyes take on that dreamy, faraway look. Where were you?"

"Neverland." She glanced away as they pulled into Brighton Heath.

"Where little boys never grow up?"

"Yes." *Or men either.* She felt an acute sense of loss.

Nothing else was said until Nick parked the mini-van in the garage. The overhead door protested with the rattle and groan of its chains as it went down behind them. Nick cut the engine and the quiet grew oppressive. Kathryn was reaching for the door handle when she felt Nick's hand on her arm.

"I've grown up, Kate." Gone was all semblance of his previous humor.

At the gentle persuasion of Nick's hand upon her chin, Kathryn turned slowly. Their gazes met and melded at once; the jolt of the connection awakened senses and feelings best left alone. He'd read her mind and now he was reading her body, lowering his lips to hers at the beckoning of the quickening pulse in her ears.

Kathryn's fingers tightened on the pull of the door, but the rest of her would not retreat. Conscious objection clashed with involuntary surrender. Nick's harmless kisses when she'd been sick had been comforting, warming, offering security. This heady assault, however, threatened to push her over the brink of insanity, beyond retreat. Not that she really wanted to retreat...

A bright light swung across the wall in front of them, flooding the interior of the car through the garage-door windows. Kathryn could hardly breathe when Nick withdrew his lips from hers, much less process what was happening amid the confusion in her brain.

"The kids are here." Nick's voice was low and husky.

"The toys!"

"I'll put them in the garage loft after they're in bed."

He stole one last hasty peck and then slid across the plush leather seat to open the door. Lights flashed on in the interior of the car, dousing the last sweet remnant of

Nick's kiss. Back in the real world with kids shouting as they ran up the front walk, Kathryn gathered up her purse and hurried into the house after Nick.

Once inside the kitchen she tossed aside her designer bag and leaned against the counter, feeling for all the world as though her legs were about to go out from under her. *Oh, God, help me. It's happening.* What she feared most had come true. Nick was winning her heart just as he had those of her children. She was a fool to think she could live in the same house, even for a few weeks, and remain immune to the Egan charm.

God, you kept Nick alive, brought him home... for what? For this? Haven't you shaken my world enough? I'm not ready for this! I'm not! She closed her eyes, fighting the fear and near desperation tugging at her heart.

"Hey, Dad, did you know you and Mom were on the news?" Jeremy's breathless question grabbed Kathryn's attention instantly.

"What were you doin' down on the floor at the toy store? You looked like some kinda dingbat or somethin'." Jason wasn't nearly as impressed as his brother.

"What did they say I was doing?"

"Shopping madness!" Karrie Anderson spoke up, bringing up the rear of the entourage. "It was one of those news clips about the holiday rush."

Kathryn sank down on one of the cushioned bar stools in disbelief. Did someone with a camera follow Nick around twenty-four hours a day?

The boys stampeded up the steps, blocking out half

of what her neighbor was saying. "Look, I gotta run...got a cake in the oven. But I had to tell you, I nearly laughed my head off when I saw you crawling after Kathryn and her trying to hide behind the checkout counter. Frankly, I thought it was romantic. Which ring did she pick?"

"None of them." Nick shrugged.

How on earth could he be discussing their relationship so casually with someone he'd only known a couple of weeks? Karrie Anderson was *her* friend, not his.

"But the night's not over yet."

Kathryn jumped back to her feet, reinforced with indignation over Nick's presumption. He wasn't the least bit ruffled that his ridiculous behavior had been seen by thousands in and outside the beltway.

"Well, good luck, neighbor!"

"Thanks...and thanks for watching the kids. Feel free to leave yours here anytime."

Kathryn listened as Nick closed and locked the front door. In a moment he walked into the kitchen, smiling. "Guess we made the news."

"You always do." Kathryn brushed past him. His startled look told her he'd felt her intentionally cold shoulder.

Confusion clouded his eyes. "Hey, where you going? I thought..."

She didn't stop until she reached the stairs. With one hand resting on a newel post and a foot poised on the first step, she turned to glare at him, ready to spring into full retreat if he so much as took one step closer.

"The night may not be over for you, Nick, but it definitely is for *us!*"

Before he had a chance to react, to change her mind, she set a new speed record in reaching the second floor and the safety of her room.

Kathryn sipped black coffee the following morning, her mind a fog from a restless night's sleep. A locked bedroom door did not compare to the security of sleeping in Nick Egan's arms. It was a case of the cure being worse than the malady. Nick and the boys had gone to church for a last-minute practice for the Christmas service that evening. Jason had a reading and Jeremy was in the children's choir. She'd promised to attend, but her anticipation was laced with mixed feelings.

Was she ready for this? For being in church again? Was she ready to face those who had tried so hard to befriend her during her struggles with Nick and after his disappearance—people whose well-intentioned comments and offers of help had only served to make her feel more abandoned than ever? Abandoned by Nick…by love…by God…

I will never leave you nor forsake you.

She shook the remembered verse away. It wasn't true. God had left her. He didn't talk to her. He hadn't told her what to do or cleared her confusion any more before than he was doing now. He'd let Nick be taken prisoner. Let her think her husband was dead. Left her on her own to raise her children.

I will never leave you...

Tears stung at Kathryn's eyes at the words she couldn't shut off. It wasn't true! It couldn't be. If God hadn't left her, then that meant one thing. *She'd* been the one to walk away.

Cutting off her self-analysis in frustration, Kathryn focused on the real estate section of the paper spread before her on the counter, but the listings simply were not registering. The realtor she'd contacted had asked her to look over what was available and circle those she might be interested in, but Kathryn hadn't had time until now. So far, out of hundreds of homes and condos, not one appealed to her. If the location was right, the price wasn't. If the price and location were right, the accommodations weren't. Then there was the consideration of schools.

Why are you leaving me alone like this? If you love me like you say, why aren't you guiding me? Her silent scream at heaven went unanswered. A long-repressed anguish rose, stinging Kathryn's eyes.

Okay, so I know I'm not perfect. But I don't deserve this! God, I need help. I don't know what to do! Crossing her arms over her chest, Kathryn rocked back and forth on the stool. *I'm tired, Lord. I'm sick...and I'm so lonely.* She felt as though her heart were breaking, flayed by nerves snapping like the tail of a whip.

The sound of the garage door opening announced the arrival of Nick and the boys. Kathryn glanced at the clock, realizing it was after noon. Jeremy was the first to burst into the house, proudly holding up a toy from a child's fast-food meal. It was some cartoon character dressed in holiday garb.

"It's an ornament for our tree! Dad said after we clean up our rooms, we can go buy a *real* tree! He's got a secret formula to keep it alive, and I'm gonna feed it every day so you won't have to worry about needles.".

"A secret formula, huh?" Her eyebrows rose.

"You cryin', Mom?"

"No, honey." She blew her nose. That was the only good thing she could say about crying. It worked better than the most expensive decongestant. "It's this cold. I've honked and honked until not just my nose but my eyes are red too."

"Need a kiss to make it better?"

Kathryn's aching heart swelled with love as she looked at her youngest's earnest expression. "I think that is just what I need!" She leaned down and received three wet pecks, one for her nose and one for each eye.

"Aw, yuck!" Jason teased as he passed by them. "Baby slobber! Like Mom needs *your* germs! Now she'll never make it to the program tonight!"

Jeremy pulled away from her embrace, his blue eyes blazing with indignation. "It's better than kissin' Melissa Vandergraff!"

Jason's face flooded Christmas red in denial. "I didn't kiss her! She kissed me!"

"Slobber's slobber!" Jeremy danced away from his

brother's angry swing. "I'd rather kiss Buttons any day!"

The kitten, which had come down from the boys' room upon hearing their arrival, spied Jeremy lumbering toward it and took off in a mad scamper up the steps.

"Obviously Buttons doesn't feel the same way about you, sweet lips!" Jason sneered.

Both boys disappeared after the cat in a stampede so heavy it sounded as if the stair treads were coming up behind them. Kathryn folded the paper and stacked it as Nick came in with a bag of groceries. Wearing a festive sweater over slim-fitting jeans, he looked like he belonged in a ski lodge more than a kitchen. Instead of acting out of his element, however, he went straight to putting the food items away.

"Someone rob you of your beauty sleep?"

Kathryn grimaced. "Thanks, you're looking well too."

All of her cupboards were now rearranged according to male preference. Canned fruit and vegetables were categorized by color and personal taste, as were the boys' clothes, which were coordinated by the color chart now hanging on the back of their door for quick reference. Dishes and glasses were moved to a lower level so that the boys had no trouble reaching anything they needed. Poor Ruth Ann was going to have a conniption when she returned.

Nick drew out a box of tissues and tossed them over to Kathryn. "Figured we needed to restock." He stared at her face, his smile fading. "Are you all right?"

"Had a sneezing marathon." She wiped the makeup she'd put on that morning off with a new tissue. "What's this about Jason getting kissed?"

"Oh, some kid brought in mistletoe at the practice, and a certain young lady put it to work over our son's head. I'm afraid it's going to take more than some parasitic plant to warm him to the idea. It's a one-sided relationship. Know just how she feels."

Kathryn let his comment slide and started reading the newspaper column in front of her. Why did *she* feel like the guilty party in this mess? She wasn't the one who was gone all the time. She hadn't put her career ahead of her family.

Lord, if you're trying to tell me something, don't use Nick as a messenger. He's cried wolf too often.

What was the point? Kathryn stared blankly at the black print in front of her. God wasn't speaking to her. She'd cut him off when Nick disappeared, and now he was doing the same to her. Maybe she deserved it.

Kathryn's thoughts halted abruptly as an article about a real estate scandal caught her eye. It was written by Lev Chandler, a reporter Nick had gone to school with. In fact, Lev had been at the party the other night. It wasn't Chandler's name that snagged her interest as much as the name of the mortgage company being investigated. Capital One was the company through which she had developed Nick's family land. Paul Radisson was a member of the board of directors and had secured a loan for the project. She frowned and focused on the article, feeling the color drain from her face as she read that Paul's company was part of a scheme to defraud sellers through Lands End Developers.

"I can't believe it!" Kathryn shook her head.

"What's that?"

She glanced up to see Nick thumbing through a cookbook.

"I did such a bang-up job at the school party that I was elected to make some punch for the snacks after the church program," he said.

It took Kathryn a moment to recover from the shock. It sill amazed her to think of Nick Egan picking out recipes. Game plans, maybe. Research on a hot story, definitely. But *recipes?* Until recently she would have said he thought food came already prepared in little boxes. Either that or on a waiter's tray. But he really impressed her with his homemade meals.

She glanced back at the article. "Um…it says here that the company who bought and developed Brighton Heath and the mortgage company that financed it are charged with real estate fraud. I wonder if Paul knows anything about this? He's on both boards, which is why I went with their proposal."

Nick looked up from the book and shrugged. "I don't know. But I'd better have my attorney take a look at the transactions and books, just to be on the safe side."

"Nick, Paul would not be party to anything like this, especially when it involved my children's trust."

"Yeah, you're probably right. But only because he

planned to have that trust in his pocket anyway by marrying my beautiful widow. I mean, why share with his partners in crime?"

Kathryn sat, mouth agape at Nick's reply. "I can't believe you said that!"

"Come on, Kate. Don't tell me that you'd go off for a weekend with a man you didn't intend to marry. I know you. You don't play games!"

"I am *not* marrying Paul Radisson!" Kathryn jumped to her feet. "And I would have had my own room at the Malchows, for your information, which is really *none* of your business to start with, mister. And something else that is none of your business—" she halted in her tracks as she headed for the hall—"I told Paul he would never be more than a friend, and he accepted it a whole lot more graciously than you have!"

"Was that before or after he handled the development for you?"

Kathryn squared her shoulders and lifted her chin. "I will not dignify that with a reply. I'm going to take a nap. I keep getting these headaches whenever you're around!"

It wasn't until she closed the bedroom door behind her that she realized she'd left her medicine downstairs along with the real estate section she really needed to examine more closely. Exhaling in frustration, she yanked the bedroom door open, only to find Nick standing there, a glass of water in one hand and her medication in the other.

"Medicine time."

Kathryn snatched the pill from him and tossed it down with the water.

"Thanks, Floyd Nightingale." She handed him back the glass.

"You're welcome, Katie girl. Want me to tuck you in?"

Kathryn thought she'd rather wrap the blanket around the neck of the man standing before her, clearly nonplussed by her irritation. Instead, she answered by closing the door between them.

"And stop calling me *Katie girl!*" She turned the lock on the knob in defiance.

If only she could lock him out of her heart as easily.

Thirteen

IT WAS WITH SOME TREPIDATION THAT KATHRYN ENTERED THE massive wreathed oak doors of St. John's. After Jason and Jeremy ran off to the Sunday school rooms where the program cast was assembling, she walked stonelike beside Nick down the wide carpeted aisle toward the poinsettia-filled sanctuary. The family pew was to the right. Kathryn had grown up in that small enclosed cubicle, as had her father before her. She'd pledged her love to Nick, until death do them part, at the altar. Later, she'd said her final good-byes to him here at a funeral service.

She glanced at Nick, who'd turned in the pew to speak to one of the parishioners. Kathryn didn't recognize the couple, whom her husband introduced to her as the DeSantis. Aware that several heads were turned her way, she nodded with a stiff smile to those she recognized.

If they hadn't read Faye Ramsey's column about the hero who exchanged a civil war for a domestic one, they'd surely seen the ridiculous clip on TV of her and Nick's shopping trip. She could imagine what they must be thinking: *There's that Kathryn Sinclair, a woman with a devoted husband come back from the dead, the long-lost father to her sons, and she had the nerve to deny him her love and his family.*

Or was that her conscience speaking?

The church bell announcing the arrival of the seventh evening hour startled her. She felt like a basket case. It had to be this flu or cold working on her nerves. All she wanted to do was cry, and that was not like her. She was too strong for that. She'd had to be.

The congregation quieted with the lowering of the lights. Now it was candlelight that illuminated the room. The small singular flames in each stained-glass window and at the end of each pew cast an ethereal glow on the wooden arches above. Angels painted on the ceiling almost looked alive, waiting in anticipation of the service. As Kathryn sat there, she felt an odd sensation, almost as though a presence surrounded and blanketed her.

She glanced at Nick, but he was focused on the stage, watching with eyes that glowed with anticipation and pride. Kathryn bit her lip as the sensation of being cloaked—no, *embraced*—grew even stronger. It was as though someone was wrapping her in strong, comforting arms.

God?

Goose bumps traveled up her back and along her arms. *God, is it you?*

Be still…

The words washed over her.

Be still…and know.

A calming peace settled over her, soothing her nerves. Her breath caught in her throat with anticipation, just as it had when she was a child squirming with the excitement of the season and on a candy high. Something sacred was about to take place—something sacred and more beautiful than anything man could conjure with divine direction. The humble, unaccomplished players were but instruments in God's theater, a means of delivering his Word, the same Word that was, is, and forever will be in all time and place. She was as sure of it as she'd ever been of anything in her life.

No heart was immune, not even Kathryn's scarred one. The nameless dread she'd felt was gone. In its place was a sense of foolishness for having avoided not just God's house, but God himself. Dare she hope there might be a word for her after so long an absence?

The kindergarten class came in first. Then in single file, Jeremy's Sunday school class marched into the room, little angels too solemn for their characteristic mischief. Even the smallest cherubs were on their most reverent behavior. Kathryn sat a little taller in her seat and waved when she saw her youngest straining to see her.

"And ye shall be led by a child…"

The Scripture crossed Kathryn's mind as Nick's camera went off beside her, starting a storm of flashes all around. The music started and two dozen or so small pairs of blinded, blinking eyes sought out the choir director decked out in Christmas red and green with her hand raised to give the signal to begin singing.

"Away in a Manger" never sounded sweeter. That was a mother's unbiased opinion. Kathryn basked in the parental pride she shared with Nick when, as the children filed out, Jeremy pointed to them and announced in a stage whisper, "See, Scott. That's my mom and dad!" She felt her cheeks pinken at the resulting titter of laughter around them, but the overwhelming sense of oneness with the man at her side lingered long after the warmth left her face.

Jason's class took turns reading the Christmas story from Scripture. With his father's flair for the dramatic, her oldest son read in a strong, mature voice, as if he felt every word. In the background, the organ softly played carols for each verse. It wasn't so long ago that Kathryn herself had been up there at the podium reading, while her mother sang in the choir loft. She knew the story by heart, yet it was as though she were hearing the words for the first time, especially in candlelight with the music of angels echoing in the rafters.

"Behold, I bring you good tidings of great joy which shall be unto all people. For unto you is born this day in the city of David a Savior, which is Christ the Lord...."

The words rang out, echoing in her heart and mind,

washing over and through her. *Good tidings of great joy…*
Unto you is born a Savior.…

The heaviness in her heart grew lighter as each
scene unfolded and the words and music became a
cleansing balm to her spirit. Suddenly she was a child
again, a little girl captured in the marvel of God's gift, the
joy of a season so filled with hope and promise. She
closed her eyes and drank her fill of the wonder. Then
the minister stood up to share his message.

"Can you feel it?" His question seemed to be directed
right at her, and Kathryn found herself nodding, fighting
back tears.

Yes, she felt it.

"It's the Holy Spirit. He's surrounding us, my
friends. He's ringing out the news again for all of us to
hear. The Savior has come; the long night is over. And
we, his people, are free indeed!"

Kathryn answered wholeheartedly with the congregation, "Amen!"

The pastor smiled at them. "It's a beautiful story, isn't
it?"

Again she chorused, "Amen."

"But not all of the Christmas story was beautiful."

Silence fell over the spirit-rich gathering. Kathryn
felt more than saw that every eye was riveted on the minister, every heart was waiting.

"There were snags. Serious snags. Herod's cruel
murder of firstborn sons, his plan to have the wise men
reveal the whereabouts of the newborn King so that he

could have the baby killed.... Even a godly man like Joseph was a problem for a while. Remember, he didn't want to marry Mary or trust her word that the Spirit of God had come upon her."

Kathryn was drawn into the sermon like a moth to a flame. The minister might just as well have been speaking about her and Nick. He went on to discuss how hard it was to trust even those we love, and how easy it was to doubt. "So God sent an angel to Joseph to show him the way."

Kathryn drew a steadying breath. If only God would send *her* an angel. She clasped her hands in her lap, yearning with all her heart for the guidance she so desperately needed.

Be still...

The whisper came again, stirring her heart even as it calmed her. She nodded, ignoring the tears that wanted to fall. Stillness wasn't her strong suit. Not by a long shot. But if that's what God was calling her to—and she believed it was—she would obey.

As best she could, anyway.

At the end of the service, there was an altar call. Kathryn started when Nick stirred, then stood. She watched as he moved past her to the aisle and went forward, his strides long and sure. She almost followed, wanted to do so with all her heart...but she simply couldn't—not in front of all these people. To walk to that altar would mean giving up her last shred of composure, her pride.

So she sat there, motionless, gripping her hands together and feeling as though an invisible rope were wrapped about her heart, pulling her. Her throat ached and her eyes stung. *Jesus, I can't. I just can't.*

At long last, the lights came on overhead and the service was dismissed.

"I have to go serve punch downstairs. Are you coming?" Nick asked after most of the congregation had dispersed.

Kathryn nodded, distracted. All she wanted to do was leave. She didn't want to be around people, not now, when she was a veritable volcano of emotion. "I'll stay here for a while. You and the boys go on. I'll join you later."

Nick's eyes studied her carefully. "You okay? Do you want me to take you home?"

Kathryn shook her head. "No, I just want some time alone in here. It's so beautiful."

"Well, you're in good company."

With an understanding wink, Nick rounded up Jeremy and Jason and headed for the festivities in the basement.

Kathryn watched as the janitor snuffed out all the candles and assured him, when he asked her to turn off the lone altar light when she left, that she'd be certain to. As the older man closed the door to the entrance hall behind him, she faced the front of the church, where a manger scene was bathed in soft light on the satin-draped altar.

There had been no more peace in Judea two millennia ago than there was today at Egan Court. Yet God's love overcame the obstacles of doubt, of fear, of mistrust...it was all there, in the story that endured as one of joy and celebration.

Bracing herself with a deep breath, Kathryn rose and stepped out into the aisle. No longer could she hold back. She knew what she had to do. Tears spilling over her cheeks, she started forward. Her destination— Bethlehem.

When Nick saw Kathryn wander into the church basement, the party was winding down. He could tell she'd been crying but afforded her the privacy of her thoughts. He once again offered to leave, but she insisted on staying and helping the adults clean up. Her smile was shaky and her blue eyes overly bright, a sign of the emotional turmoil that had made life so difficult for both of them of late.

He knew Kathryn still loved him. He knew it, yet inside he was terrified of losing her. He'd tried leaving it at the altar, but there was a part of him that wouldn't let go. He'd made his confessions to God, but there were too many secrets he harbored from the woman he loved—destroying all chance of the survival of their marriage. God surely had to understand that.

Since it was his turn to give the Andersons an evening to catch up on their Christmas preparations, the car ride home after the party was filled with encores performed by Kyle Anderson and Jeremy. All the way in the back of the minivan, Jason and Keith had their heads together, a sure sign for Nick to be on the alert. Keith's mother had reveled in telling him some of their sons' more sordid escapades, like rearranging Christmas lawn decorations for the neighbors or building fires in barbecue pits in midwinter, to mention a few.

Once home, the boys dispersed immediately to fetch sleeping bags for the campout in the family room Nick promised them, while he took out the prerequisite hot dogs and marshmallows. They'd eaten a ton of brownies and decorated cookies earlier, but, like he'd been at that age, Jason and Jeremy were bottomless pits when it came to food.

"You want me to take out one for you?" Nick asked Kathryn, who walked into the kitchen after hanging up coats.

"No, thanks."

She looked tired despite her quiet smile. The circles under her eyes were puffed from crying, and her shoulders looked as though the weight of the world were balanced on them. "I'm glad I went tonight."

Nick continued to make preparations for the indoor cookout. He wanted to ask her why, to see what she thought of the sermon, which was surely a direct answer to his prayers. Instead, he held back. He'd been where he suspected she was. This was something to be worked out between her and her Maker.

"Me, too. The kids were great."

She slid onto a bar stool and crossed her legs in ladylike fashion. Distracted by the long, shapely display, Nick nearly lost one of the wieners. He caught it before it rolled off the edge of the counter. The first time he'd seen Kathryn, she'd been at a pool party in a swimsuit. He'd misstepped on the pool ladder and nearly took the skin off his chin as he watched her stretch out on a chaise, aloof but nonetheless breathtaking.

"They always have been, Nick." She was as oblivious to his admiration now as she'd been then. "You've missed so much."

There was no sign of accusation in her voice or expression. If anything, Nick perceived melancholy.

"I know." She seemed to want to talk. "But I pray I'll not miss anything else. That's why I don't want to share the boys, Kate. I want them and you with me full time."

Kathryn squared her shoulders and Nick groaned inwardly. *Lord, please. I just want her to see that I mean what I'm saying! Please, let her see that. Don't let her shy away from me...from my love.* Whatever had happened back there in church, whatever had put that quiet glow in her gaze, he didn't want to undo it.

To his astonishment, she put her hand over his. "I know, Nick. I just—"

She broke off and struggled for words. Suddenly, she pointed to the answering machine, looking almost relieved for the distraction. A bright red digit blinked that there was a message waiting. Nick ignored it. He held his breath, hoping, praying, she'd go on, that she'd say what he longed to hear.

"There's a message."

Retreating both physically and emotionally from the confrontation, Kathryn pushed the Play button.

"Nick, this is John Waters. Good news, buddy. I have another offer for your book from Pitney-Hamilton. We're talking six digits and a major promo tour, so hope you can take off for a few months when it hits the shelves. I'm in Manhattan so call me tonight at..."

Grabbing a pencil, Nick listened for the number and jotted it down. This was an entirely new ball game from what Grossman had offered. He'd thought his agent was overly enthusiastic when he insisted on putting the proposal out for bid.

"Did you hear that?" He looked over at Kathryn, wanting to share his excitement. But she wasn't there. Her retreating steps sounded on the stairwell and ended with the closing of her bedroom door. Nick felt as if a heavy theater curtain had fallen...on him. Shut out again! Muttering silently, Nick jabbed the Delete button with his finger as if it were responsible for the interruption. Silence was allegedly golden, but he was beginning to wonder just how much more he'd have to endure of this passive nature, which did not come naturally to him.

The day before Christmas Eve, Kathryn was physically, if not emotionally, improved. She'd asked God to send her an angel and instead, she'd gotten a static-filled message on the answering machine. Ah, the wonders of progress!

The look on Nick's face when he heard about the fantastic offer only validated the one fear that would not give her peace. She'd seen that look before when he got a particularly good assignment, one that would take him away from her and his family. Cabin fever was showing its signs, despite Nick's claim that he wanted to be a permanent fixture in her life.

After spending the morning at the Emporium catching up on business, which had gone on well without her, Kathryn met her realtor for lunch. She'd delayed the inevitable long enough. It was one thing to want to believe in fairy tales. It was something else entirely to base your life on them. Paul was behind her. Soon, Nick would be also. Appointments for the showings were set for that afternoon.

Half listening to Barbara Hearn rave about the compliments she'd received on Kathryn's work from common clients, Kathryn could not shake the accusing words Jason left her with that morning. In searching for the comic section of the paper, he'd seen some houses she'd circled.

"Whatever happened to give it the old American try, Mom? Or you can't win if you don't try?"

Those sayings had meant something when she'd encouraged him to tackle a difficult subject or task. How could she make him understand this was different?

Is it?

She pushed the irritating question away, wishing she could dispense as easily with her memories of this morning.

"You just don't wanna try!" Jason had charged angrily, running away before she had the chance to defend herself.

"Ready to hit the road?" Mrs. Hearn asked from across the restaurant table, bringing Kathryn back to the present.

Her mind drawing a blank, Kathryn looked at the realtor. She'd no idea what the woman was talking about. "I'm sorry. What were you saying?"

The smartly suited woman held up the check. "I've taken care of the bill. Are you ready to go or should we stop at the ladies room first?"

"Never hurts to be safe!" Her response sounded a little too light, no doubt to compensate for the heaviness in her heart.

As Kathryn gathered her purse, she felt a vibration at her waist. Glancing down at the pager fastened to her belt, she recognized the office number flashing. What on earth could David want with her? He'd practically shoved her out the door with the declaration that she was not to come back until she'd settled her personal-life crisis. Like that could be done over the holidays, she thought wryly.

"You go ahead. I need to make a quick phone call."

"Kathryn! Thank God! I've been waiting—I mean, it's going to be all right...that is, don't worry about anything."

Kathryn was grateful she was sitting down on a bench by the phone. The near panic in David's voice made her so weak in the knees she was sure she would have ended up on the floor otherwise. David struggled valiantly to soften the news that there'd been a minor accident until she demanded sharply, *"Who* is going to be all right? What happened?"

Had Nick and the boys been the *minor* accident he mentioned? She clenched her jaw, willing David to hurry up and explain.

"Jeremy was struck on his bike by a car in front of the development on State 371. But he was conscious when the paramedics took him away."

"What was he doing riding outside the development?" Kathryn fought the panic that invaded her voice. Nick and the boys were supposed to cut the tree down to size and set it up in the living room! Nick was *supposed* to be watching them.

"Where did they take him?" Her heart sank further into despair. His agent must have called and set up an appointment.

"Georgetown."

"Thanks, David. Call and tell them I'm on my way."

Feeling as though her chest were in a vise, Kathryn hung up the phone. It wasn't the first emergency she'd faced alone. Except that she wasn't, she realized later, after explaining what had happened to Barbara and hailing a cab. God was with her. He was all that kept her from going to pieces.

Kathryn leaned back against the seat as the vehicle took off into the thick traffic, and closed her eyes. *God, please, don't let this be serious. Please God.*

The fare was only seven dollars, but it felt as if it should have been ten times that, judging from her perception of the time it took to reach the front of the hospital emergency-room entrance. People scurried about, much like her thoughts, all with a purpose—though what exactly that purpose *was* eluded her. The antiseptic smell of the polished halls invaded her nostrils as she waited to speak with a clerk at the information desk.

Where was her baby? Her attention swung to the large double doors that opened and closed automatically with the passing of patients and personnel into the restricted area.

"May I help you?"

Kathryn had to look closely at the nurse sitting behind a large computer to ascertain if the flat-line voice had come from her or the machine. After all, the woman's eyes were fixed on the screen, rather than Kathryn.

"I'm Jeremy Egan's mother. He was brought in by—"

"Egan…E-g—"

"A-n," Kathryn finished.

The nurse never glanced up or acknowledged her.

Once again it seemed as though the computer itself spoke. "Room 17, through the double doors and to your left."

After walking past a row of drawn curtains, which sealed off the various compartments of the immediate-care facility, Kathryn reached the one numbered 17. Pushing it aside, she stepped into the cubicle.

"Jerem—?" Her voice choked at the sight of an empty stall. In a rumpled ball on a stool nearby were the baggies and sweater her youngest son had chosen to wear that morning. His worn sneakers were under the stool, their dingy white stained with an ominous red.

God! she prayed, unable to think beyond his name.

Kathryn swayed unsteadily, unable to cry for more help. Suddenly there were arms about her. Desperate for reassurance, she turned into Nick's embrace, staring up at him wildly. With shaking hands, she grasped his grim face.

"Where…?"

"He's in X ray. He's going to be okay."

Okay. Kathryn seized upon the word, savoring it a moment before confusion gained sway again.

"But I thought you were putting up a tree!"

"I got a call from John Waters this morning after you left…"

Nick's admission was like a slap in the face. She'd been right! The fear and frustration of the car ride to the hospital, of not knowing how her son was, erupted in an outburst of anger. Kathryn shoved Nick away, her eyes snapping in accusation.

"I knew it, Nick! I knew you'd let me down. I knew it!"

She knocked away the arms he attempted to put about her and crossed her own, but Nick managed to herd her into the protection of the curtain, away from curious stares drawn by her emotional display. He caught her by the shoulders and gave her a rough shake.

"Jeremy is going to be all right! Now calm down!"

Stunned at the harshness in Nick's tone and behavior, Kathryn blinked away her runaway emotions so that she could see his face. Once her hysteria subsided, he gentled his voice.

"He had his helmet on. They're checking now just to see if there's anything broken."

"But his shoes...the blood..."

"He struck his nose with his arm or something and has some scratches and bruises. I've had worse run-ins on the football field. The car had just made a turn. The bike took the brunt of the damage."

The fight seeped out of her as relief swept in, and Kathryn sat down in the chair Nick pulled up for her. *Thank you, Jesus.*

"I left the boys with Karrie Anderson because the publisher was flying in this afternoon just to meet me and discuss the deal."

The deal.

"You took it." She stated, rather than asked. At that moment the curtain was hauled aside by a nurse to make way for a rolling gurney. Lying small among the hospital white sheets was Jeremy. His nose was horribly swollen. It was hard to tell where it ended and his forehead and eyes began. Remembering Nick's assurance and recalling times when she'd seen him looking worse than he really was, Kathryn rushed to the bedside and took Jeremy's hand.

"Mommy's here, darling."

Dark lashes fluttering, Jeremy looked up at her through heavy-lidded eyes. The corners of his mouth twitched.

"Hi, Mom."

"The doctor will be with you in just a minute, Mr. and Mrs. Egan," the attending nurse informed them. She hung Jeremy's chart on the end of the bed and left.

"How are you feeling, sweetie?"

His hands and fingers were warm. That was a good sign, since she'd read somewhere or seen on some emergency show how the blood left the extremities when there was internal damage or trauma.

"Like I was runned over."

A chuckle of relief shook her. "Honey, what were you doing out on the main road?"

No answer. Instead he closed his eyes.

"Jeremy!"

Her alarmed exclamation brought them open again. "Goin' to church."

Startled, she exchanged glances across the bed with Nick.

"Church?"

The boy nodded. "I needed to get closer to God."

Not quite sure where this was going, Kathryn pressed him further. "Why didn't you ask your dad or me to take you?"

"You guys were busy an—"

"Mr. and Mrs. Egan?" A young man in a green medical uniform stepped into the cubicle and extended his hand, first to Kathryn and then to Nick. "I'm Dr. Stephanos, Jeremy's attending physician."

"How is he?" Kathryn asked.

"We've got a hairline fracture of the radius, not serious. Can't make a judgment on the nose until the swelling goes down."

"Do I get a cast?" Jeremy's dazed eyes widened with excitement.

"Will a brace do?"

"Cool!"

The doctor grinned and pointed a pistol finger at the boy. "You can still take baths that way."

Even Kathryn laughed at the way her son wrinkled his nose, until he winced in pain.

"That shot the nurse gave you should be helping with that discomfort anytime now, sport," Dr. Stephanos assured the boy. "Meanwhile, we want to keep you overnight for observation. You were kind of out of it when you came in. Good thing you had on a helmet."

"I always wear a helmet."

"Smart people protect their brains!" the doctor told him before turning back to Kathryn and Nick. "I'm going to finish up the paperwork to send him upstairs. One of you needs to go to admissions and handle things there while we transport him. They'll have a room number by the time you get there."

"Thank you, sir." Nick shook the doctor's hand again.

"Looking forward to your column in the *Journal*, man!"

"Thanks, Doc. And thanks again for taking care of my son."

Was there anywhere Nick went that he wasn't recognized? Kathryn turned back to Jeremy.

"I'm going to have to get you admitted, sweetie, but—"

"I'll do it. I've got my new medical card. The boys are on it."

One thing Kathryn could say about Nick. He was always full of surprises. In the past few weeks he'd pulled his life back together remarkably well…as efficiently as he'd pulled hers apart.

"Deal." She was grateful not to have to leave her son. Only God knew what she'd been through on that interminable cab ride across town, the horrible scenarios of losing him that would not let her be.

A few moments after Nick left, orderlies came in to take Jeremy up to the children's floor. Kathryn accompanied them, listening to how her son didn't mind needles because they gave them in the tube attached to the big needle in his hand. It hurt when they put it in, but not as much as his nose hurt. He'd thrown up in X ray, clear across the table, he bragged.

By the time he was settled in a room with another boy his age, who was in for pneumonia, Jeremy's words were becoming slurred. The nurse assured Kathryn that sometimes the pain medication made little ones groggy and not to worry.

Alone at last with her baby in the curtained half of the room, she bent over and kissed his forehead, moving aside his thick dark hair with her lips.

"Darling, why did you think you needed to go to church to get closer to God?"

For a second, she thought he was asleep. Suddenly he cracked open his eyelids and mumbled. "'Cause Kyle said asking Santa wouldn't make you stay married to Dad an' that God was closer in church." He paused and yawned. When he picked up his conversation again, it was fainter. "An' I wanted to be sure God heard…"

Jeremy didn't have to finish his sentence. Kathryn knew the rest. *He'd wanted to be sure God heard his prayer that she and Nick stay together.*

"And ye shall be led by a child…"

The Scripture gripped her soul as she bent over and tenderly gathered her son in her arms. God *had* sent her an angel after all.

"Honey, God is with us *all* the time. He hears us wherever we are…even when we can't see him."

"Like now?"

"Yes," Kathryn whispered brokenly. "Like now."

287

"Mom?" Jeremy's voice grew fainter as the sedative took effect. "Will you pray it for me?" He yawned. "I think I'm gonna go to sleep right now."

Her tears won out at last, flowing down her cheeks and falling onto the crisp white sheet covering her son. "Yes, Jeremy, I'll pray it for you."

And closing her eyes, she did what she now knew she should have done long ago. She gave up her fears to God, whose answer could not be denied, and claimed his grace for herself, her sons, and her marriage to Nick.

Fourteen

"TELL MR. RAFETTO I'LL SPEAK TO HIM BY PHONE OR WE C[
meet in the hospital cafeteria, but I am not leaving [
wife and son."

Nick tried to keep his voice hushed, so as not to [
turb the boy lying on the bed or the boy's mother, wh[
nodded off in a nearby recliner, which was provided[
the hospital for the comfort of parents staying over[
with their children. He wasn't successful. Kathryn [
her head. The defeat in her voice cut Nick to the c[

"Go, Nick. This is important. Jeremy and I are [
She shifted in the chair, bringing it upright. "Have [
per meeting; then pick up Jason, stop by the hous[
pick up a few things for me, and come back."

"Hold on, John." Nick put his hand over the m[
piece of the phone. "I'm staying, Kate. You've do[
alone for too long."

"Nick, you're helping me! Remember, we have two sons. I can't be in two places at once. I know the Andersons will keep Jason, but I feel like we've burdened them enough already."

"Divide and conquer, huh?"

Kathryn smiled wearily. "Teamwork."

Nick removed his hand and spoke, not quite convinced. "Okay, John. I'll meet Rafetto at his hotel after dinner at eight, but only for an hour or so. And I'm not agreeing to anything right now. I don't exactly trust my judgment at the moment."

If he hadn't changed his plans, he, Kate, and the boys would be trimming the tree in the family room. That was what he'd had in mind. She was a sucker for holiday music and Christmas decorating, always had been. Nick wanted to see her relax and enjoy herself, rather than drive herself to the point of collapse. It seemed as if everything he tried to do to win Kate over backfired.

He hung up the phone. "Look, I think *you* should take Jason home when I come back and let me stay over. You're just over that nasty cold and need your rest. All I need is *two* patients."

"You'll have to get Laine again."

Both Nick and Kathryn turned to see Jeremy had awakened also.

"Laine?" Kathryn arched her brow, looking at him.

Nick stood at his full six-feet-plus height, but it felt like his spirit had slumped to the floor, shot down by Jeremy's inadvertent slip.

The boy cut his swollen eyes at his mother, then back to Nick in panic. Suddenly tears added another dimension to his dismay. "Sorry, Dad!"

"Who's Laine?"

"It's okay, sport. When all is said and done, honesty is the best way."

"Even about Mr. Paul?"

Kathryn was on her feet, suspicion mirrored on her face. "What about Paul?" There was no sign of fatigue now. She was a lioness, ready to pounce, and he was the victim du jour.

Nick held up his hand as though to check her first assault. "First let me say it was all relatively harmless."

"We didn't mean to make him go to the hospital, Mom."

"*What?*" Kathryn glared across the bed at Nick. "What have you done?"

"I hired a temporary housekeeper to help out while you were at work. But when you got sick, the boys and I took it over, all of it." There. Nick was glad it was out. He'd felt guilty about it from day one, but wanted Kate so much he hadn't listened to his conscience. Or the Lord. *Okay, Father, now it's time to pay the piper.*

Kathryn rolled her eyes. "I should have known!"

"I was wrong, okay? I admit it!"

"All's fair in love and war, Mom!"

"What else? What did you do to Paul?" She ignored Jeremy's stab at his dad's defense.

"Dad didn't know anything about it! It was me and Jason's idea."

291

That seemed to knock the wind from her sails. Kathryn turned to Jeremy. *"What* was your idea?"

From the look on her face, Nick wondered if she wasn't afraid of the answer.

"Me an' Jason gave him some of Miss Karrie's diet tea so he couldn't leave a bathroom long enough to take you away for the weekend."

Nick jumped in. "It was an accident. They made it too strong. They meant well, Kate. They didn't want you going away with Radisson any more than I did."

Kathryn swung away from the bed and marched to the window, her arms folded across her chest in indignation. "I can't believe what I'm hearing! You are home for less than a month and already you have my boys plotting behind my back. All's fair in love and war!" She spun about, erupting in accusation. "Isn't that a lovely thing to be teaching them? That it's okay to lie to their mother and make someone else sick just to get their way!"

Nick felt he was being sucked under the angry flow, and not all of it was Kathryn's doing. It was his own. He'd taken matters into his own hands. He'd set a bad example for his boys. Now he was paying the price.

"When I found out what they'd done, I told them that we all were wrong. That from now on, we had to be up-front, nothing but the truth."

"That's what he said, Mom," Jeremy chimed in from the bed. "You don't have to be a kid to make a mistake. An' God says we're s'pose to forgive, right?"

Good call, son. But the look on Kathryn's face told Nick she didn't think so.

Not by a long shot.

Kathryn steeled herself against Jeremy's plaintive words. He didn't understand. He didn't know just how close she'd come to believing in miracles, only to have them shattered before her.

"Is there anything else, Nick? Anything else you haven't bothered to tell me? Any more secrets?" *God, what are you doing to me? Just when I think I know what you'd have me do...*

"Isn't that enough, Kate?" Nick glanced at his watch. "I'd best get going. Traffic is heavy at this hour."

He leaned over the bed and kissed Jeremy on the forehead.

"I'm sorry, Dad."

"It's for the best, sport. I know you only did what you did because you loved us."

That's right, make *her* the bad guy, Kathryn fumed, her expression hardening as Nick gave her a short "See you later" and left the room. Just when she was beginning to trust him.

"Honest, Mom, that's the only reason all us guys did what we did. We love you and don't want to lose you."

Against Nick her rigid fury might prevail, but not against Jeremy. Her son hadn't learned the art of manipulation and deceit yet, although he'd had an effective

293

lesson. Kathryn took Jeremy's hand and gently stroked around the intravenous needle. Nick deserved retaliation. Her baby didn't.

"I know you meant well, darling, but what you did to Paul was dangerous."

"We didn't think goin' to the bathroom was dangerous."

"You caused him to be in severe pain, severe enough to go to the hospital. We thought he had food poisoning."

"But wasn't it good that you didn't go away? You were really sick."

"That has nothing to do with right and wrong," Kathryn insisted firmly. "You and Jason were very wrong. You will have to be punished, and you'll certainly have to apologize to Mr. Radisson."

"Don't tell him, Mom, please! You can send Santa away this year, but please don't tell Mr. Paul! He already hates us."

Jeremy was on the verge of frightened tears, but it was his statement about Paul that made Kathryn waiver. Why hadn't she seen how serious the antagonism was between Paul and the boys before?

"I'll think about it. Meanwhile, I think I hear the food cart coming down the hall. Are you hungry?"

As she helped Jeremy with the electric controls to move the bed into an upright position, an aide came in carrying a tray. With a flourish, she unveiled a piece of oven-fried chicken with nutritious, if not delicious, trimmings. The moment she was gone, Jeremy started spooning the green peas into his mashed potatoes and gravy.

"Good thing I got more smashed potatoes than peas." He focused on his task of disguising the vegetable. "If there's enough good stuff, the bad's not hard to swallow." With that, he added a dollop of applesauce.

If Kathryn had had any appetite, the sight of the mush on her son's plate banished it. She watched as he took a spoonful of it and downed it with a chaser of milk.

"See?" A milk mustache stretched over his wide smile.

Kathryn nodded, but she was lost in thought. *"If there's enough good stuff, the bad's not hard to swallow."*

Lord, am I listening to an angel or just a precocious child?

She recalled the hasty retreat Nick made when she'd asked him if there was anything else he hadn't told her; the nervous glance at his watch; the way he'd sidestepped answering. Bad *stuff* could be dealt with if it was confessed. It was the hidden things that ate away at a soul like a cancer, destroying trust, burying hope. Nick had misled her. He'd set a poor example for his sons in doing so.

Diet tea. Poor Paul!

Were it anyone else's kids, she'd be tempted to at least chuckle, but that wasn't the case. There was a matter of trust, of something very fragile and precious to her, being violated. And there was the matter that Nick had not confessed to, that sent him eagerly off for an appointment he'd at first been reluctant even to make. A myriad

295

of suspicions raced through her mind, but Kathryn was at a loss to imagine what could be worse than what he'd already admitted to.

Maybe, she thought, her heart sinking even lower, *I don't want to know.*

An evening spent in a recliner, even if it was as plush as those Kathryn sold to her clients, did not make for a good night's sleep. Add to that bells, buzzers, announcements, and rattling medicine carts, and Kathryn didn't even fight collapsing on the couch for a much-needed nap after they'd brought Jeremy home the following day. While she rested, Nick, Jason, and Jeremy, with his one free arm, tackled the task of trimming the fresh spruce sitting in the family room in front of one of the patio doors. The other door had to be left accessible for bringing in the wood from the pile Nick had had delivered a few days earlier. Heaven forbid there be Christmas without a fire in the hearth.

A picture conjured in Kathryn's mind: their family gathered in the fire's glow about the first fresh tree in the house since it had been remodeled. Her heart twisted as she listened to the holiday music playing on the stereo. Trustworthy or not, Nick was firmly entrenched in her perception of family. Neither her mother nor Paul had come close to filling the void in the pictures of holidays past—only Nick would do.

Not the polite Nick who'd picked up her and

Jeremy at the hospital that morning and assured her that everything was under control, so she could get some sleep. Nor the Nick who'd stiffly admitted to serious consideration of the book offer, which would take him away from home for a month or so. In the picture-book setting she longed for, however, there was no arm's length between them, either physical or emotional, as there was in reality.

They drifted through dinner at an Italian restaurant and the Christmas Eve church service that followed as if in different dimensions connected only by Jason and Jeremy. She listened for a message and pleaded silently for some sign that God intended to save their marriage, but all she heard was the age-old story in the beautiful carols, and all she saw through the glaze plaguing her eyes were the happy faces of other families gathered there for worship and celebration. On the surface, the Egan clan appeared the model family unit, but Kathryn felt their hearts were miles apart.

And hers was breaking.

Later, while Nick got the boys ready for bed, Kathryn struggled with the Christmas turkey she intended to bake overnight. A fire lapped around sizzling wood in the hearth and the tree lights twinkled, giving the family room a fairylike glow. It was the perfect setting for a story-book family Christmas. Aggravated by the way things were, rather than how they appeared, Kathryn took her frustration out on the bird, slamming it about on the counter as she seasoned it.

They'd cleaned the house up beautifully, her big and little men, putting away all the empty tree trimming boxes and running the sweeper to pick up hazards to bare feet. They'd done their best to make this a perfect Christmas Eve, even dressed for dinner and church without complaint. It all looked perfect. If only it *felt* that way.

The telephone rang, startling Kathryn from her troubled thoughts. Wiping her hands on a towel, she walked to the wall unit and answered.

"Merry Christmas, sweetheart!"

"Mother!" Kathryn exclaimed in surprise. "Are you home?"

With Jeremy's accident and her quandary about Nick, Kathryn had nearly forgotten her mother was to arrive home today from her cruise. *Please, God, don't let her want to come over tonight.*

"No, I've had a change of plans. I do hope you and the boys will forgive me, but a group of us decided to fly on to Las Vegas."

"Las Vegas?" Kathryn hoped she didn't sound too relieved or surprised by the quick answer to her frantic prayer. The fact was, her mother's arrival would only make matters worse between her and Nick. Kathryn needed to make her decision about the future without her mother's and Nick's antagonism toward each other complicating everything.

"There comes a time in one's life, Kathryn, when one has to stop doing what is expected of them and start doing what they want to do."

"When have you ever not done what you wanted to, Mother?" Stella Sinclair was the most single-minded woman Kathryn knew. Not only did she run her own life according to her notion, but she tried to run everyone else's as well. Especially Kathryn's. It had taken her a long time to cut the well-intentioned strings her mother held her with.

"You'd be surprised, Kathryn. Maybe this old gal has learned a few new tricks."

Intuition came to full alert. There was more to this than Stella was saying, but with her own problems, Kathryn wasn't sure what lay between the lines.

"Mother, are you trying to tell me something?"

"I'm saying I'm tired of living according to accepted ways. I may be a senior citizen, but I'm also a woman."

"I never doubted that, Mother." How could she? Stella was a grande dame in the beltway society.

"I'm not about to fade into life as a gracious widow. I intend to make a grandstand play."

"Grandstand play?" What on earth? Kathryn was amazed Stella even knew what the term meant, let alone used it! Had she swallowed a sports manual on her cruise?

"Oh, for heaven's sake, Kathryn, stop repeating after me like a parrot. I'm getting married in Las Vegas. I met this wonderful..."

The tale came rushing out. Her mother was going to marry a retired sportscaster whose vocabulary had infected her as much as his romantic nature. They were flying to Las Vegas to get married and would be home by the New Year...maybe.

299

"Kate, are you all right?"

Kathryn started at the sound of Nick's voice. Nodding, she sat down on the bar stool, listening as her mother bubbled over with the details of her meeting this Ed Hunter and how he'd made her feel like a carefree woman again instead of a stiff-mannered matron.

"It's Mother," Kathryn whispered, her hand over the phone. At least it was her mother's voice. But the words were someone else's.

"I only have one drawback."

Stella's blithe comment made Kathryn smile. It wasn't a prenuptial agreement. She'd already covered that. "What's that, Mother?"

"I feel guilty being so happy after what's happened between you and Paul. Kathryn, I was dumbfounded when I heard."

"Heard what?"

Kathryn had forgotten about her mother's indefatigable gossip chain, although to her knowledge, aside from Nick—who certainly was not her mother's confidant—no one knew that Kathryn had ended her relationship with Paul. Had Paul told someone? Surely he hadn't called Stella himself!

"Kathryn, I know Paul is on the lam. I read all about it in the papers. That mortgage company has lawsuits all over the East Coast!"

Slapped from yet another direction, Kathryn shook her head in disbelief. "On—on the lam?"

"I'll bet he went to that place he invested in in Barbados."

"Mother, I don't know what you're talking about! I haven't seen a paper in two days." Kathryn held back the story of Jeremy's injury. There was no sense in upsetting her mother when she was so…what? happy? crazy?

As if he'd tuned in to the conversation, Nick picked up the morning paper from the hall and spread it on the counter in front of Kathryn. There in bold print beneath the headlines about government scandal was an article titled "Capital Attorney Flees Charges of Fraud." Next to it was Paul Radisson's picture. Her mother filled Kathryn in on the details.

"You'd best have Nick check on the development that rascal handled for you. It could have bought his little getaway. As I recall, he purchased it about the same time you remodeled the house."

"I think Nick is already checking on that."

"It just goes to show you, you never know," Stella went on. "And *this* lady is forgetting what she knows and going with her heart. Wish me the best, darling! I know you'll like him."

"Who?" Kathryn was still stuck on "forgetting what she knows and going with her heart."

"Ed, of course! He reminds me a bit of Nick, good looking, charming, full of that boyish mischief."

Stella hated Nick! Kathryn glanced out in the garage where Mr. Boyish Charm was dutifully hauling down Santa's loot.

"Speaking of that devil, where is he?"

"In the garage."

301

"You're making him sleep in the garage? Good for you! Make him beg before you take him back."

Now Kathryn knew someone else had possessed her mother's body. "I don't think that's going to happen." She clamped her mouth shut, mortified at the disappointment echoing in her voice.

"That's not what I hear."

"Mother..."

"Don't try to fool me, Kathryn, and for heaven's sake, don't fool yourself! I've heard all about the two of you at Jason's soccer game, at the mall, at church, just the four of you in our family pew..."

Dumbfounded, there was nothing for Kathryn to do but listen.

"And what on earth took you on the roof of your house?"

"Buttons."

"Who?"

"The cat." Kathryn wondered if this conversation was for real. She pinched herself and winced.

Nick, who'd just squeezed through the door with two armloads of packages, looked at her, a slight frown evidence of his concern. "You sure you're okay?"

Kathryn shook her head. She didn't know whom she was really speaking to, much less what her mother was talking about.

"I just want you to be happy, darling. I suppose I've known you never stopped loving that rascal. I was ready to fly home and put an end to his nonsense, but Ed stopped me. He made me see that it was none of my business and, moreover, just because I was a dried-up, stiff old prune, that wasn't any reason to make you one."

"A…dried-up prune?"

"You're parroting again, dear. Is Nick there? Maybe I should be talking to him."

"No!" She was in enough confusion as it was without compounding it by whatever Stella and Nick could conjure. "No, I'm fine, Mother. I'm just…I'm just happy for you if this is what you want."

"Now *you're* sounding like the mother."

They laughed together. Kathryn couldn't remember the last time they'd shared a laugh. Her mother was usually too busy trying to run everyone's life to be funny.

"Well, Ed's waving. That must be our flight. I have to go, darling. Merry Christmas!"

"Merry Christmas, Mother…and best wishes! I mean that from the bottom of my heart."

"Give my love to the boys, but don't tell them I'm bringing them a new grandpa."

"No—"

"And hug that rascal of a husband of yours."

"Okay—"

"Bye, darling, and remember, if you're afraid to take risks, you're afraid to live."

Kathryn put down the phone after muttering some sort of good-bye, but her mother was already gone, off to a new marriage—her *mother,* the woman whose idea of spontaneity was reservations made a week in advance.

"Where do you want me to put this stuff?" Nick dragged the last of the bags into the kitchen. Protruding from the top was the space station Jason and Jeremy both wanted. "You said you wanted to wrap it," he reminded her as she stared at the fierce space battle depicted on the label.

"I'm not sure...but I think that was my mother." Kathryn wondered if she hadn't been struck by a stun gun. "She's getting married, Nick...in Las Vegas...to a retired sportscaster!"

"Anyone I know?"

The least he could do was look surprised!

"Ed somebody. I can't remember. I was so shocked."

"Well, your mom's not unattractive, and she can be charming when she wants to. Even the Huns got lonely." Nick put the packages down and dodged Kathryn's playful kick at him. "So Stella the Hun's got herself a man. Not Ed Hunter, is it?"

"That's it."

"Nice guy. Wife died of cancer right after we worked together at the Winter Olympics." Nick chuckled. "Hard to picture Stella with a sports fanatic."

Kathryn walked over to Nick and placed her hands on his sweater, a soft red cashmere lightly scented with his cologne. "Harder still to imagine her saying to give you a hug for her."

Reaching around his neck, Kathryn pressed against him. Maybe she had been shot by a stun gun or maybe, just maybe, she was finally beginning to understand where God wanted her to go. At least Nick's embrace seemed the right place. Her head was in a fog, but her heart had never wavered. Nuzzling against his neck, she kissed the pulse quickening there.

Instead of holding her or responding, however, Nick stepped away, kicking a bag of toys as he did so. "You're right. That couldn't have been Stella. Maybe it was a wrong number."

His mouth curled up with a humor absent from his eyes. Bending over, he picked up the bags again and put the food bar between them.

"Okay, Mrs. Claus. So what do we wrap and what do we assemble? This is your forte, my being new at this."

"Assemble the station. I'll wrap the vehicles and figures."

How Kathryn kept her voice steady when she was still reeling inside from his deliberate evasion was beyond her. She fought an overwhelming urge, but couldn't decide if it was to laugh or cry. She left Nick unpacking the loot while she retrieved the special Santa paper she'd hidden in the hall closet.

Well, what had she expected? True, Nick hadn't been able to keep his hands to himself at first. But since Jeremy had let the cat out of the proverbial bag about the housekeeper and the terrible trick the boys played on Paul—and since she'd demanded to know if there were other secrets Nick had kept from her—things had changed.

Trying to act as if nothing were amiss, Kathryn began to wrap the action figures and the various attack vehicles with names she could hardly pronounce. After an hour, the space station was assembled and she had to marvel over every gizmo and flashing light it boasted while Nick tried it out. Just to see if it would work, of course.

Jeremy's presents went on the left side of the tree, Jason's to the right. Nick added a new soccer ball, knee pads, and elbow guards to the display. The task that normally kept her up to the wee hours of Christmas morning was finished shortly after midnight.

"How about some eggnog?" Nick volunteered as they surveyed their handiwork with a degree of pride. "I sprinkled nutmeg in it myself, but the rest was pre-mixed."

When Kathryn arched an exasperated eyebrow at him, he held up both hands.

"Just keeping things honest!"

"Everything?" She followed him into the kitchen.

Aside from the lights on the tree and the light over the counter, they were cloaked in the magical luster of Christmas Eve. A traditional carol faded on the stereo and a contemporary one started as Nick poured two glasses of the holiday mixture. He put hers on the counter and pointed to the stool in front of it.

"Belly up, partner."

Kathryn's patience snapped. "This isn't funny, Nick. I mean it. Is there anything else you need to tell me before—"

She broke off, unable to complete her sentence. Before what? Before she made a fool of herself and took the leap of faith? Before she confessed that, even though he'd hurt her, she loved him and always would? That she couldn't give up on this marriage until she gave it a fighting chance? She owed that much to the boys…and to herself.

God, if this is what you want, help us, please!

"All right. Sit down, Kate."

The look on his face chilled her, but not nearly so much as the flat, dispassionate words that came next.

"You wanted the whole truth. Well, I hope it's worth it."

Fifteen

Jesus, help us.

It was all Kathryn could think of as Nick eased down on the stool beside her, his obvious contemplation fixed on the tree at the opposite side of the adjoining family room. His jaw was taut, even when he took a sip of the eggnog. The slight trace of a vein pulsed at his temple, as though something terrible churned inside, brewing rapidly to a boiling point. Yet it wasn't anger. Anger she could deal with. This nameless threat was far more unsettling.

Kathryn had to steady her hand as she lifted her glass to her lips. The creamy liquid splashed on her upper lip, but she was too distracted to worry with it. Nick had her undivided attention, whether he met her gaze or not. She'd never seen Nick struggle for words. She'd never seen him afraid. As if an unseen force guided her, she put a compassionate hand over his clenched one.

"Ah, Katie girl." His acknowledgment was razed with emotion. "I loved you the first day I saw you, and…" He swallowed, his Adam's apple bobbing above the turned collar of his sweater. "And I've never stopped."

Her heart surged at the fervent admission. She tightened her hand upon his. Whatever this was, they'd face it together. *With your help, Lord. Please.*

Tell him.

She swallowed hard at the urging, resisting for a heartbeat, then giving in with a sigh. It was time to stop running. Time to give as much honesty as she was asking to be given.

She drew a steadying breath and plunged in. "If we're going to confess all, then I have to say the same. I…I didn't want to love you, Nick. But I can't help it."

"What about Paul?"

"He never…I mean, we never…I just couldn't, Nick!" *Thank you, Father, for that. How could I have been so stupid?* Neither she nor Nick needed any more obstacles to overcome. "I was so selfish. I should have broken off what relationship we had long ago, but you were dead and I kept… I kept thinking maybe, just *maybe,* things would work out, for the boys' sake more than mine. Nick, I know now I can't do this alone, raise the boys without a father—*their* father. I've been guilty of the same thing I wanted to divorce you for—loving my family so much that I practically abandoned them to provide for them. My priorities…I have been so confused!"

Nick buried his face in his hands. His broad shoulders shook once, as though the monster were about to burst free of constraint, but he made no sound.

Instinctively, Kathryn put her arm around him. She'd never comforted Nick before. It had always been the other way around. But even this wasn't enough. She wanted to hold him, to kiss him, to reassure him that there was nothing they couldn't face together for the sake of their sons. She turned him toward her, and his arms absorbed her into a starved embrace.

Nick squeezed her until she could hardly breathe, pressing her face against his chest. He kissed the top of her head in a desperate frenzy, as if he expected her to run away as she had in the past.

Instead, it was he who withdrew from the intimate closeness, the bond of unrequited longing broken. A chill swept through the chasm between them as he looked down at her, his face a mirror of dread. It was infectious, with long, icy fingers it crept across to ensnare Kathryn's chest, her very breath.

"The LORD is my light and my salvation; whom shall I fear…" Or what?

"I wish I could say I was as innocent as you, Kate. I wish to God I could!" Nick licked his lips and chewed them, as if to glean some courage to go on.

Dear God, not now. Not now that I finally feel as though I know what's right.

Infidelity had crossed her mind once in a while, but she'd never been able to believe Nick capable of doing that to her. Their problems were based on what he *didn't* do, not what he did.

"*The LORD is my strength of my life…*" She mustn't be afraid!

"I thought I could go on and leave this in the past, but I can't. Everything I've held back to keep from losing you has only driven us further apart. I took false credit for running the house—"

"But you stopped when you realized it was wrong," she argued, remembering Jeremy's words.

"*After* I'd led my sons astray as well."

"But you didn't know!"

"Kate, I had an affair."

Kathryn shrank away from the admission, but the additional space between them was no help. Her thoughts reeled in spiritual combat, reason against hurt, faith against fear. Help came from a voice within. "*By grace are ye saved…and that not of yourselves…*"

It was true. But for God's grace, she might have done the same thing. Paul was charming and attractive. She might have—

"At least, I'm pretty sure I did." Nick's face was the picture of misery.

Pretty sure I did?

The rampant chaos screeched to an abrupt halt. Kathryn's gaze questioned when her lips could not.

Nick turned away, unable to look her in the eyes. "I was drunk. I'd just received the divorce papers." He got up and paced over to the sink. He poured out the eggnog with a frustrated sling. "I didn't even think I'd live to see the week's end anyway with the interview I'd just lined up. Turns out, I got captured instead of killed."

"Why'd you agree to such a risk?" While Kate wondered about the answer to this, another question pressed more heavily on her mind. *Who?* But that was one she couldn't bring herself to ask, not yet. *God, we've come so far. Not now...please!*

He looked at her through the reflection in the window over the sink, a cynical twist contorting his mouth.

"I'd lost you and Jason. What did I have to live for?"

Her confusion escalated. He'd been so composed, so cool when they'd hacked their lives in two over the lawyer's table. He might as well have been conducting an interview for all the emotion he showed. She absorbed the bitterness in his voice only to discover her own anguish was not quite as buried in the past as she'd believed. It actually helped to form the "So who was she?" on her lips, but Nick beat her to the punch.

"Kit had a sympathetic ear and a comfortable bed." He raked his hand through his hair. "It happened. So help me, Kate, I've regretted it ever—"

"*Kit?* Kit Cody?" Relief washed over her and seeped into her voice as she recalled the exonerating conversation she'd overheard between the photographer and her coworker.

When Nick nodded in confirmation, Kathryn laughed. It was a high-pitched, hysterical release. She couldn't help herself. Gleeful voices chorused in her ears and would not be contained, despite the shocked, scolding look on Nick's face. Bless his dear, loyal heart!

"I'm ten years older, Kate, but believe it or not, I turned her head."

Tears trickled down her cheeks, but she was beyond caring. Nick was carrying an imaginary devil on his back, one she was determined to relieve him of as soon as her own emotional landslide subsided. She loved Nick so much! If only she'd trusted her heart...and God's messengers!

"Blast it, Kate, it's not funny! Did you hear what I said?"

Kathryn soothed his wounded male ego in the only way she could at the moment. Throwing her arms about his neck, she planted a salty kiss on his mouth with a loud smack.

"I love you, Nick Egan!"

With an emotional hiccough, she tried to kiss him again, but he grabbed her by the shoulders and shook her. "Did you hear me? I said I had an affair...*with another woman!*"

"Well, I should hope it would be with a woman!"

Furious, most likely because he couldn't get a sensible response from her, Nick gave her another shake, but his viselike fingers gave way to his desperation. Instead, he stroked the length of her upper arm in a plea, drawing her close.

"I need you to forgive me, Kate! God knows I've never forgiven myself!"

"For boring a young woman all night long yakking about your love for me?"

Kathryn's heart fluttered back to some semblance of normalcy in her chest. As to whether her feet were touching the ground, she'd not venture to guess. Clasping Nick's confounded face between her hands, she gazed up at him, letting her eyes sparkle with all the love she no longer wanted to hold back.

"You didn't sleep with her, Nick. You passed out on the bed while waiting for your pants to dry after she spilled developing fluid on them."

The stunned look on his face almost triggered her hysterical laughter again. He straightened, and she felt his muscles tense. Her sweet clueless darling!

"How do you know all this?"

"Girl talk." Kathryn gave him a devilish grin and smoothed out the skeptical lift of his brow with her fingers. "I overheard your Miss Cody in the restroom lamenting to a friend over her exciting night with *the* Nick Egan. Your reputation is shot, Romeo!"

Nick ran his fingers through his hair as if to make certain her meaning was sinking in. The sandy brown locks were as attractive tousled as they were groomed to camera perfection, she mused, dizzy with happiness. He reminded Kathryn of Jason after his first goal, reeling in joy and disbelief at the same time.

"Aww, man!" He dropped onto the bar stool as the truth finally settled in. "I wish I'd 'fessed up sooner. You don't know what I've been through since—"

He broke off as Kate moved to lean against his chest.

"It's not been easy for either of us, Nick. We've *both* made mistakes. I couldn't see beyond my own—"

Nick reached out, took hold of her, and pulled her close, claiming her confession with a tummy-curling kiss of forgiveness. His caressing fingers reveled in the silkiness of her hair, wrapping in first one lock and then another until his palms pillowed her head in worshipful affection. There was no holding back for either of them, not anymore.

Kathryn molded her body against his, as if to push out everything that had kept them apart—pride, hurt, bitter memories, fear…

And the bar stool.

Its wooden legs scraped on the floor in warning. Suddenly Nick was groping to catch himself on the counter as the stool went out from under him. The crossbar caught Kathryn across the shins, driving her in the opposite direction. Frozen, despite the desire heating their veins, they held each other's startled gazes. The final crash of the bar stool between them hardly phased them.

Kathryn recovered first, instinctively bending over to rub the front of her legs, but the sight of Nick, the athlete extraordinaire, hanging by his elbows from the counter like a dazed overgrown rag doll, was too much to bear. A renegade giggle erupted when she truly meant to ask if he was all right.

The feminine prick to his manly ego brought him

back to his senses. Struggling to gain his footing, he gave her a perfectly wicked look, the kind Kathryn imagined flashed in the eyes of the Big Bad Wolf when he realized Little Red Riding Hood was his for the taking.

She forgot her aching shins and backed away, not the least threatened. In fact, the very thought of the revenge Nick had in mind nearly took her knees out from under her. It was just that no self-respecting heroine would simply fall into the wolf's arms without *some* semblance of resistance. The game demanded a chase.

She dodged the grasp of Nick's hand and snickered when his fingers missed the satiny material of her blouse. As she made a mad dash for the steps, a distant inner voice, one belonging to her organized, practical nature, reminded her that some of the lights were still on. The sound of Nick's growl less than a breath behind her, however, spurred her onward and upward, as if the hounds of hades were on her heels.

The lights would wait.

The little girl in her thrilled to the game, fleeing to the master bedroom, seeking the safety inside, but it was the woman within who left the door open. Spinning around, breathless with anticipation, Kathryn watched as Nick came through the door, giving it a slam behind him. It was hard to hold her ground when he looked at her with those intense whiskey-colored eyes.

The time for running away was over. Kathryn couldn't if she wanted to…and she didn't want to.

A long drawn out "Mo-om!" sounded in alarm the following morning, invading the cozy security of Kathryn's slumber. With a mother's instinct she was instantly awake, bolting upright and out of the warm embrace of the man sleeping next to her. The door to the room burst open. At the same time, she snatched the bedclothes up over her chest, realizing that she'd not donned her nightgown as usual. But then nothing about last night had been usual.

"Dad's—"

"Gone!" Jeremy finished when Jason halted abruptly in front of him.

The younger boy crashed into his brother, jarring him from his openmouthed stare.

"We...we thought Dad had gone." Jason's face turned crimson as he took in the scene of scattered clothing leading up to the bed where Nick stirred groggily beside her. "He wasn't in his room."

Kathryn's mind went blank, at a loss as to how to begin explaining. Not that Jason appeared to need much. She wondered which of them was more embarrassed.

Nick, his wits somewhat gathered, sat up beside her. "You guys ever hear of knocking?" The possession of his arm about her warmed her cooling shoulders. The temperature must have dropped during the night...not that she had noticed until now.

"Sorry, Dad. It's just—well, you were gone and I didn't

think Mom…" Jason heaved a sigh of exasperation, no better able to think than his mother.

Nick came to his rescue. "So, you guys think Santa has been here?"

"I *know* he has!" Not the least discomfited by the situation, Jeremy sprinted toward the foot of the bed to join them, but Jason caught him by the pajama bottoms, hauling him up short.

"C'mon, jerkface! Ever heard of *privacy?*"

"You're gonna stay married now, aren't you!" the younger boy declared confidently, ignoring the fact that he was being dragged backward out of the room. "I asked God *and* Santa! I knew it would work. I just knew it!"

"Man, Jer, you are so stupid!"

"Am not!"

Disgruntled, Jeremy turned and, with his good arm, took a swipe at Jason. The older boy promptly pulled down the smaller one's pajama bottoms and took off running down the hall.

"They *got* to stay married now 'cause they're *naked!*" Jeremy tugged one-handed at his waistband as he tore off in hot pursuit of his nemesis.

"You guys go stay in your room till we come for you!" Nick called after them.

"We'll be right with you!" Kathryn chorused.

The door at the opposite end of the hallway slammed, was yanked open, then slammed again, muffling the ensuing tussle, which no doubt involved pillows. Despite being flushed with embarrassment,

Kathryn exchanged an amused glance with Nick when Buttons scampered into the room and up on the bed, which was part of the kitten's habitual morning run. Discovering that people were still in it, however, sent her off in startled retreat, heralded by a descending ruckus in the stairwell, as if she were falling down head over all four feet.

"So much for catlike grace," Kathryn quipped. "As for modesty…"

She turned into Nick's waiting embrace.

"Guess we *got* to stay married, Mrs. Egan," he whispered, bussing her nose with his lips. "'Cause, unless I'm badly mistaken, the boy is right."

Kathryn giggled, enjoying the present warmth as well as that from the memory of the previous night together. It had been a night of passion, yes, but it had been more. Their souls had been purged of guilt and reunited, taking together the leap of faith and trust in the One who'd blessed their union years before.

"What God has joined together, let no man put asunder." Nick had repeated his vows, punctuating each one with a kiss, a caress, an embrace. "Mrs. Egan…"

"I'm going to have to get used to that name again." She sighed, not particularly averse to the idea.

"Ah, Katie girl, it doesn't matter what you call yourself. Keep your maiden name, if you like. Just so you are mine, heart and soul, like I'm yours."

Kathryn ran her fingers over the span of Nick's chest, staring up at his stubble-shadowed face with the rakish tousle of hair curling just above his eyes. Now there was a whiskey she could never drink enough of.

"And don't forget body," she reminded him with an impish grin.

The fires of the night before had only banked while they rested, for she saw them rekindle in Nick's gaze, sparking her own response. As he lowered his mouth to hers again, however, a crash resounded on the other side of the house, dousing them like a bucket of cold water. She'd heard it before. The stackable bookshelf between the boys' beds had collapsed during the roughhousing. If boys were going to continue being boys, she was going to have to ask Nick to anchor it to the wall!

Chuckling, she shoved him away and reluctantly rolled out of bed.

"Ah, the unparalleled joys of parenthood." He grinned, throwing himself back against the pillow with his hands locked behind his head and watching as she cold-footed it across the polished wooden floors to fetch the thick terry cloth robe hanging inside her closet.

"Get up, lazy bones. We have to see if Santa has been here." She shrugged it on, shivering, and checked the temperature on the thermostat. Just as she suspected; it wasn't a drop in the temperature, it was her body's protest at leaving Nick's arms.

"I agree with Jeremy." Nick was in no particular hurry. "I know the fat man's been here 'cause I talked to God too. I got what I wanted for this Christmas and for all those to come—the woman I love."

Kathryn stopped at the bathroom door. Even from across the room, she felt the embrace of Nick's declaration of love. She wondered if anyone had ever fainted of sheer happiness. "I love you, Nick Egan. I've always loved you. I guess I was just afraid."

"What changed your mind, Kate?"

A smile tugged at her lips as well as her heart. Her memory came to life with images and words, delivered by the messengers she'd prayed for but had been slow to recognize: Jeremy with his childish coloring of the prodigal son's lesson in forgiveness on her dresser; her minister with the heart-gripping sermon about Joseph's dilemma and struggle with his faith; God's own Word on the well-worn page in Nick's Bible, pointing out the foolishness of fear when one claimed God's Word; even her mother with her uncharacteristic behavior and advice!

It was all so timely, every encounter coming just when she needed it most. God had heard and answered her furtive prayer for messengers when she knelt alone at the altar after the children's Christmas program. He'd heard her confess her desperation and fear, responded to her plea for him to take control of her life. There was only one answer Kathryn could give to Nick's question. Love poured from her very soul as she responded softly.

"Angels. God sent me angels."

Epilogue

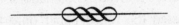

THE RUSH AND TUMBLE OF THE WATERFALL BESIDE THE CAMP-
site was as soothing to the soul as the smell of the fish
Nick was frying in a pan over the fire. Kathryn put a pri-
ority-mail envelope with the approval of David's latest
Emporium order in the compact car that was attached
with a tow package to the back of the motor home. The
latter had been the family lodging for the last two weeks.
Kathryn had managed to conduct whatever business
was essential via cellular phone, laptop, and express mail
ever since Nick started his book tour with his family in
tow in late August.

"Hey, guys, I need some more firewood! Who's got
the detail?"

Freshly showered from the early fishing venture that
morning, not to mention the fish-cleaning episode that
followed, Jeremy emerged from the motor home door.

"Me, mee!"

"Here, you can burn this paper." Cleaning out the vehicle, Kathryn handed the boy last week's edition of the *Journal* containing the latest story on the development scandal. While Paul hadn't swindled Kathryn personally in handling Nick's estate, some questionable fees had been turned up by Nick's auditors. Since Paul either took or destroyed a number of his files before fleeing the country, there were no ready explanations.

Jeremy tossed the rolled paper onto the fire and, after watching it curl and burn, skipped merrily into the brush, looking as carefree as Kathryn felt. She glanced over at Nick and caught the kiss he blew her.

Over a year and a half had passed and she still melted inside at the smallest show of affection from her husband. A mischievous wink, the warmth of his breath against her ear as he whispered words for her alone, that wolfish growl of his when he caught her in his arms…she tingled at the memories.

"And what are you grinning about, Mrs. E.?" Nick held up his hand. "Wait, don't tell me. You're thinking about the revenge you're going to take when I go on that buying tour with you this fall."

"Not even close." Kathryn sniffed. "Although I have to admit, I am looking forward to wearing dresses instead of jeans and khakis and seeing you in a tuxedo next to me at the London theater."

Ruth Ann was going to keep the boys while Kathryn and Nick went to Europe for a few weeks. Combining business with pleasure was fast becoming a way of life for them. One they all thrived on.

"Actually, I'm looking forward to stepping out on the town with my two ladies."

Kathryn ran a self-conscious hand over her blossoming stomach. The little girl she carried was due just before Christmas. It was a toss-up who was more excited about the prospective addition to the family—she, Nick, or the boys.

"Hope Caitlin likes fish," she remarked, the scent making her mouth water. Kathryn was starved. A cup of black coffee no longer satisfied her for breakfast, now that she was eating for two.

"If she let you eat that dinner you had last night, that kid'll eat anything. Chocolate-smothered ice cream and fried dill pickles!"

Kathryn laughed at Nick's shudder. She'd been very lucky with this pregnancy, no morning sickness or any other discomfort, unless one counted outgrowing her wardrobe. She walked up behind him and hugged him.

"Ever since Mom and Ed brought those fried dill pickles back from the Mississippi River cruise, I've been craving them!"

"I knew that woman was warped."

"Nick!"

Nick flinched from her playful pinch. "I mean it! She's not only been civil to me, but she went to a Redskins game! Stella the Hun at a football game!"

"But she had the best seats in the house and wore a Bartot original." Kathryn giggled. Some things about her mother would never change.

It was hard to imagine Stella attending sports events, but she had changed so much since marrying Ed Hunter. Maybe she'd been afraid to live beyond her accepted role as the widow of Kathryn's father. Perhaps her lifestyle was so ingrained that change never occurred, much less appealed to the woman. The fact was, her mother had discovered a whole new world through the eyes of love.

Much like her daughter, Kathryn thought, planting a kiss atop Nick's head.

"What was that for?"

"Having the patience to show me the wonders of the all-outdoors. I've never been happier, Nick."

Kathryn meant every word. No matter where she was or what she was doing, so long as it was with Nick, she was in her glory. Absently, she massaged his shoulders, more than twice the full span of her fingers. He leaned against her.

"Just be glad I have a signing this afternoon, lady, or I just might have to introduce you to love in a waterfall."

This time, it was Kathryn's turn to shudder. The idea was as chilling as it was warming. "With the kids around?" She hugged him.

"Tonight there's a hayride at the campground."

With the last of the evenly fried fish on a platter, Nick removed the pan from the fire and set it aside.

"Tonight, huh?" she echoed as he rose and pulled her into his arms.

"Tonight."

"Won't it be cold?"

He kissed her fully on the mouth and broke away with a rakish grin. "I promise you won't notice. Trust me, Katie girl."

Kathryn basked in the glow of love enveloping them. Just like God, that love had always been there for them. All they'd had to do was reach for it. All they'd had to learn was to *trust*.

And Kathryn did. Her faith had never been deeper, her relationship with God never more solid. She knew as never before that he was there, watching over her, loving and caring for her and her family. And she knew with a heart filled to overflowing that, at long last, her fondest prayer had been answered.

Nick was home for good.

Dear Reader,

When I started writing, some sixteen historical and contemporary romances ago, inspirational romance never entered my mind. My ministry was the music my husband and I performed for church and charity. Being a slow learner when applying biblical lessons to my life, it took me two years to figure out that, when God has a plan for one, one doesn't ignore it.

Of course, I had more excuses than Jonah had not to go to Nineveh. I wasn't "holy or good" enough or "informed" enough to write inspirational romance. Besides, a human editor was intimidating enough, but *God?* After two years of resistance, of ignoring the advice of friends who insisted this is what I should be doing, of clinging to past success in the secular romance market, I finally caved in.

I realized God didn't expect me to be perfect. He just expected me to try my best for Him. He'd been grooming me for this all along and, by golly, I was going to Nineveh. Thank goodness I was spared the gastric juices of a whale!

Hi Honey, I'm Home is my leap of faith into this new genre with heart *and* soul. It has made me laugh, cry, and relive the wondrous and humbling moment of discovery that the God of my childhood, the Savior I'd turned away from for a while, still loved me in spite of all my faults—both past and present. I pray that reading

Kathryn and Nick's story has moved you as much as writing it did for me.

In His love,

Linda Windsor

Write to Linda Windsor
c/o Palisades
Multnomah Publishers, Inc.
P.O. Box 1720
Sisters, OR 97759